BOOKS BY
GIORGIO BASSANI
Translated into English

THE GOLD-RIMMED SPECTACLES   1960

A PROSPECT OF FERRARA   1962

THE GARDEN OF THE FINZI-CONTINIS   1965

THE GARDEN
OF THE
FINZI-CONTINIS

GIORGIO BASSANI

THE GARDEN OF THE FINZI-CONTINIS

*Translated from the Italian
by Isabel Quigly*

ATHENEUM

New York

1965

To Micòl

Certo, il cuore, chi gli dà retta, ha sempre qualche cosa da dire su quello che sarà. Ma che sa il cuore? Appena un poco di quello che è già accaduto.

I PROMESSI SPOSI

Of course the heart always has something to say, for one who knows how to hear it. But what does the heart know? At most, a bit about what is already past.

THE GARDEN
OF THE
FINZI-CONTINIS

Foreword

F or years I have wanted to write about the Finzi-
Continis – about Micòl and Alberto, professór
Ermanno and signora Olga – and the others who
lived or like me spent time at the house in Corso
Ercole I d'Este, at Ferrara, shortly before the last war
broke out. But the urge, the impulse to get down to
doing so, I had only a year ago, one April Sunday in
1957.

It was during one of the usual week-end outings. A
group of us, divided between two cars, had gone out
along the Aurelia highway straight after lunch, without anything very definite in mind. A few kilometres
from Santa Marinella, attracted by the towers of a
medieval castle that sprouted suddenly on the left, we
turned down an unpaved country lane and ended up
spread about the desolate sandy waste at the foot of the
castle: which, looked at more closely, was a lot less
medieval than it had promised from a distance, when
we saw it from the highway, outlined against the light,
on the dazzling blue expanse of the Tyrrhenian Sea.
Buffeted by the wind, with sand in our eyes, unable
even to visit the inside of the castle without written
permission from some God-forsaken institute in Rome,
deafened by the roaring surf, we felt thoroughly irri-
tated and put out at having left Rome on such a day,

which now, at the seaside, turned out so raw as to be practically wintry.

We walked up and down for about twenty minutes, following the curve of the beach, the only cheerful one among us being a small girl of nine, the daughter of the young couple who had brought me in their car. The wind, and sea, and wildly whirling sand, sent Giannina into transports of excitement which, with her gay, expansive nature, she made no effort to control. Although her mother tried to stop her, she had taken off her shoes and socks, and kept dashing up to the waves as they crashed on to the shore, wetting her legs up to the knee. In fact, she seemed to be enjoying herself no end, so that when we got into the car again, a bit later, I saw her vivid dark eyes, that glowed above the hot, tender cheeks, clouded over with obvious disappointment.

Back on the highway, in five minutes we were in sight of the road branching off to Cerveteri. As we had decided to go straight back to Rome, I was certain we would carry straight on. But instead, our car slowed down at this point more than it had to, and Giannina's father put his arm out of the window. He was signalling to the second car, which was about thirty yards behind us, that he meant to turn left. He had changed his mind.

So we found ourselves on a small smooth paved road that in a moment took us to a group of houses, most of them new, and from there, winding round towards the hills of the hinterland, to the famous Etruscan necropolis. No one asked for an explanation, and nor did I.

After the houses the road was slightly uphill, and slowed us down. We were now a few yards from the

tumuli called *montarozzi*, which are strewn all over the
province north of Rome as far as Tarquinia and beyond, more on the hills than near the sea, thus making
the whole of it into one vast, almost uninterrupted
cemetery. Here the grass grows more greenly, and is
thicker and darker than it is on the plateau below, between the Aurelia highway and the sea: which shows
that the everlasting sirocco that blows in across the sea
has lost most of its saltiness by the time it gets up there,
and that the dampness of the mountains not so far away is
beginning to have a good effect on everything growing.

"Where are we going?" asked Giannina.

Husband and wife were both sitting in front, with
the child between them. Her father took his hand off
the steering-wheel and laid it on Giannina's dark curls.

"We're going to take a look at some tombs that are
more than four or five thousand years old," he said, in
the tone of someone about to tell a story, and so not
fussing much about the accuracy of his figures. "Etruscan tombs."

"How gloomy!" sighed Giannina, laying her head
on the back of the seat.

"Why gloomy? Haven't they told you at school
who the Etruscans were?"

"In our history book they're right at the beginning,
near the Egyptians and the Jews. But who d'you think
were older, Papa, the Etruscans or the Jews?"

Her father burst out laughing.

"Try asking him," he said, jerking his thumb at me.

Giannina turned round. Her mouth hidden by the
edge of the seat, she glanced at me quickly, looking
severe and suspicious. I waited for her to repeat the
question. But nothing happened: she turned round
again at once and looked ahead of her.

Down along the road, which still sloped slightly and was flanked by a double row of cypresses, groups of country people, boys and girls, were coming down towards us. It was the Sunday stroll. Some of the girls walked arm in arm, and spread across into the middle of the road, and as we met them, we could feel them staring at us through the windows, their laughing eyes full of curiosity and of a kind of strange pride, or barely concealed scorn.

"Papa," Giannina asked, "why are old tombs less gloomy than new ones?"

A larger group than the others, taking up most of the road, and singing in chorus without bothering to get out of our way, had almost brought the car to a stop. Her father went into second gear.

"Well, of course, people who've just died are nearer to us, so we love them more," he said. "You see, the Etruscans have been dead for such ages"—and again he was telling a fairy-tale—"that it's as if they'd never lived, as if they'd *always* been dead."

Another pause, longer this time. At the end of which (we were now very near to the open space outside the entrance to the necropolis, full of cars and motor coaches), it was Giannina's turn to teach us a lesson.

"But, now you've said that," she said gently, "you've made me think the Etruscans did actually live, you know, and I love them as much as everyone else."

Our visit to the necropolis, I remember, was wrapped round in the remarkable tenderness of what she had said. It was Giannina who made us ready to understand. It was she, the youngest, who in a way led us on.

We went inside the most important tomb, the one

that belonged to the noble Matuta family: a low underground hall with twenty funeral beds arranged in as
many niches in the tufa walls, and decorated with
closely packed polychrome plaster casts of the beloved, trusted objects of everyday life: stoppers, ropes,
hatchets, shears, spades, knives, bows, arrows, even
hunting dogs and marsh birds. And meantime, I had
cheerfully abandoned my last philological scruples, and
was trying to imagine concretely what their frequent
visits to this suburban cemetery can have meant to the
late Etruscans of Cerveteri, the Etruscans after the time
of the Roman conquest.

They would come from their nearby homes, probably on foot–I imagined–family groups, troops of
young people like those we had met just now in the
road, pairs of lovers or friends, or else alone; just as
today, in Italian villages, the cemetery gate is still the
place where every evening stroll is bound to end. They
came among the cone-shaped tombs, which are as
solid and heavy as the bunkers the German soldiers
strewed vainly all over Europe during this last war
(gradually, through the centuries, the iron cart-wheels
have cut two deep parallel furrows in the paved road
that crosses the cemetery from one end to the other):
tombs that, even inside, obviously resembled the for-
tress-houses of the living. The world changed, admittedly–they must have said to themselves–it was no
longer what it once had been, when Etruria, with its
confederation of free aristocratic city-states, dominated
nearly the whole of the Italic peninsula. New civiliza-
tions, rougher and more plebeian, but stronger and
more warlike as well, now held sway. But what did it
matter?

Once inside the cemetery where each of them owned

a second home, and in it the bed on which he would soon be laid to rest with his fathers, eternity must no longer have seemed an illusion, a fairy-tale, a priests' promise. Let the future overturn the world, if it cared to; but there, whatever happened, in that small space sacred to the family dead; in the heart of those tombs where they had the foresight to take, not only their dead, but everything that made life beautiful and desirable; in that sheltered, well defended corner of the earth, there at least nothing would change, and their thoughts, their madness, still hovered round the conical mounds covered in coarse grass after twenty-five centuries.

When we left it was dark.

It isn't far from Cerveteri to Rome, barely twenty-five miles. But it was not a short journey. Half-way back the road became jammed with cars coming from Ladispoli and Fregene. We had to crawl along, almost at walking speed.

But once again, in that peace and torpor (even Giannina had gone to sleep), my memory kept going back over my early years in Ferrara, and to the Jewish cemetery at the end of via Montebello. Again I saw the large tree-strewn ground, the plaques and monuments set close together along the walls – the outer and inner, dividing walls – and, as if I had it actually before my eyes, the monumental tomb of the Finzi-Continis; an ugly tomb, admittedly – since I was a child I had always heard it called so at home – and yet imposing, a sign of the family's importance, if nothing else.

And my heart was wrenched as never before by the thought that in that tomb, which seemed to have been set up to guarantee the everlasting repose of its first customer – his, and that of his descendants – only one of the Finzi-Continis I had known and loved in fact achieved that everlasting repose. The only one actually buried there was Alberto, the elder child, who died in 1942 of lymphogranuloma. But where Micòl, the second child, and professór Ermanno, the father, and signora Olga, the mother, and signora Regina, signora Olga's very old paralysed mother, all deported to Germany in the autumn of '43, found their burial place is anyone's guess.

PART
ONE

Chapter One

The tomb was large, solid, really imposing: a kind of vaguely ancient and vaguely oriental temple, the kind you saw in the productions of *Aïda* and *Nabucco* fashionable in our opera houses until a few years ago. In any other cemetery, for instance the municipal graveyard next door, a pretentious tomb of the kind would not have been the least bit surprising, and in fact, lost among so many others, might even have gone unnoticed. But in ours it was the only one: and so, although it arose quite some distance from the entrance gates, in fact at the far end of an abandoned stretch of ground where no one had been buried for over half a century, it seemed a thing apart, and hit you in the eye straight away.

A distinguished professor of architecture, responsible for many other contemporaneous outrages in Ferrara, had been entrusted with the building of it by Moisè Finzi-Contini, Alberto and Micòl's great-grandfather, who died in 1863, shortly after the northern provinces of the papal states had been annexed by the kingdom of Italy; as a result of which the Jewish ghetto in Ferrara was abolished, once and for all. A big landowner, "reformer of Ferrarese agriculture" – according to the plaque the Jewish community had set up on the synagogue wall in via Mazzini, on the third landing, com-

17

memorating his virtues "as an Italian and as a Jew" – but
obviously without a very highly developed artistic
taste, once he had decided to set up a tomb *sibi et suis* he
must have let the architect do what he pleased. Things
seemed fine and flourishing in those days: everything
about the times encouraged hope and daring. Swept up
into a mood of euphoria by his newly acquired civil
equality, the same that as a young man, at the time of
the Cisalpine Republic, had allowed him to reclaim his
first substantial piece of land, the unbending patriarch
understandably, in those solemn circumstances, spared
no expense; very likely, in fact, he gave the distinguished professor of architecture *carte blanche*. And with
so much marble at his disposal, and such marble, too! –
white from Carrara, red from Verona, grey flecked
with black, yellow, blue, pale green – the architect had,
in his turn, lost his head.

An incredible mess came out of it, echoes of the
mausoleum of Theodoric at Ravenna, the Egyptian
temples at Luxor, Roman baroque, and even, as the
stocky pillars of the peristyle showed, archaic Greek of
Cnossus, all jostling one another. But there it was. And
gradually, year after year, time that in its way always
settles everything, somehow managed to harmonize
this unlikely mixture of styles. Moisè Finzi-Contini,
here called "austere example of unceasing toil", died in
'63. His wife Allegrina Camaioli, "the angel of the
house", in '75. In 1877 their only son, Menotti the
engineer, died still young, and he was followed twenty
years later by his wife Josette, who belonged to the
Treviso branch of the family of baron Artom. After
which the upkeep of the chapel, which had taken in
only one more member of the family, Guido, a child of
six, in 1914, had obviously fallen into the hands of

people who were less and less inclined to keep it clean
and tidy and repair any damage there might be, and
above all keep a check on the endless incursions of the
surrounding greenery. Tufts of dark, almost black,
practically metallic grass, ferns, stinging nettles,
thistles, and poppies had been allowed to grow and
press forward more and more freely. So that in 1924
and '25, about sixty years after its inauguration, when
I saw it for the first time as a child, the Finzi-Continis'
tomb ("A real horror," my mother never failed to say,
as I held her hand) already looked more or less as it
does now that no one has been directly concerned with
looking after it for such a long time. Half buried in the
rank growth around it, the surfaces of its polychrome
marbles, once smooth and shining, now opaque under
their dark patina of dust, its roof and outer steps visibly
decayed by wind and weather: even then it already
seemed changed into something rich and strange, the
way any long-sunk object always does.

How anyone is drawn to solitude, and why, nobody
knows. But the fact remains that the same isolation, the
same separation with which the Finzi-Continis had
surrounded their dead surrounded their *other* house as
well, the house at the end of corso Ercole I d'Este.
Immortalized by Giosue Carducci and by Gabriele
d'Annunzio, this Ferrarese street is so well known to
lovers of art and poetry all over the world that any
description of it is superfluous. As everyone knows, it
is in the heart of the northern part of the city that was
added to the small medieval town during the Renaissance by duke Ercole, and named after him. Wide and
straight as a die from the Castle to the Wall of the
Angels, with dark, imposing dwelling-houses on either
side of its entire length, and, high in the distance, a

backdrop of brick red, leafy green, and sky that seems
to lead you into infinity: Corso Ercole I d'Este is so
fine, and such a tourist attraction, that the left-wing
town council that has been running Ferrara for nearly
fifteen years has realized it must be left as it is and
strictly protected against speculative builders and shop-
keepers; in fact, that its aristocratic character must be
preserved exactly as it was.

The street is famous: and besides, substantially un-
changed.

Even today, the house of the Finzi-Continis must be
approached from Corso Ercole I–except that today,
to reach it, you must cross more than half an extra
kilometre across a huge stretch of mostly untilled
ground; although it still includes the historic ruins of
a sixteenth-century building, at one time a residence or
"pleasure ground" of the Este family, bought by the
same Moisè in 1850, and later, through successive
alterations and restorations, transformed by his heirs
into a kind of neo-Gothic manor-house, English style:
in spite of so much that is of interest in it still, who now
knows anything about it, I wonder, and who still
remembers it? The Touring Club guide has no mention of it, and this justifies tourists passing through the
town. But in Ferrara itself, even the few Jews left who
make up the languishing Jewish community seem to
have no memory of it.

The Touring Club guide does not mention the
house, and this is no doubt quite wrong of it. But let's
be fair: the garden, or, to be more precise, the great
park that surrounded the Finzi-Continis' house before
the war, and stretched for many acres right up to the
Wall of the Angels on the one hand, and to Porta San
Benedetto on the other, was in itself something quite

rare and remarkable (in the early years of the century the Touring Club guide never failed to mention it, in a curious tone, half lyrical and half worldly), but today it no longer exists, quite literally. All the large trees, limes, elms, beeches, poplars, plane trees, horse chestnuts, pines, firs, larches, cedars of Lebanon, cypresses, oaks, holm oaks, and even palms and eucalyptus trees, planted in hundreds by Josette Artom, were cut down for firewood during the last two years of the war, and the land is slowly going back to what it once was, when Moisè Finzi-Contini bought it from the family of marchese Avogli: just another of the many large gardens within the city walls.

The house itself should be considered. But this big, odd building, pretty badly damaged in an air raid in 1944, is still occupied today by fifty evacuee families belonging to the same beggarly sub-proletariat, not unlike the Roman slum-dwellers, that still keeps thronging the passages of the office in via Mortara: rough, embittered, intolerant folk (showers of stones, I heard, greeted the municipal sanitary inspector when he rode out on his bicycle to have an official look round, a few months ago), who, to discourage any notions about eviction that might occur to the Superintendent of Monuments in Emilia and Romagna, have hit on the bright idea of scraping the last remnants of the old painting off the walls.

Well, why endanger the poor tourists?–I imagine those who compiled the latest editions of the Touring Club guide wondered. And in fact, to see what?

Chapter Two

Y ou might call the Finzi-Continis' tomb "a horror" and smile at it, but you could not, even after fifty years, manage to smile at their house, isolated over there among the mosquitoes and frogs of the Panfilio canal and the drains, and enviously nicknamed the *magna domus*. Oh, you could pretty nearly feel sore about it still! Suppose you just–say–walked along the endless wall that ran round the garden on the Corso Ercole I d'Este side, a wall interrupted about half-way round by a portentous dark oak gate, without any handles at all; or else, on the other side, peer through the woody tangle of trunks and branches and the leaves below them from the top of the Wall of the Angels where it beetles over the park, till you caught a glimpse of the strange spiky outline of the house, and behind it, very much farther away, at the edge of a clearing, the dun-coloured stain of the tennis court: then the old discourtesy of their disdain and separation would come back hurtfully all over again, almost as searing as it used to be.

What an absurd, upstart idea!–my own father used to say, with a kind of passionate rancour, every time the subject came up.

Yes, of course–he admitted–the old owners, the family of marchese Avogli, had the bluest possible blood in their veins; garden and ruins rejoiced *ab*

antiquo in the highly decorative name of Barchetto del
Duca: all very fine, admittedly!-and all the more so
since Moisè Finzi-Contini, who deserved full credit for
realizing he was on to a good thing, had obviously got
it for the proverbial song. So what?- he continued,
straight away. Did Moisè's son Menotti, rather poin-
tedly nicknamed "the crazy apricot", after the colour
of an eccentric fur-lined overcoat he wore, really have
to transfer himself and his wife Josette to a part of town
that was so much out of the way, so unhealthy even
now, so imagine what it must have been like then!-
and so deserted, besides, so melancholy, and above all,
so very unsuitable.

Well, it was all very well for the parents, who belonged to a different age, and in any case could perfectly well afford the luxury of investing whatever they
liked in old stones. And it was especially all very well
for Josette Artom, who came from the Treviso branch
of the family of baron Artom (a magnificent creature,
in her time: a busty, blue-eyed blonde whose mother
came from Berlin, an Olschky). Apart from being
so crazy about the house of Savoy that in May 1898,
shortly before she died, she took it on herself to send
an admiring telegram to General Bava Beccaris, who
had fired on the Milanese socialists and anarchists, poor
devils, and a fanatical admirer of Germany in the days
of Bismarck's spiked helmet, she had never bothered,
since her husband Menotti, eternally at her feet, had
installed her in her Valhalla, to disguise her own dislike
of the Jewish world of Ferrara, which was too narrow
for her-so she said: or, however grotesque such a thing
might appear, *her own fundamental anti-semitism*. But
professór Ermanno and Signora Olga (he a scholar, she
a Herrera from Venice: which means she was born into

a *very* good Sephardic family, of course, but one that was financially not too sound, although fearfully orthodox): what sort of people did they think they'd become? Real, top-level aristocrats? Of course, of course, they had lost their son Guido, their first child, who died in 1914, aged only six, after a lightning attack of American-type infantile paralysis, against which even Dr. Corcos could do nothing; and what a terrible blow this must have been to them: to her, signora Olga, especially, who never went out of mourning from that time on. But apart from this, wasn't it really that, what with one thing and another, living exclusively on their own had made them swollen-headed too, and had given them the same absurd whims as Menotti Finzi-Contini and his good lady had had? Aristocracy, my eye! Instead of giving themselves such airs, they'd have done very much better not to forget who they were, and where they came from, since there's no doubt that Jews—Sephardic and Ashkenazi, western and eastern, Tunisians, Berbers, Yemenites, and even Ethiopians—whatever part of the world, under whatever sky history might have strewn them, were and would always be Jews, which means closely related. Old Moisè certainly gave himself no airs! No delusions of grandeur for him! When he was living in the ghetto, at 24 via Vignatagliata, in the house where he had wanted to end his days, come what might, resisting the pressure of his haughty Trevisan daughter-in-law, who was impatient to move to Barchetto del Duca as soon as possible, he went out shopping himself every morning in piazza delle Erbe, with his shopping-basket tucked cosily under his arm. And it was he, for this very reason nicknamed *al gatt*,* who had pulled the family up from

* "The cat": Ferrarese dialect.

nothing. Because if it was quite true that "that" Josette
came down to Ferrara with a big dowry, consisting of
a villa in the province of Treviso with frescoes by
Tiepolo, a fat cheque, too, and of course jewels, plenty
of them, which on first nights in the theatre, against
the red velvet background of her private box, drew
the eyes of the entire theatre on her and her glittering
bosom, it was equally true that *al gatt*, and he alone,
had got together the thousands of acres in the *bassa*,*
between Codigoro, Massa Fiscaglia and Jolanda di
Savoia, on which even today most of the family's
wealth was based. The monumental tomb in the
cemetery: that was the only mistake (of taste, above
all) of which you could accuse Moisè Finzi-Contini.
But besides that, nothing.

This was the way my father talked: especially at Passover, during the long dinners that still took place in our
house even after the death of my grandfather Raffaello,
which about twenty relations and friends attended; but
at Kippúr as well, when the same friends and relations
came to us to end their fast.

But I remember a Passover supper in the course of
which, to the usual criticisms – bitter and general and
always the same, and made above all for the pleasure
of reviving the old stories of the Jewish community –
my father added something new and surprising.

It was in 1933, the year when the Fascist Party was
opened to everyone.

Thanks to the "clemency" of the Duce, who suddenly, as if inspired, had decided to open his arms to
every one of "yesterday's agnostics and enemies", the
number of Fascist Party members had risen suddenly
to 90 per cent, even in the circle of our Jewish com-

* The part of the Po delta which is in the province of Ferrara.

munity. And my father, who was sitting there at his
usual place at the head of the table, the place in which
my grandfather Raffaello had presided for many years
with a very different authority and severity, had not
failed to welcome the event. The rabbi, Dr. Levi–he
said–had been quite right to mention it in his sermon
recently at the Italian synagogue, when, in the presence
of the highest city authorities–the Prefect, the
Federal Secretary, the *Podestà*,* the commander of the
local garrison–he had commemorated the granting of
the constitution.†

And yet Papa wasn't entirely happy about it. In his
boyish blue eyes, brimming with patriotic ardour, I saw a
shadow of disappointment. So something must be need-
ling him, some small unexpected and unpleasant obstacle.

And, as a matter of fact, having started counting on
his fingers how many of us, how many of us *judím* in
Ferrara were still "outside", and having at last reached
Ermanno Finzi-Contini, who had never joined the
party, it was true, but considering what an important
landowner he was, it wasn't really very easy to see why
not; suddenly, as if sick of himself and his own discretion, he decided to tell us about two odd things that
seemed to have no connection–he said–but were no
less significant for all that.

The first was that when Geremia Tabet, the lawyer,
had, as a Sansepolcrista‡ and intimate friend of the

* The head of the municipal administration under the Fascists.
 † This was the Constitution granted in 1848 by Carlo-Alberto,
King of Sardinia, to his Piedmontese and Sardinian subjects and
then adopted in 1861 by the kingdom of Italy.
 ‡ Those who had become fascists before the March on Rome
in 1922 were referred to by this name, which is derived from a
meeting held in piazza San Sepolcro in Milan in 1919; in a
sense this meeting marked the birth of Italian fascism.

Federal Secretary, gone to Barchetto del Duca just to offer professór Ermanno a membership card, already filled in, it had not only been returned to him, but shortly afterwards, very politely of course, but quite firmly, he had been shown out.

"But how did he get out of it?" someone asked plaintively. "I never heard that Ermanno Finzi-Contini was all that tough."

"How did he get out of joining?" said my father, laughing violently. "Oh, the usual stuff: that he's a scholar (I'd like to know what the hell he's working at!), that he's too old, that he's never taken any part in politics, etc. etc. Anyway, he was pretty cunning about it, our friend was. He must have noticed Tabet's black look because suddenly, wham!—he slipped five thousand lire into his pocket."

"Five thousand lire!"

"Exactly. For the party's holiday camps of the O.N.B.* Pretty smart, don't you think? Listen to what comes next, though."

And he went on to tell everyone at the table that a few days before professór Ermanno had written to the council of the Jewish community through Renzo Galassi-Tarabini (could he possibly have picked a more hypocritical, *halto*† old humbug of a lawyer than that?) and officially asked permission to restore at his own expense, "for the private and exclusive use of his family and of those who might possibly be interested", the small ancient Spanish synagogue in via Mazzini, which had not been put to religious use for at least three centuries and was now used as a storeroom.

* Opera Nazionale Balilla: Fascist youth organization.
† 'Bigot' in the dialect of Ferrara Jews.

Chapter Three

In 1914, when the child Guido died, professór Ermanno was forty-nine, and signora Olga twenty-four. The child felt ill, was put to bed with a high fever, and fell into a deep torpor right away.

Dr. Corcos was sent for urgently. He examined the child silently, interminably, frowning deeply; then he raised his head abruptly, and looked gravely at the father and then at the mother. He looked at them for a long time, stern and oddly scornful; while under his thick Umberto-style whiskers, already completely grey, his lips tightened bitterly, almost angrily, as they did in desperate cases.

"There's nothing more to be done," that look and that face meant to say. But perhaps something else as well. That he himself, that is, ten years before (and perhaps he spoke of it that same day, before leaving, or else, as certainly happened, only five days later, turning to my grandfather Raffaello as they slowly followed the imposing funeral) that he, too, had lost a child, his own Ruben.

"I have known this torture myself, I know what it is to see a child of five die," Elia Corcos said suddenly.

Head drooping, hands on the handle-bars of his bicycle, my grandfather Raffaello was walking beside him. He seemed to be counting the cobble-stones of

Corso Ercole I d'Este, one by one. At these highly un-
usual words from his sceptical friend, he turned in surprise to look at him.

And, indeed, what did Elia Corcos himself know
about it? He examined the child's inert body for a
long time, made his own gloomy prognosis of what
was likely to happen, and then looked up into the stony
eyes of the parents: the father an old man, the mother
still a girl. How could he possibly get down into their
hearts, and read them? And who else ever would, in
the future? The inscription on the giant tomb in the
Jewish cemetery (seven lines not very noticeably cut
and coloured on a plain rectangle of white marble),
was to say only:

Alas,
GUIDO FINZI-CONTINI
(1908–1914)
choice form and spirit
your parents were ready
to love you more and more
and not weep for you so soon

More and more. A soft sob, that was all. A load on
the heart, not to be shared with anyone else on earth.

Alberto was born in 1915, Micòl in 1916: my contemporaries, pretty nearly. They were not sent to either
the Jewish primary school in via Vignatagliata, where
Guido had been without even finishing the first form,
or later to the state high school, *G. B. Guarini*, the melt-
ing-pot of all the most promising youngsters in town,
Jewish and non-Jewish, and so just as hallowed a
choice. Instead both Alberto and Micòl were taught
privately, with their father occasionally interrupting
his own solitary studies in agriculture, physics, and the

history of the Jewish communities in Italy, to keep a
close eye on their progress. These were the foolish but
in their way generous early years of fascism in Emilia.
Every action, all behaviour, was judged–even by
people who, like my father, liked to quote Horace and
his *aurea mediocritas*–through the rough sieve of patriot-
ism or defeatism. Sending your children to the state
schools was considered patriotic, on the whole. Not
sending them was defeatist: and so, as far as anyone
who did send them was concerned, definitely offensive.

But, although they were kept so much apart, Micòl
and Alberto always kept up a very flimsy contact with
the outside world, with children who, like us, went to
the state schools. Two teachers we had in common,
both from the *Guarini* school, acted as go-betweens.

There was Meldolesi, who taught us Italian, Latin,
Greek, history and geography in the fourth form at
school, and every second afternoon, from the district
of small houses that had grown up outside Porta San
Benedetto in those years, where he lived alone in a
furnished room the view and aspect of which he used
to tell us about, rode out on his bicycle to Barchetto
del Duca, and sometimes spent three hours on end
there. And signora Fabiani, who taught mathematics,
did the same.

Nothing very much, to be honest, ever leaked out
through signora Fabiani. She was from Bologna, a
widow over fifty without children, and terribly pious;
while we were being questioned we would see her
withdrawing, whispering to herself and rolling her
Flemish blue eyes continuously, as if she was just about
to be carried away in an ecstasy. She was praying. For
poor souls like us, no doubt, most of us quite hopeless
at algebra; but also very likely to hasten the conversion

of the wealthy Jews to whose house–and what a house it was!–she went twice a week. The conversion of professór Ermanno and signora Olga and of the two children above all, Alberto so intelligent and Micòl so lively and so pretty, must have seemed to her too important and too urgent a task for her to risk the chance of success by gossiping at school.

Meldolesi, on the other hand, was far from silent about them. He came from a peasant family at Comacchio, and was educated entirely at a seminary (and there was a great deal of the priest about him, the little sharp, almost feminine country priest), and afterwards at Bologna University, where he read and was in time for the last lectures of Giosue Carducci, whose "humble pupil" he boasted of being: the afternoons spent at Barchetto del Duca, in an atmosphere steeped in Renaissance memories, and five o'clock tea taken with the whole family–signora Olga very often came back from the park just then, her arms full of flowers–and later on in the library, perhaps, enjoying professór Ermanno's learned conversation until it was dark: those extraordinary afternoons were clearly something precious to him, and they provided him with material for everlasting chat and digressions with us as well.

Since professór Ermanno had revealed to him one evening that in 1875 Carducci had been his parents' guest for ten days on end, and had then shown him the room he had occupied, had let him touch the bed he had slept in, and had finally given him to take home and look through at leisure a sheaf of signed letters written by the poet to his mother, Meldolesi's excitement and enthusiasm knew no bounds. He actually got to the point of persuading himself, and trying to

persuade us as well, that the famous line in the *Canzone
di Legnano*:

> *O bionda, o bella imperatrice, o fida**

in which the even more famous lines:

> *Onde venisti? Quali a noi secoli†*
> *si mite e bella ti tramandarano . . .*

are clearly foreshadowed, and the poet's famous conversion to the "charm of royal womanhood" of the
house of Savoy, were all inspired by the grandmother
of his pupils Alberto and Micòl Finzi-Contini. Oh,
what a splendid subject it would be – he sighed in class
once – for an article to send to the *Nuova Antologia*, in
which Alfredo Grilli, his friend and colleague Grilli,
had for some time been publishing his sharp-witted
pieces on Renato Serra!‡ Some day, with all the necessary tact, of course, he would try mentioning it to the
owner of the letters. And God willing, if only – considering the number of years that had passed, and the
importance and, obviously, the perfect correctness of
letters in which Carducci addressed the lady only as
"dear baroness" and "kind hostess", and such-like – if
only he didn't refuse! In the happy event of professór
Ermanno agreeing he, Giulio Meldolesi, would at once
– supposing he were given explicit permission to do so
by the one person who had the right to give or with-
hold it – copy the letters one by one, and add to those
sacred fragments, those venerable sparks from the great
hammer, a minimum amount of comment. What, in-

---

* O fair, beautiful and trusted empress.

†Whence came you?What centuries passed you on to us, so
mild and lovely.

‡ A critic (1884–1915).

deed, did the text of the letters require? Nothing but
a general introduction, possibly with a few historico-
philological footnotes. . . .

But apart from the teachers we had in common,
there were also the exams for those who were taught
privately–exams that took place in June, at the same
time as the ones for the pupils at the state schools–and
these brought us into direct contact with Alberto and
Micòl at least once a year.

These were, perhaps, the very happiest days for us at
school, especially if we had been moved up a form. As
if suddenly regretting the lessons and homework just
done with, we found no better place to meet as a rule
than the big entrance hall, where we hung about in the
cool, crypt-like gloom, standing before the big white
sheets of paper with the results on them, fascinated by
our names and those of our friends, which, when we
read them like that, set down in beautiful handwriting
under glass, behind a light wire grating, never ceased
to amaze us. It was fine to have no more to fear from
school, fine to be able to go out soon afterwards into
the limpid blue light of ten o'clock in the morning,
that winked at us through the private way in, fine to
have long hours of idleness and freedom before us to
spend however we liked. Everything was fine, everything was marvellous, in those first days of the holidays.
And then there was the joy of thinking, as we kept
doing, of our coming departure for the sea or the
mountains where work, which wearied and worried
so many others still, would hardly be a memory!

And there, among those *others* (big, clumsy, country
louts, for the most part, peasants' sons prepared for the
exams by the village priest, who, before they came inside the school, looked bewilderedly about them, like

calves led to the slaughter), were Alberto and Micòl
Finzi-Contini: not the least bit bewildered, since for
years they had been turning up and sailing through,
faintly ironical, perhaps, especially towards me, when
they saw me across the hall among my friends and
greeted me from a distance with a wave and a smile.
But always polite, even a bit too polite, and friendly:
just like guests.

They never came on foot, still less on bicycles. But in
a carriage: a dark blue brougham, with large rubber-
tyred wheels and red shafts, and gleaming all over with
varnish, glass, and chromium.

It waited there outside the school's front door, for
hours and hours, not moving except to follow the
shade. And I must say that examining it close up, in
every detail, from the large powerful horse with its
docked tail and cropped mane, that occasionally kicked
out calmly, to the tiny coat of arms gleaming silver
against the blue background of the doors, even occasionally getting permission from the indulgent coachman, who was not in full livery but sat up on the box
as if on a throne, to mount up on one of its foot-rests
at the side, so that we could gaze comfortably, noses
glued to the panes, at the shadowy upholstered grey
interior (it looked like a drawing-room: there were
even flowers in a corner, in a slim goblet-shaped oblong
vase): this could be really something, in fact it certainly was: one of the many adventures and joys those
marvellous late spring mornings of adolescence poured
out on us.

Chapter Four

As far as I personally was concerned, in any case, my relations with Alberto and Micòl had always been rather more intimate. The understanding looks and familiar waves they gave me every time we met at school alluded only to this, as I knew perfectly well, and were something to do with us and us alone.

Rather more intimate. But how, in fact?

Well, of course, in the first place we were Jews, and this would have been more than enough, apart from anything else. Let me make myself clear: we might have had nothing at all in common, not even the little that comes from having sometimes chatted a bit. But the fact that we were what we were, and that at least twice a year, at the Passover festival and at Yom Kippur, we appeared with our respective families all at once at the same street door in via Mazzini–and it often happened that, having gone through the door together, the narrow hall beyond it, half in darkness, obliged the grown-ups to much hat-doffing, hand-shaking, and polite bowing, although for the rest of the year they had no other occasion for it: as far as we children were concerned, this was quite enough, whenever we met elsewhere, and above all when there were other people about, to make our eyes cloud or laugh with a quite special feeling of complicity and connivance.

The fact that we were Jews, though, inscribed in the
registers of the same Jewish community, in our case
hardly counted. Because what on earth did the word
"Jew" mean? What meaning could terms like "community" or "Israelite universality" have *for us*, since
they took no account of the existence of that more basic
intimacy–a secret intimacy that can be properly appreciated only by those who have had it–derived from the
fact that our two families, not from choice, but
through a tradition older than any possible memory,
belonged to the same religious rite, or rather to the
same "school"? When we met at the synagogue door,
generally as darkness was falling, after our parents had
exchanged embarrassed greetings in the shadowy porch,
we nearly always ended up mounting the steep steps
to the second floor together, where, crammed with all
kinds of people, echoing like a church with organ
music and singing–and so high up, among the roof-
tops, that on some May evenings, when the side windows were wide open to the sunset, we would find ourselves steeped in a kind of golden mist–was the large
Italian synagogue. Only we, being Jews, of course, but
Jews brought up in the very same religious rite, could
really understand what it meant to have our own
family pew in the Italian synagogue, up there on the
second floor, and not in the German synagogue on the
first floor, which, with its severe, almost Lutheran
gatherings of prosperous Homburg hats, was so very
different. Nor was that all: because, even supposing
people outside strictly Jewish circles might know that
there was an Italian synagogue different from the German one, with all the subtle distinctions this implied,
socially and psychologically, who, apart from us, could
have been in a position to give precise details about,

say, "the via Vittoria lot"? This referred, as a rule, to
the members of the four or five families who had the
right to use the small separate Levantine synagogue,
also called after the city of Fano, on the third floor of
an old dwelling-house in via Vittoria: the Da Fanos of
via Scienze, in fact, the Cohens of via Gioco del Pal-
lone, the Levis of piazza Ariostea, the Levi-Minzis of
viale Cavour, and a few other odd families: all rather
peculiar people, in any case, faintly ambiguous and inclined to keep themselves to themselves, people whose
religion, which in the Italian synagogue had become
popular and theatrical in an almost Catholic sense, a
fact that was clearly reflected in the character of the
people, who were mostly open and optimistic and
what you might call very "Po Valley", had remained
essentially a half-secret, exclusive cult best practised at
night, by a few people gathered together in the dark-
est, least known alley-ways of the ghetto. No, no: only
we, born and brought up *intra muros*, as you might say,
could know and really understand these things: which
were terribly subtle, of course, and maybe quite beside
the point in everyday life, but none the less real for
that. As for the others, all the others, not excluding
school friends, friends played with as children and
loved incomparably more (at least by me), it was hopeless to think of bringing them into anything so private.
Poor souls! As far as this sort of thing was concerned
they just weren't in the running at all, they were all
sentenced for life, every one of them, to a rough, simple
existence at the bottom of chasms, unscalable chasms
of ignorance, or–as even my father said, grinning
amiably–the life of "*negri goim*".*

So, when we happened to meet, we went up the

* "Poor perishing Catholics" in the dialect of Ferrara Jews.

stairs together, and all went into the synagogue together as well.

And since our seats were next to each other, up there,
close to the semicircular enclosures surrounded by a
marble banister in the middle of which arose the *tevà*,
or lectern, of the rabbi officiating, and both with a
good view of the imposing black carved wooden cupboard where the scrolls of the Law, called *sefarím*, were
kept, we clattered together across the resonant pink and
white lozenges of the synagogue floor. Mothers, wives,
aunts and sisters had parted from us males in the entrance hall. They vanished, one behind the other,
through a small door in the wall that led into a dark
little room, from which a spiral staircase led up to the
women's enclosure, and very soon we would see them
peering out through the holes in their hen-coop grating, right up under the ceiling. But even like that,
reduced to the males–which meant me, my brother
Ernesto, my father, professór Ermanno and Alberto;
and sometimes signora Olga's two bachelor brothers
came from Venice for the occasion, the engineer
and Dr. Herrera–we were quite numerous. In any
case we carried some weight, we mattered: so much
so that at whatever moment in the ceremony we
appeared in the doorway, we never managed to get
to our seats without arousing the liveliest curiosity all
round.

As I have said, our seats were close together, one behind the other; we in front, the Finzi-Continis behind.
So that even if we had wanted to it would have been
very hard to ignore each other.

Attracted by their difference just as much as my
father was repelled by it, I was always very careful to
notice any movement or whisper from the seat behind

us. I was never still for a moment. Either I would be whispering to Alberto, who was two years older than I was, it was true, but still had to "go into the *mignàn*", yet in spite of this hastened, the minute he arrived, to wrap himself up in the great *talèd* of white wool with black stripes that had at one time belonged to his grandfather Moisè; or professór Ermanno, smiling kindly at me through his thick spectacles, would with a movement of his finger invite me to look at the copper engravings illustrating an old Bible he had got out of the drawer especially for me; or else I would listen, fascinated and open-mouthed, to signora Olga's brothers, the railway engineer and the T.B. specialist, chatting together half in Venetian dialect and half in Spanish ("Cossa xé che stas meldando? Su, Giulio, alevantate, ajde! E procura de far star in pie anca il chico . . ."*) and then stopping suddenly to join loudly in the rabbi's Hebrew litany: in fact, one way or another I was nearly always facing backwards. There were the two Finzi-Continis and the two Herreras, in a row in their seats, not much more than a yard away, yet terribly far, quite intangible, as if protected by a wall of glass around them. They were not alike. Tall, thin, bald, with long pale bearded faces, always in blue or black, and, apart from that, putting an intensity, a fanatical ardour into their devotions which their brother-in-law and nephew—all you need do was look at them to see it—would never be capable of, the relations from Venice seemed to belong to a civilization completely foreign to that of Alberto's tobacco-coloured sweaters and thick, sporty socks, or Professór Ermanno's scholarly, country gentlemen's clothes—English wool, yel-

*"What are you reading? Come on, Giulio, get up! And try and make the child stay on his feet too. . . ."

lowish linen. All the same, in spite of their differences, I felt their profound solidarity. What was there in common – all four of them seemed to say – between them and the distracted, whispering, *Italian* rank and file, that, even in the synagogue, before the wide open Ark of the Lord, was still taken up with all the trivial cares of everyday life, business, politics, even sport, but never with the soul or with God? I was a child in those days, it was true, between ten and twelve years old, yet I felt a confused but searing scorn and humiliation at my equally confused but basically accurate guess that I belonged there in the rank and file myself, among those vulgar folk to be kept at a distance. And what about my father? Up against the glass wall behind which the Finzi-Continis and the Herreras, always pleasant but remote, continued to all intents and purposes to ignore him, he behaved in a way just the opposite from mine. Instead of trying to approach them, as I did, I saw him in reaction against them; with his medical degree, freethinker, war volunteer, fascist whose membership went back to 1919, sports enthusiast, in fact modern Jew – he exaggerated his own healthy intolerance of any overservile and obvious exhibition of faith.

When the gay procession of the *sefarìm* passed by the seats (wrapped in their rich mantles of embroidered silk, silver crowns askew and small bells tinkling, the sacred scrolls of the *Torah* seemed like a series of royal infants shown to the populace to bolster some tottering monarchy), the Herreras were all agog to leap out of their seats and kiss whatever scarlet bits of mantle they could get hold of, with practically indecent greed. True, professór Ermanno, followed by his son, simply covered his eyes with a piece of the *talèd*, and softly whispered a prayer, but even so!

"What mawkishness, what *haltúd!*"* my father would comment later at the table, disgustedly: not that this prevented him–quite the contrary, in fact–from returning straight afterwards, yet again, to the question of the Finzi-Continis' hereditary pride, to the absurd isolation they lived in, or even to their persistent, sub-terranean, aristocratic-type anti-semitism. But while we were there, having no one on which to vent him-self, he took it out on me.

As usual, I had turned round to look.

"Will you please shut up and behave yourself?" he whispered through clenched teeth, his angry blue eyes glaring exasperatedly at me. "Even in the synagogue you can't behave. Look at your brother here: he's four years younger than you, and could certainly teach you manners!"

But I never listened. Soon afterwards, his orders quite forgotten, I had turned again, my back to Dr. Levi singing the psalms.

Now, if he wanted to have me under his control for a few minutes–his physical control, of course, nothing more–all my father could do was wait for the solemn benediction, when all the sons were gathered under the fathers' *taletod*, as if inside as many tents. And here at last (Carpanetti, the verger, had finished going round with his rod, lighting up the thirty silver and gilt bronze candelabra one after the other: the room was blazing with lights) here, anxiously awaited, Dr. Levi's voice, as a rule so colourless, would suddenly take on the prophetic tone suited to the supreme, final moment of the *berachà*.

"*Jevarehehà Adonài veishmerèha*," the rabbi solemnly intoned, bending almost prostrate over the *tevà*, after

* "Bigotry" in the dialect of Ferrara Jews.

covering his towering white berretta with the *talèd*.

"Come along, boys," my father would say then, gaily and quickly, snapping his fingers: "Come along in!"

Escape, in actual fact, was perfectly possible. My father's hard sportsman's hands could grab us by the scruff of our necks, and me in particular, very efficiently. Although grandfather Raffaello's *talèd*, which he used, was vast as a tablecloth, it was too worn and too full of holes to guarantee that his dreams were hermetically sealed. And in fact, through the holes and tears the years had wrought in that immensely frail material that smelt so old and stuffy, it wasn't hard, at least for me, to watch professór Ermanno as, there beside me, one hand on Alberto's dark hair and the other on the fine, blonde, fluffy locks of Micòl who had dashed down from the women's enclosure, he repeated, one after the other, and keeping behind Dr. Levi as he did so, the words of the *berachà*. Above our heads my father, who knew about twenty words of Hebrew, the usual ones used in everyday speech, and would never have bowed down, anyway, was silent. I imagined his face looking suddenly embarrassed, his eyes, half sardonic and half intimidated, looking up at the unpretentious plaster-work on the ceiling or at the women's enclosure. But meantime, from where I was, always newly envious and newly surprised, I watched from below professór Ermanno's wrinkled, sharp face that looked transfigured at that moment and his eyes that, behind the glasses, I would have said were full of tears. His voice was thin and melodious, perfectly in tune; his Jewish pronunciation, frequently doubling the consonants, and with the z, s and h much more Tuscan than Ferrarese, came filtered, at two removes, by his culture and his class. . . .

I looked at him. Below him, for as long as the blessing lasted, Alberto and Micòl never stopped exploring the loopholes of their tent as well. And they smiled and winked at me, both of them oddly inviting: especially Micòl.

Chapter Five

Once, all the same, in June of 1929, the day the results of the exams were put up in the school hall, something special happened.

My exam results were far from satisfactory, and I knew it.

Although Meldolesi had done all he could for me, and had even, quite against the rules, managed to question me himself, in spite of this I hadn't managed to get anything like the marks that usually appeared in my school report. Even in literary subjects I ought to have done very much better. Questioned in Latin on the *consecutio temporum*, I tripped up over a hypothetical sentence of the third type, that is "of unreality". And in Greek I had stumbled just as badly on a passage of the *Anabasis*. Well, of course, I caught up later in Italian, history and geography. In Italian, for instance, I did well on *The Betrothed*, and on the *Ricordanze*.* And I recited the first three verses of *Orlando Furioso* without

* *Memories*, a famous poem by Leopardi.

a single slip, and Meldolesi, dead keen, let rip with such a loud "Fine!" that it made not only the other examiners smile, but me as well. But on the whole I must admit that even in literary subjects my results weren't up to my reputation.

The real disaster, though, was in maths.

Since the previous year, in form IV, algebra had simply refused to get into my head. And besides, I had always behaved pretty meanly with signora Fabiani. I did the small amount of work needed to get the minimum marks, and often not even that minimum, relying on Meldolesi's unfailing support for my results at the end of term. What could mathematics possibly matter to someone like me who had already declared his intention of reading literature at the university?–I kept saying to myself that morning, as I cycled to school along corso Giovecca. Actually I'd hardly opened my mouth in the algebra or the geometry orals. Well, so what? Poor signora Fabiani, who'd never, during the past two years, dared give me less than six out of ten, would never do so at the final session with the other teachers; and I avoided the word "failed", even mentally, for the very notion of failing in a subject, with the consequent trail of depressing, dreary coaching I'd have to put up with at Riccione for the entire summer, seemed absurd when referred to me. To think of me, me of all people, who'd never once undergone the humiliation of having to take an exam over again, and had, in fact, in the first, second and third form of high school been decorated "for good work and good conduct" with the much-prized title of "Guard of honour to the Monuments of the Fallen and the Garden of Remembrance", to think of *me* failing an exam, being reduced to mediocrity, lost

among the rabble, in fact! And what about my father?
Suppose, just suppose signora Fabiani did fail me (she
taught maths higher up in the school as well: this was
why she had questioned me herself–she had a right
to!), how would I have the courage, a few hours later,
to go home and sit down at table opposite my father,
and start eating? Maybe he'd smack me: that would be
best, after all. Any punishment would be better than
the reproach of his terrible, silent blue eyes.

I went into the school hall. A group of boys, among
whom I noticed several friends right away, was standing calmly in front of the notice-board. I leant my bike
against the wall by the front door, and went up to it,
trembling. No one seemed to have noticed my coming.

From behind a hedge of backs turned obstinately to
me I looked. My eyes clouded over. I looked again:
and the red five, the only red ink figure in a long black
row of them, seared my mind as viciously as a red-hot
branding-iron.

"Hey, what's up?" said Sergio Pavani, giving me a
friendly slap on the back. "You're not going to make
a tragedy out of a five in maths now. Look at me," he
said, and laughed. "Latin and Greek."

"Come on, cheer up," added Otello Forti. "I've
failed in one thing too: English."

I stared at him, stupefied. We had been in the same
form and had sat side by side since we started school,
and had always worked together, alternating between
our two homes when we did our prep, and both convinced of my superiority. There had never yet been a
year when I hadn't passed in all subjects in June, whereas he, Otello, always failed in something and had to do
it over again in October: English sometimes, or Latin,
or maths, or Italian.

And now, suddenly, to hear myself compared with a *mere* Otello Forti, and the comparison made by him, what's more! To find I'd suddenly shot down to his level!

What I did and thought in the four or five hours that followed isn't worth telling in detail, starting from the effect on me of my meeting, as I left school, with Meldolesi (he was smiling, hatless and tieless, with an open-necked striped shirt, Robespierre style, and quick to confirm, as if there was any need to, signora Fabiani's "pig-headedness" with regard to me, and her categorical refusal to "close an eye once again") and continuing with a description of my long, desperate, aimless wanderings after Meldolesi had given me a friendly, encouraging tap on the cheek. All I need say is that about two in the afternoon I was still going along the Wall of the Angels, on my bike, in the neighbourhood of corso Ercole I d'Este. I hadn't even rung them up at home. Face streaky with tears, heart bursting with self-pity, I was pedalling along scarcely realizing where I was, and making confused plans for suicide.

I stopped under a tree: one of those old trees – limes, elms, plane trees, chestnuts – which a dozen years later, in the freezing winter of Stalingrad, were to be sacrificed for firewood, but which in 1929 still raised their great leafy umbrellas high above the city walls.

Completely deserted, all round. The unpaved lane I had cycled along like a sleep-walker from Porta San Giovanni wound on among the tree trunks towards Porta San Benedetto and the railway station. I lay on the grass, face downwards beside the bicycle, my burning face hidden in the crook of my elbow. The warm breeze lapped me round as I lay, wishing for nothing but to stay there, eyes closed, like that. Only a few sounds managed to penetrate the cicadas' narcotic chorus: the crowing of a cock from a nearby garden, the beating of linen, some washerwoman working late in the greenish water of the Panfilio canal, and finally, very close, just by my ear, the tick-tock of the bike's back wheel, growing gradually slower as it neared stillness.

By now–I thought–they'd certainly have heard, at home: from Otello Forti, very likely. Had they sat down at the table? Maybe they had, behaving as if nothing had happened; and then they had had to stop eating, unable to go on. Perhaps they were looking for me. Perhaps they had put Otello himself on the scent, Otello my good, inseparable friend, telling him to search the whole town, including the Montagnone and the Walls, on his bike, so that at any moment I might see him appear before me, looking suitably gloomy, but at the same time simply delighted, as I knew perfectly well, to have failed only in English. No, but: maybe, overwhelmed with grief, my parents hadn't been satisfied with Otello alone, and had got to the point of sending the police out as well. My father had gone to talk to the chief at police headquarters in the Castle. I could just see him: stammering, tousled, alarmingly aged, a shadow of himself. He was weeping. Ah, but suppose he'd seen me two hours ago gazing into the river at Pontelagoscuro from high above it on the iron bridge (ages, I'd been up there, looking down! How long? Oh, twenty minutes at least, at the very least . . .) that'd really have shaken him . . . that'd really have made him see . . . that'd . . .

"Hey!"

I woke up with a start, but without opening my eyes right away.

"Hey!" I heard again.

I raised my head slowly, turning it to the left, against the sun. Who was calling me? It couldn't be Otello. Then who?

I was about half-way down the three kilometres of city wall that start where corso Ercole I ends, and finish at Porta San Benedetto, opposite the station. It has always been remarkably solitary there. Thirty years ago it was so and it still is today, in spite of the fact that on the right especially, on the industrial zone side, that is, dozens and dozens of small many-coloured working-class houses have sprouted up in the last few years, with a background of factory chimneys and goods sheds, in comparison with which the dark, wild, bushy, half-ruined buttress of the fifteenth-century rampart seems to grow progressively more absurd.

I gazed about, searching, and half-shut my eyes against the glare. At my feet (it was only then I noticed) the foliage of its noble trees filled with midday light, like that of a tropical forest, Barchetto del Duca was spread before me: enormous, really boundless, with, half-hidden in its green centre, the turrets and pinnacles of the *magna domus*, and entirely surrounded by a wall interrupted only a little way ahead, where the Panfilio canal flowed through.

"Goodness, you're pretty blind, aren't you," a girl's voice said gaily.

From the blonde hair, that special streaky Nordic-looking blonde of the *fille aux cheveux de lin*, which was hers alone, I immediately recognized Micòl Finzi-Contini. She appeared at the garden wall as if at a window-sill, leaning forward on folded arms; not more than twenty-five yards away. She looked up at me from below: near enough for me to see her eyes;

which were light and large (too large, perhaps, in those days, in her small thin child's face).

"What are you up to, down there? I've been watching you for ten minutes. Sorry if I woke you, though. And . . . bad luck!"

"Bad luck? Why?" I stammered, feeling my face turn red.

I had hauled myself up.

"What's the time?" I asked, more loudly.

She glanced at her wrist watch.

"I make it three," she said, with an attractive grimace, and then:

"Bet you're hungry."

I was completely at a loss. So they knew too! For a moment I even thought they must have heard of my disappearance straight from my father or mother: by telephone, of course, like an endless lot of others. But Micòl put me right at once.

"I was at the school this morning, with Alberto, to see the results. You must have felt pretty sick about it, didn't you?"

"What about you, did you get through?"

"We don't know yet. Maybe they're waiting to see how all the *other* outsiders have done before they put up the marks. But why don't you come down? Come nearer, so I shan't have to shout myself hoarse."

It was the first time she had spoken to me; in fact, it was the first time, to all intents and purposes, I had ever heard her speak. And from the start I noticed how much her pronunciation resembled Alberto's. They both talked in the same way: slowly, as a rule, underlining particular and quite unimportant words, the real meaning and weight of which they alone seemed to know, and slurring oddly over others, which you might have thought much more important. This they considered their *real* language: their own special, inimitable, wholly private deformation of Italian. They even gave it a name: Finzi-Continian.

Slithering down the grassy slope, I ended up at the bottom of the garden wall. Although it was shady–a shade that stank high of stinging nettles and dung–it was hotter down there. And now she looked at me from above, her blonde head in the sun, as calm as if ours were not a casual, absolutely chance meeting, but as if, since we were small, we had met there more often than you could count.

"You're fussing," she said. "What does it matter, having to take an exam again in October?"

Obviously she was teasing me, and even despising me a little. It was pretty much what you might expect, after all, to happen to someone like me, the son of such commonplace, such "assimilated" parents: a semi-*goi*, in fact. What right had I to make such a fuss?

"I think you've got some rather funny ideas," I answered.

"Have I?" she said, and grinned. "Then will you just tell me, please, why you haven't been home for lunch today."

"How d'you know that?" I let slip.

"Aha, our spies told us. We've got our network, you know."

It was Meldolesi, I thought, it couldn't be anyone else (and in fact I was right). But what did it matter? Suddenly I realized that this business of my failure had slipped into second place, a childish matter that would settle itself.

"I say, how d'you manage to stay up there?" I asked. "Like at a window."

"I'm standing on my dear old ladder," she said, accentuating the syllables of "my dear old" in her usual possessive way.

A loud barking arose at this point from beyond the wall. Micòl turned her head and glanced over her left shoulder with a mixture of boredom and affection. She pulled a face at the dog, then turned to look at me.

"Bother," she remarked calmly. "That's Yor."

"What breed is he?"

"He's a Great Dane. He's only a year old but he practically weighs a ton. He's always trailing after me. I often try and cover up my tracks, but he always finds me after a bit, you can count on that. It's *ghastly*."

Then, as if following straight on:

"Would you like me to let you in?" she said. "If you like, I'll show you what to do right away."

Chapter Six

How many years have gone by since that remote June afternoon? Over thirty. And yet, if I shut my eyes, Micòl Finzi-Contini is still there, looking over the garden wall, watching me, talking to me. She was little more than a child in 1929, a thin fair thirteen-year-old with large light magnetic eyes, and I a stuck-up, dandified, extremely middle-class brat in short trousers, whom the first whiff of

trouble at school was enough to throw into the most
childish despair. We stared at each other. Above her
the sky was blue, all of a piece, a warm, already summer sky without a trace of cloud. Nothing could
change it, and nothing has, in fact, changed it, at least
in my memory.

"Well, d'you want to or don't you?" said Micòl.

"I . . . I'm not sure . . ." I started to say, pointing to
the wall. "It seems terribly high to me."

"Because you haven't seen it properly," she retorted
impatiently. "Look there, and there, and there," and
she pointed to make me see. "There are masses of
notches, and even a nail up here, at the top. I stuck it in
myself."

"Yes, there are footholds all right," I murmured
uncertainly, "but . . ."

"Footholds!" she broke in at once, and burst out
laughing, "I call them notches."

"Well, you're wrong, because they're called footholds," I said, acid and obstinate. "Anyone can see
you've never been up a mountain."

I have always suffered from dizziness, since I was a
child, and, although there was nothing to it, the climb
bothered me. When I was a child and my mother,
carrying Ernesto (Fanny was not yet born), took me
on to the Montagnone, and sat down on the big grassy
space opposite via Scandiana, from the top of which
you could make out the roof of our house, only just
distinguishable in the sea of roofs around the great hulk
of the church of Santa Maria in Vado, I was, I remember, always very scared when I escaped my mother's
vigilance and went over to the parapet that surrounded
the field on the side of the open country, peering
over into a gulf ninety feet deep. Someone was nearly

always going up or down those sheer, dizzying walls:
young labourers, peasants, bricklayers, each with a
bike across his shoulders; and old men too, whiskery
fishermen after frogs and catfish, loaded with rods and
baskets: all of them from Quacchio, Ponte della
Gradella, Coccomaro, Coccomarino, and Focomorto,
and all in a hurry, so that instead of going through
Porta San Giorgio or Porta San Giovanni (because in
those days the bastions were still all of a piece on that
side, with nowhere you could get through for at least
five kilometres), they took instead what they called the
Wall road. If they came out of town, having crossed
the field, they passed quite near me without looking
my way, then climbed over the parapet and dropped
over on the other side till the tips of their toes found a
foothold in the decrepit wall, and so got down to the
field below in a few minutes. If they came in from the
country, their eyes, stretched wide open, seemed to be
staring into mine, as I peeped timidly over the edge of
the parapet; but of course I was wrong to think so,
since all they were interested in was finding the best
foothold. In any case, while they were hanging over
the abyss like that—usually in pairs, one behind the
other—I would hear them chatting peacefully away
in dialect, just as if they were walking along a path
through the fields. How calm and strong and brave
they were!—I said to myself. After they had climbed
right up, till they were quite near my face, so near that
often, apart from being mirrored in their eyes, I
was submerged in their stinking wine-laden breath,
they grabbed the inner rim of the parapet with their
thick calloused fingers, and, emerging straight out of
space—oops!—there they were, safe and sound. I
should never manage such a thing—I said to myself

each time, as I watched them move away: filled with
admiration, but with a powerful dose of the creeps as
well.

Well, I felt something similar now, as I faced the
garden wall from the top of which Micòl Finzi-Contini
had invited me to climb. It certainly wasn't as high as
the bastions at the Montagnone. But it was smoother,
much less corroded by time and weather; and the
notches Micòl had pointed out to me barely showed.
And suppose–I thought–my head started spinning as I
climbed and I came crashing down? I might be killed
just the same.

And yet this wasn't really the reason why I still hesitated. What kept me back was a revulsion that differed
from the purely physical one of dizziness: it was ana-
logous, but different, and stronger. For a moment I
managed to regret my recent despair, my silly childish
tears at failing an old exam.

"And I can't quite see," I said, "why I should start
mountaineering right here. If you're inviting me in,
thanks very much, I'll accept with pleasure; but quite
honestly, it seems very much more comfortable to
go in through there"–and I raised my arm in the
direction of corso Ercole I–"through the gate. How
long will it take? With my bike I'll be there in a
minute."

I realized at once that my suggestion had not gone
down too well.

"Oh no, no . . ." said Micòl, twisting her face into an
expression of intense annoyance. "If you go through
there Perotti's bound to see you, and then it's good-bye
to all the fun."

"Perotti? Who's he?"

"The porter. You know, you may have noticed him,

he acts as our coachman and chauffeur as well. . . . If he sees you–and he can't help seeing you, because apart from the times he goes out with the carriage or the car, he's always there on guard, the old pig–I'll just have to take you to the house, afterwards. . . . And just tell me if . . . what d'you think?"

She looked straight into my eyes: serious, now, although very calm.

"Right," I said, turning my head, and jerking my chin at the bank, "but where shall I leave my bike? I can't possibly just leave it here abandoned! It's new, a Wolsit: with an electric lamp, a tool-bag, a pump, just think . . . if I let my bike be taken *as well*. . . ."

I said no more, suffering again at the thought of the inevitable meeting with my father. That very evening, as late as possible, I'd have to go home. I had no choice.

I turned to look at Micòl again. Without a word, she had sat up on the wall as I was talking, with her back to me; and now she lifted a leg decisively and sat astride it.

"What are you up to?" I said, surprised.

"I've got an idea, about the bike. And at the same time I can show you the best places to put your feet. Watch where I put mine. Look."

She vaulted nimbly over the wall, up there on top of it, and then, grabbing the big rusty nail she had shown me before with her right hand, she started coming down. She came slowly but surely, looking for footholds with the toes of her tennis shoes, first one and then the other, and always finding them without too much trouble. She came down beautifully. But before touching the ground, she missed a foothold and slithered. Luckily she fell on her feet; but she had hurt her fingers; besides which, as it scraped against the

wall, her pink linen dress, a kind of beach affair, had
torn a bit at one of the armpits.

"How stupid," she grumbled, blowing on her hand.
"It's the first time that's happened to me."

She had grazed her knee as well. She raised a piece
of her dress and showed an oddly white, strong thigh,
already a woman's, and leant over to examine the
graze. Two long blonde locks, among the lightest of
her hair, which had slipped out of the band that kept
it in place, fell forward and hid her forehead and her
eyes.

"How stupid," she repeated.

"Needs surgical spirit," I said mechanically, without
going near her, in the rather gloomy tone everyone in
my family used in similar circumstances.

"Surgical spirit my foot."

She licked the wound, fast: a kind of little affectionate kiss; and stood up again at once.

"Come on," she said, all red and dishevelled.

She turned and started climbing obliquely along the
sunny edge of the bank. With her right hand she pulled
herself along, hanging on to tufts of grass; while with
her left she kept taking the circular hairband on and
off, as fast as if she were combing her hair.

"See that hole over there?" she said to me, as soon
as we got to the top. "You can easily hide the bike in
there."

She pointed about fifty yards ahead, to one of those
grassy conical mounds, not more than two yards high,
and with the opening nearly always covered with
earth, found fairly often along the walls at Ferrara.
They looked a bit like the Etruscan *montarozzi* of the
Roman campagna; on a much smaller scale, of course.
But the often huge room below ground, which any

one of them may open into, has never been used to house the dead. The old defenders of the wall once kept their arms there: cannon, arquebuses, powder, and so on–and maybe those strange cannon-balls of rare marble that in the fifteenth and sixteenth century made the Ferrarese artillery so much feared in Europe. You can still see at the castle, decorating the main courtyard and the terraces.

"Who on earth would guess there was a new Wolsit under there? You'd have to know. Ever been inside?"

I shook my head.

"No? I have, hundreds of times. It's *gorgeous*."

She moved decisively, and I picked the Wolsit up from the ground, and followed her in silence.

I joined her at the opening. It was a sort of vertical crack, cut straight out of the neat grass cover of the mound: and so narrow that only one person could go in at a time. Immediately inside the floor sloped down; and you could see it for eight or ten yards, not more. Beyond that was shadowy. As if the tunnel ended against a black curtain.

Micòl leant forward to look, and then suddenly turned.

"You go down," she whispered, and smiled faintly, embarrassed. "I'd rather wait for you up here."

She stood on one side, her hands clasped behind her back, leaning against the grassy wall by the opening.

"You don't mind it, do you?" she asked, almost in a whisper.

"Oh, no," I lied, and leant down to lift the bike up on my back.

Without another word, I went past her into the mound.

I had to go slowly, because of the bicycle, apart from

everything else, and its right pedal kept banging into
the walls; and at first, for three or four yards at least,
I was quite blind, couldn't see a thing. About ten yards
from the opening, though ("Look out!" Micòl's
already distant voice shouted behind me at this point:
"Mind the steps!"), I began to make things out a bit.
The tunnel ended a little farther ahead: the floor
sloped down for a few yards, not more. And it was
from there, in fact, starting from a kind of landing
round which, before I got there, I could make out
something completely different–the steps Micòl had
told me about.

When I reached the landing, I paused a moment.

The childish fear of the dark and the unknown that
I had felt when I moved away from Micòl was gradually replaced, as I went below, by a no less childish
feeling of relief: as if, having got away from Micòl's
company in time, I had escaped a greater danger, the
greatest danger a boy of my age ("A boy of your age":
it was one of my father's favourite expressions) could
meet. Oh, yes–I thought now–when I went home
that evening my father might smack me. But I could
now face his whacks quite calmly. An exam to take
again in October: Micòl was right to laugh at me.
What was an exam in October compared with what–
and I trembled–might have happened to us down
there in the darkness? Maybe I'd have dared to kiss
Micòl: kiss her on the lips. And then? What would
have happened afterwards? In the films I'd seen, and in
novels, kisses just went on and on, long and passionate!
But in actual fact, in comparison with *the rest*, it
was only a moment, a moment that was really quite
unimportant, since, once lips had come together, and
mouths pretty well interpenetrated each other, the

thread of the narrative couldn't as a rule be taken up
until the following morning, or even until several days
later. All right, all right: but suppose Micòl and I had
got to the point of kissing like that–and the darkness
would obviously have made it easier–time would
have run quietly on after the kiss, with no providential
intervention from outside to help us land up suddenly
on the morning after. However should I have filled the
minutes, the hours? Oh, but it hadn't happened,
luckily. Just as well I'd saved myself.

I started going down the steps. A little light filtered
feebly in: I noticed it now. And partly through sight,
and partly through hearing (it didn't take much: a
bump against the wall with the bike, a heel slithering
down one of the steps, and the echo enlarged and multi-
plied the sound right away, giving an idea of spaces and
distances), I soon realized how enormous the place was.
It must have been a room about forty yards across, I
calculated, round, and with a dome-shaped roof at
least as high. A kind of overturned funnel. And who
knows: maybe through a system of secret passages it
was linked with other underground rooms of the same
kind–there must have been dozens of them inside the
bastions. Nothing easier.

The floor was an earth one, smooth, damp and com-
pact. I tripped over a brick, and then, groping my way
along the curve of the wall, trod on straw. I leant the
bike against the wall and sat down, one hand grasping
its wheel and the other arm round my knee. Only the
odd squeak and rustle broke the silence: rats, very
likely, or bats. . . .

And suppose it had happened? I thought. Would it
really have been so frightful, if it had?

It was pretty well certain I'd not have gone home

again, and my parents, and Otello Forti, and Sergio
Pavani, and all the others, including the police, would
have had a high old time searching for me! At first
they'd have dashed around, looking everywhere. Even
the newspapers would have talked about it, and fished
out all their usual notions: kidnapping, accident,
suicide, a secret dash abroad. Then little by little things
would have subsided. My parents would have calmed
down (after all, they'd still have Ernesto and Fanny
left), and the search would have been called off. And
the person who'd have paid for it most in the end
would be that stupid old crawthumper Fabiani, who'd
be packed off "to another seat of learning", as Meldolesi would put it, for a punishment. Where? Oh, to
Sicily or Sardinia, of course. And serve her jolly well
right! That way she'd learn, to her cost, not to be such
a sneaky old bitch.

As for me, as the others took it quietly, I'd take it
quietly myself. Outside, I could count on Micòl: she'd
see to bringing me food and anything else I needed.
She'd come to me every day, climbing the garden
wall, summer and winter. And every day we'd kiss,
in the dark: because I was her man, and she was my
woman.

And anyway, there was no law against my ever going outside again! In the daytime I'd sleep, of course,
breaking my slumbers only when I felt my lips
brushed by Micòl's, and then afterwards sleeping
again, with her in my arms. But at night, why at night
I could perfectly well make long sorties outside,
specially if I chose the early hours of the morning,
around one or two o'clock when everyone was asleep,
and practically no one was left in the streets. How
strange and terrible, but what fun as well, to go along

via Scandiana, and see our house again, see the windows of my bedroom, now used as a sitting-room;
hidden in the shadows some way away, peer at my
father coming home from the club at that very
moment, without the faintest glimmer of an idea that
I was alive, and watching him. He'd take the keys out
of his pocket, open the door, go inside, and then, quite
calmly, just as if I, his eldest son, had never existed,
slam the door shut.

And what about my mother? Couldn't I try, some
day or other, to let her know, through Micòl maybe,
that I wasn't dead? And see her again, before I got sick
of my underground existence and left Ferrara for
good? Why not? Of course I could!

How long I stayed there I don't know. Ten minutes,
maybe; maybe less. In any case I remember quite
definitely that as I went up the steps, and back into the
tunnel again (without the weight of the bike I was now
going fast), I kept on thinking, imagining. And what
about my mother?—I wondered. Would she, like
everyone else, forget me?

In the end I found myself out in the open; and Micòl
was no longer there, waiting for me where I'd left her
a bit before, but, as I saw almost at once, shielding my
eyes against the sunlight, she was up again astride the
garden wall of Barchetto del Duca.

She was arguing away with someone who was waiting at the bottom of the ladder, on the other side of
the wall: the coachman Perotti, very likely, or even
professór Ermanno himself. It was obvious: they'd
noticed the ladder leaning against the wall and had
realized at once how she'd been slipping off. Now they
were asking her to come down. And she wouldn't
make up her mind to obey.

At last she turned and saw me on top of the bank
and blew out her cheeks as if to say:

"Phew! At last!"

And her final look, before she disappeared on the
other side of the wall (a look that went with a smiling
wink: just like those she'd given me in the synagogue,
when she peeped at me under my father's *talèd*), was
for me.

PART
TWO

Chapter One

The time I managed to get properly inside, beyond the garden wall of Barchetto del Duca, and to push on among the trees and clearings of the great private wood until I reached the *magna domus* and the tennis court, was quite a lot later, almost ten years.

It was in 1938, about two months after the racial laws had been introduced. I remember it very well: one afternoon towards the end of October, a few minutes after we had got up from the table, I had a telephone call from Alberto Finzi-Contini. Was it true or wasn't it, he asked me at once, without any preamble (and the fact was we had had no chance of exchanging a word for over five years), was it true or wasn't it that I and "all the others" had had letters signed by marchese Barbicinti, vice-president and secretary of the *Eleonora d'Este* tennis club, expelling the lot of us from the club: in fact, "chucking us out"?

I denied it sharply: it wasn't true, there'd been no such letter; not to me, anyway.

But straight away, as if he thought my denial completely valueless, or actually hadn't been listening, he suggested I should come along to their house right away and play. If I didn't mind a plain earth court—he said—without much surround; if, above all, as I was

sure to be a much better player than they were, I'd
"deign to knock a ball about a bit" with him and Micòl
both of them would be delighted and "honoured".
And any afternoon would do for them, if I liked the
idea, he went on. Today, tomorrow, the day after tomorrow: I could come whenever I pleased and bring
along anyone I pleased, on Saturdays as well, of course.
Apart from the fact that he'd be staying in Ferrara at
least another month, as his term at the Polytechnic in
Milan wouldn't be starting before November 20th
(Micòl took it all much more calmly than he did, as a
rule: and this year, what with the excuse that she was
*fuori corso,** and had no need to turn up and get things
signed, heaven knows if she'd ever set foot in the university), wasn't this simply marvellous weather? As
long as it lasted, it would be a crime not to take advantage of it.

These last words were spoken with less conviction:
it seemed as if some unhappy thought had come to him
all at once, or else that, quite suddenly and without
reason, he was bored by the thought of my coming,
and hoped I'd take no notice of his invitation.

I thanked him, without promising anything definite.
Why had he telephoned? I wondered, with astonish-
ment, as I put back the receiver. Since he and his sister
had been sent to study outside Ferrara (Alberto in '33,
Micòl in '34: about the time professór Ermanno had
had permission from the Jewish community to do up

---

* *Fuori corso* is the name given to students who for some reason
do not manage to finish their course in the prescribed number of
years, but continue to attend the university while waiting to
pass their exams. The signatures Micòl no longer has to worry
about are those which the students have to obtain from their
teachers at the end of each term.

"for the use of his family and of those who might possibly be interested", the ex-Spanish synagogue incorporated in the buildings of the synagogue via Mazzini, since when the seat behind ours, in the Italian synagogue, had remained strictly empty) we had seen each other only very rarely, and always fleetingly and from a distance. We had become such strangers, during that time, that one morning in 1935, on the station at Bologna (I was in my second year at the university, reading Italian, and went there and back every day by train), when a tall dark pale youth with a plaid rug over his arm and a porter loaded with suitcases at his heels hurtled violently into me on platform one as he dashed for the just-leaving Milan express, I didn't even faintly recognize Alberto Finzi-Contini right away. When we reached the end of the train he turned to hurry the porter, at the same time giving me an absent-minded glance as I turned to protest and vanishing into the carriage. That time–I kept thinking–he hadn't even felt the need to greet me. And so why such smarmy friendliness now?

"Who was it?" asked my father, the minute I got back into the dining-room.

There was no one else in the room. He was sitting in the armchair beside the wireless, waiting anxiously, as usual, for the two o'clock news.

"Alberto Finzi-Contini."

"Who? The boy? Well, how condescending! And what does he want?"

He gazed at me with his blue, bewildered eyes, which had long ago lost hope of influencing me, or of guessing what was going through my head. He knew perfectly well–he told me with his eyes–that his questions annoyed me, that his everlasting efforts to poke his

nose into my life were indiscreet and unreasonable.
But, good God, wasn't he my father? And couldn't I
see how he'd aged, this last year? My mother and
Fanny he couldn't trust: they were women. Nor
Ernesto either: he was too small. So who was he to talk
to? Could I possibly not realize that I was just the one
he needed?

I clenched my teeth and told him what it was all
about.

"Well, are you going?"

He gave me no time to answer. Right away, warm-
ing up the way he did every time he got a chance of
dragging me into any kind of conversation – and if it
was on politics all the better – he plunged headlong into
"getting things straight".

Unfortunately it was true – he began burbling, tire-
lessly: on September 22nd, after the first official announcement on the 9th, all the newspapers had published that additional circular from the party secretary
about various "practical measures" the provincial
Federations should take right away with regard to us.
In future, "mixed marriages were to be strictly forbidden, all young people known to belong to the Jewish race were to be excluded from the state schools of
every kind and level", and denied the "high honour"
of compulsory military service; and we Jews could no
longer announce deaths in the newspaper, have our
names in the telephone directory, have Aryan servants,
or belong to "leisure-time clubs" of any kind. And yet,
in spite of that. . . .

"I hope you're not going to trot out the usual stuff,"
I broke in at this point, shaking my head.

"What stuff?"

"About Mussolini being more *good* than Hitler."

"I know, I know," he said. "But you've got to admit it. Hitler's a bloody lunatic, whereas Mussolini may be a turncoat and as Machiavellian as you like, but . . ."

I broke in again, unable to restrain an impatient gesture. Did he or didn't he agree – I asked, rather abruptly – with the thesis of Leon Trotsky's essay, which I'd handed him a few days ago?

I was referring to an article published in an old number of the *Nouvelle Revue Française,* several complete years of which I kept jealously in my room. This was how it happened: for some reason, I can't remember what, I had been rude to my father. He was hurt, and sulked, and, as I wanted to re-establish normal relations as soon as possible, I thought the best thing to do was tell him what I had been reading just lately. Flattered by this sign of my good opinion, my father didn't wait to be asked twice. At once he read, or rather devoured, the article, underlining away in pencil, smothering the margins of the pages with closely written notes. In fact – he had told me explicitly – what "that old scoundrel, Lenin's chum" had written had been a real revelation to him as well.

"But of course I agree!" he exclaimed, pleased to find me ready to discuss things, and disconcerted at the same time. "There's no doubt about it, Trotsky's marvellous at polemics. And what fire, what language! He's quite capable of having written the article in French himself. Yes, the fact is," and he smiled proudly, "those Russian and Polish Jews mayn't be terribly likeable, but they've always had a perfect genius for languages. They've got it in their blood."

"Stop worrying about languages, we're talking about concepts," I broke in, with a touch of schoolmasterish sharpness I regretted at once.

The article was quite clear, I went on more gently. Capitalism, in its phase of imperialistic expansion, couldn't help being intolerant of all national minorities, and of the Jews, who are *the* minority, by definition. Now, in the light of this general theory (Trotsky's essay was written in 1931, we mustn't forget: the year in which Hitler's real rise to power began), what did it matter that Mussolini, as a person, was better than Hitler? And was he, in fact, any better, even as a person?

"I see, I see . . ." my father kept repeating softly, while I spoke.

His eyelids drooped, his face was twisted, as if he had something painful to endure. At last, when he was quite certain I had nothing more to add, he laid a hand on my knee.

He had understood—he told me yet again, slowly opening his eyes. But just let him speak: he thought things looked too black to me, too catastrophic.

Why wouldn't I admit, in fact, that after the announcement on September 9th, and even after the additional circular of the 22nd, things, at least at Ferrara, had in fact carried on pretty well the way they'd done before? It was perfectly true—he admitted, with a melancholy smile—during the last month, out of the 750 members of our community no one important enough to deserve space in the *Corriere ferrarese* had died (just a couple of old women in the home in via Vittoria, if he wasn't mistaken: one called Saralvo, and the other Rietti; and old girl Rietti wasn't even from hereabouts, but from some Mantuan village: Sabbioneta, Viadana, Pomponesco, or something like that). But let's be fair: the telephone directories hadn't been withdrawn to be reprinted, purged; not a single *havertà*,* maid, cook, nurse, or old housekeeper, serving in any of our families, had suddenly discovered a "racial conscience" and packed her bags; the *Circolo dei Commercianti*, where the lawyer Lattes had been vice-president for over ten years – and which, as I must know, he still frequented, undisturbed, almost daily – hadn't so far asked anyone to resign. And had Bruno Lattes, Leone Lattes's boy, been expelled from the tennis club, by any chance? Without a thought for my brother Ernesto, who was always gaping at me, openmouthed, poor boy, and imitating me as if I was heaven knows what *hahàm*,† I'd stopped going to the tennis club: and I was wrong, I must really let him say it, quite wrong to shut myself away, and segregate myself, and refuse to see anyone, and then, with the excuse of the university and my season ticket, slink off to Bologna three or four times a week. (I no longer wanted to see even Nino Bottecchiari, Sergio Pavani, and Otello Forti, my inseparable friends until a year ago, here in Ferrara; and you couldn't say they'd let a month go by without ringing me up, sometimes one and sometimes another of them, poor chaps!) Whereas look at young Lattes, now. As far as one gathered from the sports pages of the *Corriere ferrarese*, he wasn't just taking part regularly in the last tournament of the season, which was now in full swing, but getting on splendidly in the mixed doubles, where he was partnered by that pretty Adriana Trentini, whose father was chief engineer of the province: they'd won three matches easily, and were now getting ready for the semi-finals. Oh, no, you could say what you liked about old Barbicinti: that he was rather too keen on

* "Maidservant" in Hebrew.
† Hebrew term meaning "sage" or "scholar".

his own (pretty modest) family arms, for instance, and
not quite keen enough on the grammar of the articles
promoting tennis which the party's Federal Secretary
got him to write every now and then for the *Corriere
ferrarese*. But that he was a man of integrity and honour,
for all that, not the least bit hostile to the Jews, and
pretty mildly fascist–and as he said "fascist" my
father's voice quivered, very slightly and timidly
quivered–no one could doubt or dispute.

Now, about Alberto's invitation, and the behaviour
of the Finzi-Continis in general: why, like a bolt from
the blue, this sudden excitement of theirs, this sudden
passionate need to get in touch?

What had happened last week at the synagogue, at
Roshashanà, was odd enough already (as usual, I'd refused to come: and once again, if I'd forgive him saying
so, I'd been wrong). Yes, it had been pretty odd
already, bang at the height of the service, and with the
pews full to bursting, to see Ermanno Finzi-Contini all
of a sudden, and his wife and mother-in-law, followed
by the two children and the inevitable Herrera uncles
from Venice–the whole tribe, in fact, male and female
all bundled in together–solemnly re-entering the
Italian synagogue after a good five years of disdainful
isolation in the Spanish synagogue: and looking so
smug and so benign, too, for all the world as if they
meant their presence to reward and *forgive* not just
everyone present but the entire Jewish community.
But, quite obviously, this hadn't been enough. They'd
now got to the pitch of actually inviting people to
their house: to Barchetto del Duca, just think of that
now, where since Josette Artom's day no outsider had
set foot, except strictly in emergencies. And would I
like to hear just why? Well, obviously, because they

were pleased with what was happening, *halti** as they'd always been (all right, all right, they'd been against fascism, but *halti* most of all), *deep down they actually liked the racial laws*! If they'd only been good Zionists, now. At least, seeing that here, in Italy and in Ferrara, they had always felt so much out of things, so much on loan as it were, they could have taken advantage of the situation to transfer themselves to Israel once and for all. But no. Apart from digging out a bit of money for Israel just occasionally – and there was nothing very odd about that, in any case – they'd never done a thing. When they really forked out, it was always for some aristocratic nonsense: like the time in '33, when, to find an *ehàl* and a *parochèt* worthy of appearing in their own personal synagogue (authentic sephardic vestments, for goodness sake, and not Portuguese or Catalan or Provençal, but Spanish – and the right size!) they pushed off by car, followed by a big lorry, no less, as far as Cherasco, in the province of Cuneo, a village where a now extinct Jewish community had lived until 1910, or thereabouts, and where only the cemetery still functioned because a few families from Turin, who'd sprung from the place, Debenedettis, Momilianos, Terracinis, still kept on burying their dead there. And Josette Artom, now, Alberto and Micòl's grandmother, in her day had kept bringing in palms and eucalyptus trees from the botanical garden in Rome, the one at the foot of the Gianicolo: and so – just so that the carts could get through easily, but for plain swank as well, quite obviously – she'd made her husband, poor Menotti, widen the way in through the garden wall of Barchetto del Duca, so that the gate was at least twice as big as any other in Corso Ercole I d'Este. Well, what

* Plural of *halto,* "bigots".

happens is that if you're crazy about collecting – things, plants, everything – you end up wanting to collect people as well. And if the Finis-Continis sighed for the ghetto (clearly that's where they'd like to see everyone shut in: and quite prepared, in view of this fine ideal, to carve Barchetto del Duca into a kind of *kibbuz*, under their own exalted patronage): well, they were perfectly free to do so, let them go ahead. But just in case they did, he'd always preferred Palestine. Or, even better, Alaska, Tierra del Fuego, or Madagascar. . . .

It was Tuesday. I could not say why a few days later, on the Saturday of that same week, I made up my mind to do exactly the opposite of what my father wanted. It was not, I think, the usual quite mechanical opposition that makes children disobey their parents: perhaps all that made me suddenly take out my racket and tennis clothes, which had been lying in a drawer for over a year, was the bright day, and the delicate caressing air of an unusually sunny afternoon in early autumn.

In any case, several things had happened in the meantime.

First of all, two days after Alberto's telephone call I think it was, which makes it the Thursday, the letter "accepting" my resignation from the *Eleonora d'Este* tennis club in fact arrived. Typewritten, but long-windedly signed at the bottom by N.H.* marchese Ippolito Barbicinti, the registered letter, sent express, indulged in nothing personal or particular. Its few dry lines, clumsily echoing the bureaucratic style, went straight to the point: simply mentioned the Federal Secretary's "definite orders", and went on to say that the future presence of my "distinguished self" was "inadmisible" (*sic*) at the tennis club. (Could marchese

* Abbreviation of *Nobil Huomo*, a title of nobility.

Barbicinti ever refrain from seasoning his prose with spelling mistakes? Obviously not. But noticing them and laughing at them was a bit harder this time than it had been.)

Secondly, the following day I think, Friday, I had another telephone call from the *magna domus*; and not from Alberto, this time, but from Micòl.

It resulted in a long, in fact enormously long conversation: the tone of which Micòl especially kept up as that of an ordinary, ironical, rambling chat between two seasoned university students between whom, as children, there might have been just a pinch of tenderness, but who now, after something like ten years, want nothing but a sober homecoming.

"How long since we met?"

"Five years or more."

"And what are you like, these days?"

"Ugly. A red-nosed old maid. And what about you? Which reminds me: d'you know that I read . . ."

"Read what?"

"In the papers. That you were in that Art and Culture racket at Venice a couple of years ago. Flying the flag, weren't you? Pretty good! But of course you were always frightfully good at Italian, right from the start. Meldolesi was just *mad* about some of the essays you wrote at school. I think he even brought some along to read to us."

"That's nothing to laugh at. And what about you, what are you doing?"

"Nothing. I ought to have taken my degree in English at Venice last June. But what the hell. Laziness permitting, let's hope I do this year. D'you think they'll let those who are *fuori corso** finish just the same?"

* See note on page 66.

"Sorry to disappoint you, but I'm perfectly sure they will. Have you picked your thesis yet?"

"Well, yes, I have: on Emily Dickinson, you know, that nineteenth-century American poet, a rather ghastly old girl. . . . But what am I to do? I'd have to trail round after the prof, and spend whole fortnights at Venice, and after a bit the Pearl of the Laguna makes me. . . . In all these years I've been there as little as possible. And besides, to be quite honest, I've never been terribly good at that sort of thing."

"Liar. Liar and snob."

"No, honestly, I *swear*. And to go and sit there like a good little girl this autumn – well, I feel less like it than ever. I say, d'you know what I'd really like to do, instead of burying myself in the library?"

"Let's hear."

"Play tennis, dance and flirt, just imagine!"

"Well, that sounds harmless enough, dancing and tennis included, but you could perfectly well do it all in Venice, if you liked."

"Oh, I bet . . . with my uncles' housekeeper always at my heels!"

"Well, tennis at any rate you can perfectly well manage. Now me, for instance, the minute I can I dash off by train to Bologna to . . ."

"Oh, come off it, you're off to see your girl friend. Confess, now."

"No, no. I've got to take my degree next year as well. I still don't know whether it'll be in the history of art or in Italian, but I think it'll be Italian, now. And when I feel like it, I just allow myself an hour's tennis. I hire a court, in via del Cestello or at the Littoriale (they're hard courts, as you can imagine: with warm showers, a bar, all mod. cons. . . .) and nobody can object. Why don't you do the same, in Venice?"

"The trouble is that for playing tennis or dancing you need a *partner,** and in Venice I just don't know a soul that's right. And then I must say, Venice is all very beautiful, I'm not arguing that, but I just don't fit in there. I feel on the hop, an outsider . . . a bit like being abroad."

"D'you sleep at your uncles' house?"

"Yes, of course: sleep and eat."

"I see. Well, I'm grateful to you for not coming to the university for that business two years ago. Honestly. I feel it's the blackest page in my life."

"Why? After all. . . . D'you know that at one point as I knew you'd be there I actually had the idea of going along to cheer . . . you know, just to raise the flag. . . . But listen: d'you remember that time on the Wall of the Angels out here, the year you failed in maths? Poor old thing, you must have been crying your eyes out: they looked like nothing on earth! I wanted to cheer you up. I even had the idea of making you climb over the wall into the garden. Well, why didn't you? I know that you *didn't* come in, but I can't remember why."

"Because someone surprised us, bang in the middle."

"Ah, yes, Perotti, that old hound the gardener."

"Gardener? Coachman, I thought he was."

"Gardener, coachman, chauffeur, porter, everything."

"Is he still alive?"

"Goodness, yes!"

"And the dog, the real dog, the one that barked?"

"Who? Yor?"

"Yes, the Great Dane."

* In English in the original.

"Oh, he's alive and kicking as well."

She repeated her brother's invitation ("I don't know if Albert's rung you up, but why don't you come here for a game with us?"); but without pressing it, and, unlike him, without referring to marchese Barbicinti's letter. She mentioned nothing, in fact, but the simple pleasure of seeing each other after so long, and of enjoying together, in spite of everything against it, whatever was enjoyable in the season.

Chapter Two

I was not the only one invited.

When, that Saturday afternoon, having avoided corso Giovecca and the middle of town, I came out at the end of corso Ercole I from piazza della Certosa, I immediately noticed a small group of tennis players in the shade outside the Finzi-Continis' gate. There were four boys and a girl, all with bikes like me; and they all, as I realized at once, were regular players at the *Eleonora d'Este* tennis club. Unlike me, they were all dressed for the game, in gaudy pullovers and shorts: only one, who was older than the others, about twenty-five, and was smoking a pipe, and whom I didn't know even by sight, was wearing white linen trousers and a brown corduroy jacket. Eager to be admitted, they must have already pressed the bell at the gate several times, but with no result, that was obvious: and in

light-hearted protest, and quite oblivious of the very
occasional passers-by, they stopped talking and laughing, now and then, and all together, rhythmically, rang
their bicycle bells.

I braked, tempted to turn back. But it was now too
late. Two or three of them had already seen me, had
stopped ringing their bells and were looking at me
curiously. One of them, whom as I approached I suddenly recognized as Bruno Lattes, was actually signalling to me, brandishing his racket at the end of a long
skinny arm. He wanted me to recognize him (we had
never been friends: he was two years younger than
me, so even at Bologna University we'd never met
very often), and at the same time was trying to urge
me on. I stopped right in front of him.

"Hello," I said. "What's this get-together about? Is
the big tournament over? Or are these all the van-
quished?"

I had talked to them all and to no one in particular,
and I think I was grinning, my left arm on the smooth
oak of the gate, my feet still on the pedals. As I did so,
I looked them over: Adriana Trentini, fine coppery
hair loose on her shoulders, long and admittedly marvellous legs, but an over-white skin curiously splotched
with red, as always happened when she was hot; the
silent youth with the pipe, linen trousers and brown
jacket (who was he? definitely not from Ferrara!—I
said to myself at once); the other two boys, very much
younger than him and even than Adriana: maybe still
at school or at the technical institute, and for that very
reason, since they had "come on" in the past year,
during which I had gradually drawn away from every
circle in town, hardly known to me at all; and lastly
Bruno, there in front of me, taller and drier than ever,

and, with his dark skin, more than ever like a young,
vibrant, worried Negro: in such a state of nervous excitement, even that day, that he managed to transmit
it to me through the light contact between the front
tyres of our bikes.

The inevitable flicker of Jewish understanding passed
between us, quickly; as, half anxious and half revolted,
I had already foreseen it would. Then I went on, looking meaningly at him:

"I hope you asked *signor* Barbicinti's permission before coming to play somewhere else."

The unknown outsider, obviously surprised by my
sarcastic tone, or perhaps uneasy, made a small movement beside me. Instead of soothing me, this excited
me even more.

"Now come on and tell me," I insisted. "Are you
allowed to do this, or have you just slunk off?"

"What are you talking about!" Adriana burst out,
with her usual thoughtlessness: it was quite innocent,
of course, but no less offensive for that. "Don't you
know what happened last Wednesday, during the
finals of the mixed doubles? Don't tell me you weren't
there: and do drop this eternal Vittorio Alfieri pose of
yours. I saw you in the audience, while we were playing, with my own two eyes."

"Well, I wasn't there," I retorted drily. "It's at least
a year since I've set foot in the place."

"And why?"

"Because I was sure I'd be chucked out sooner or
later whatever I did. And I wasn't mistaken, as it turns
out: here's the letter expelling me."

I took the envelope out of my jacket pocket.

"I expect you've had one too," I said, turning to
Bruno.

It was only at this point that Adriana seemed to remember that I was in the same condition as her partner in the mixed doubles. She was clearly upset; but the thought of having something important to tell me, which I obviously knew nothing about, quickly made her forget it.

Something very "unpleasant" had happened, she told me, while one of the two youngest boys again pressed the small sharp bell-push of black horn. Maybe I didn't know, but in the tournament that was just over at the tennis club, she and Bruno had got right into the finals, no less – which was something neither of them had ever even dreamt of. Well then: the final match was in full swing, and once again things had begun taking the most incredible turn (enough to make everyone goggle, quite honestly: Désirée Baggioli and Claudio Montemezzo, two real stars at the game, in trouble with a couple of non-classed players: even to the point of losing the first set ten-eight, and being outmatched in the second as well!), when suddenly marchese Barbicinti, who was judge and umpire of the tournament, on his own initiative interrupted the match. It was six o'clock, admittedly, and they couldn't see too well. But not so dark that they couldn't have carried on for at least another two games! Heavens, what a way to behave! At four–two in the second set of an important match, no one had the right to shout "stop" out of the blue, to march on to the court waving his arms and declaring the match suspended "because of the darkness", and putting the whole thing off till the following afternoon. Besides, the marchese wasn't acting in good faith at all, that was perfectly obvious. And if she, Adriana, hadn't noticed him, at the end of the first set, in an excited huddle with that

creep Gino Cariani, secretary of the G.U.F.* (they'd
moved a bit away from the crowd, next to the little
building where the changing rooms were); and
Cariani, perhaps so as not to be noticed, had his back
turned to the tennis court as if to say: "Carry on, carry
on with your game, it's not you we're talking about":
all she'd have needed was the marchese's face as he
bent down to open the gate into the courts, so pale and
bewildered she'd never seen anything like it–a real
proper death's-head!–to guess that the gathering darkness was only a pretext, a feeble excuse. Anyway, how
could you possibly doubt it? The interrupted match
was never even mentioned, as next morning Bruno
got exactly the same express letter as I'd had, the one
I'd wanted to show her. And she, Adriana, had been so
disgusted by the whole business–so outraged, apart
from everything else, at anyone having the bad taste to
mix sport and politics–that she'd sworn never to set
foot in the *Eleonora d'Este* club again. Suppose they'd
got something against Bruno, well, they could have
forbidden him to take part in the tournament; said
frankly: "Things being the way they are, we're terribly
sorry, but we can't accept you for it." But once the
tournament had started, in fact was nearly over and he
was within a hair's breadth of winning one of the
matches, they just shouldn't have behaved the way they
did. Four–two! What pigs! The sort of piggery you
might expect from Zulus, not from anyone supposed
to be educated and civilized!

Adriana Trentini spoke excitedly, getting more and
more worked up, and Bruno butted in occasionally,
adding details.

According to him, it was Cariani's fault the match

* Gruppo universitario fascista–Fascist university youth movement.

was broken up, and if you knew him at all it was just exactly what you might expect. It was all too obvious: an "undersized little runt" like that, with his tubercular chest and the frame of a shrimp, whose one thought, from the minute he got into the G.U.F., was to get ahead, and who never missed a chance, in public or in private, to lick the Federal Secretary's boots (hadn't I ever seen him at the Caffè della Borsa, on the rare occasions when he managed to sit down at the same table as the "old ruffians of the *Bombamano*"?* He fairly puffed himself up, cursed and swore outrageously, but the minute consul Bolognesi, or old Calamity, or some other bigwig in the group contradicted him, he'd have his tail between his legs in no time, doing the most menial jobs, like running to the tobacconist's in the theatre arcade to buy the Federal Secretary a packet of fags, or ringing up old Calamity's home to tell his ex-washerwoman wife when the great man would be home, and such, to curry favour and get himself forgiven): a worm like that obviously wouldn't lose the chance, you could bet your life on that, of cutting a dash in the party once again! Marchese Barbicinti was what he was: a distinguished old chap, no doubt about that, but rather hard up, submissive, and anything but a hero. If they kept him on to run the tennis club, it was because he looked good in the part, and above all because of his name, which they may have thought had some quite remarkable snob-value. Now it must have been ridiculously easy for Cariani to give the poor old nobleman the shakes. He may even have said to him: "And what about tomorrow? Have you thought of tomorrow evening, marchese, when the Federal Secre-

---

* "Hand grenade squad." The name of the shock troops to which the "old ruffians" had belonged.

tary will be coming here for the ball, and he'll find he's
got to give the silver cup and the Roman salute and the
rest of it to a . . . Lattes? I'd say it'll mean a scandal, and
a great fat one at that. And trouble; endless trouble. If
I was in your shoes, seeing it's getting dark, I wouldn't
think twice about stopping the match." It wouldn't
need any more than that, as sure as eggs is eggs, to
make the marchese break things up the way he had, so
grotesquely and so disagreeably.

Before Adriana and Bruno had finished bringing me
up to date on what had happened (at one point
Adriana even managed to introduce me to the stranger:
who was called Malnate, Giampiero Malnate, and
came from Milan, a newly-qualified chemist working
in one of the new synthetic rubber factories in the industrial zone), the gate was finally opened; and a fat,
thick-set man of about sixty appeared, with short grey
hair which the early afternoon sun, streaming in
through the gate's narrow vertical opening, lit with
metallic gleams, and a short grey moustache under a
fleshy, purplish nose: a bit like Hitler, it struck me, the
nose and moustache. Yes, it was old Perotti himself,
gardener, coachman, chauffeur, porter, everything, as
Micòl had told me, and on the whole not the least bit
changed since our schooldays, when he'd sat up on his
box, waiting impassively for the dark and ominous den
that had swallowed up his two fearless, smiling young
charges to give them back at last, no less serene and sure
of themselves, to the coach, all glass, varnish, nickel-
plating, padded cloth and valuable wood–really just
like a precious casket–the upkeep and driving of which
was his sole responsibility. The small eyes, for instance,
which were grey as well and sharp, glittering with
hard, peasant Venetian shrewdness, laughed good-

naturedly under the thick, nearly black eyelashes: exactly as they had done before. But what were they laughing at now? The fact that we'd been left hanging about for at least ten minutes? Or was he laughing at himself, for turning up in a striped jacket and white cotton gloves: brand new, the gloves were, and probably put on for the occasion.

So we went in, and, once inside the gate that the officious Perotti clanged straight away behind us, we were greeted by the hefty barking of Yor, the black and white "harlequin". He came trotting down the drive towards us, looking tired and not the slightest bit alarming. But Bruno and Adriana shut up at once.

"He won't bite, will he?" Adriana asked, scared.

"Don't you worry, signorina," said Perotti. "Whatever could he bite these days, with the three or four teeth he's got left? Polenta, that's about all. . . ."

And while the decrepit Yor, who had taken up a sculptural pose in the middle of the drive, stared intensely at us with his cold expressionless eyes, one of them dark and the other light blue, Perotti started to apologize. He was sorry to have kept us waiting, he said, but it wasn't his fault; the trouble was the electric power, that sometimes failed (luckily signorina Micòl had noticed and sent him straight off to see whether we'd turned up, by any chance), and the distance— over half a kilometre, no less. He couldn't ride a bike, but once the signorina got something into her head. . . .

He sighed, raised his eyes to heaven, smiled once more for some reason, his thin lips parting to show a set of teeth much sounder and more complete than Yor's; and pointed out the drive that after about a hundred yards continued through a thicket of rattan canes.

Even with a bike–he warned us–it always took three
or four minutes, just to get to the "mansion".

Chapter Three

W e were really very lucky with the weather.
For ten or twelve days it stayed perfect,
strung in a kind of magical suspense, a
glassy, glowing stillness and sweetness peculiar to some
of our autumns. It was hot in the garden: almost like
summer. Anyone who liked to could carry on playing
tennis until half-past five or later, without any risk of
the evening dampness, so lethal in November, damag-
ing the racket strings. By that hour, of course, you
could hardly see on the court. But the light still gilded
the grassy slopes of the Wall of the Angels below there,
distant slopes that, especially on Sundays, were crowded
with boys chasing balls, nurses knitting beside their
prams, soldiers off duty, courting couples looking for
a place to cuddle; and this final bit of daylight urged us
to carry on, knocking up even if we were playing
almost blind. The day was not yet over, it was still
worth staying a little longer.

We came back every afternoon, at first ringing up
beforehand, and then not even doing that; and always
the same group, with the exception, now and then, of
Giampiero Malnate, who had known Alberto in Milan

since 1933, and, contrary to what I had thought the first day when I met him outside the Finzi-Continis' gate, not only had never before seen the four young people he was with, but had nothing at all to do with the *Eleonora d'Este* tennis club or its vice-president and secretary, marchese Ippolito Barbicinti, either. The days seemed too glorious, yet somehow too much threatened by winter, now so close. It seemed a crime to lose a single one, and without arranging it, we always turned up at about two o'clock, straight after lunch. At the beginning we often met outside the gate, as we had done the first day, waiting for Perotti to come and open it. Later, after about a week, once the internal telephone and the lock that worked by remote control had been installed, we found getting into the garden was no longer a problem, and so as a rule we turned up in driblets, just as we happened to get there. I myself never missed an afternoon, even to make one of my usual bolts to Bologna. But neither did the others if I remember rightly: Bruno Lattes, Adriana Trentini, Carletto Sani, Tonino Collevatti, and, in the last few days, my brother Ernesto and three or four other boys and girls. The only one, as I said, who came less regularly was "that" Giampiero Malnate (it was Micòl who started this way of calling him, putting the "that" before his name: and soon we all did). He had to keep factory hours: admittedly they weren't very strict – he confessed one day – since the factory where he worked, which the Fascist regime had forced on the Montecatini at the time of the "iniquitous Sanctions", and kept going purely for propaganda purposes, hadn't produced a single kilo; but still, there were factory hours to keep. In any case, he was never away for more than a couple of days at a time. On the other hand he

was the only one, apart from me, who wasn't ex-
aggeratedly keen on tennis (to be honest, he played
pretty badly) and was often quite content, when he
turned up on his bike after work, about five o'clock, to
umpire a match or to sit a little way off, smoking his
pipe and talking to his friend Alberto.

However things were with us, our hosts were even
keener than we were. We might get there very early,
when the distant piazza clock was still striking two, but
however early we arrived we were sure to find them
already on the court, never playing together now, as
they had been that first Saturday when we came out on
the clearing behind the house where the tennis court
was, but checking that everything was in order, the
net at the right height, the ground well rolled and
watered, the balls in good condition, or else lying
motionless on deck-chairs wearing large straw hats,
sun-bathing. As hosts, they couldn't have been better,
quite honestly. Although obviously their interest in
tennis purely as physical exercise, as a sport, was pretty
moderate, they stayed on until the very last game—
generally both of them and always at least one or the
other–and never left early with the excuse that they
had an engagement, or something to finish off, or
weren't feeling well. Sometimes, in fact, it was they
who, in almost total darkness, kept insisting on us
having "just another knock-up, the last!" and urging
anyone who was leaving back on to the court.

The court, as Carletto Sani and Tonino Collevatti
had noticed at once the first day, couldn't really be
called much good.

Being matter-of-fact fifteen-year-olds, too young to
have ever trodden any courts but those marchese Barbicinti was so justifiably proud of, they had immedi-

ately, without even bothering to lower their voices so that the owners of the house shouldn't hear, started listing the defects of this "potato patch" (as one of them put it, making a scornful face). These were: practically no surround, particularly behind the back lines; a white surface, terribly badly drained, which the least bit of rain would turn into a swamp; and no evergreen hedge along the wire-netting fence.

But as soon as they finished their game (Micòl couldn't stop her brother catching up on her to make it five all: at which point they gave up) Alberto and Micòl outdid each other in denouncing these same defects without the slightest reserve, in fact with a kind of sarcastic, self-wounding enthusiasm. Oh, of course – Micòl said gaily, while she was still rubbing her hot face with a Turkish towel – for people like us, who were used to the red courts of the club, it must be very hard to feel comfortable in their dusty "potato patch"! And then what about the surround? How could we play with so little space behind us? It was just too bad what we'd got down to, poor dears! But she had a perfectly clear conscience about it. She'd told her father endlessly they'd got to move the netting at the ends at least three yards back, and at the sides about two yards. But there it was! Her father, with his typical farmer's outlook, that considered anything uncultivated so much waste land, kept putting it off, counting on the fact that she and Alberto had played on a dump like that since they were children, they could jolly well carry on playing there when they were grown up. But things were different now; they had guests now, "very distinguished guests": so that she'd go back into the fray with renewed energy, bothering and tormenting her "hoary parent" so much that by next spring there was a 99 per cent likelihood she and Alberto would be able to offer us "something decent" at last. She was grinning quite openly, so that there was nothing we could do but refute what she said, in chorus, and assure her that everything was fine as it was, that the court didn't matter in the least and in any case it wasn't at all bad, and to make up for it, we praised its surroundings, which meant the park, compared with which–it was Bruno Lattes who said it: at the very moment in which, their "fight to the death" suspended, Micòl and Alberto came up to us–the other privately owned parks in town, including duke Massari's, faded into prettified suburban backyards.

But, quite honestly, the tennis court was not "decent", and besides, as there was just a single one, it meant we had to rest too long between games. So, promptly at four every afternoon–above all, perhaps, to prevent the two fifteen-year-olds in our hetero-geneous group regretting the much more intensive time, sportively speaking, they might be spending under marchese Barbicinti's wing–Perotti invariably turned up, his bull-like neck stiff and red with the effort of carrying a large silver tray in his gloved hands.

And it was overflowing: with buttered anchovy rolls, and smoked salmon, and caviare, and *foie gras*, and ham; with little *vol-au-vents* stuffed with minced chicken in *bechamel* sauce; with minute *buricchi** which must have come from the expensive little kosher shop which signora Betsabea, the famous signora Betsabea (Da Fano), had kept for years in via Mazzini, to the delight and glory of the entire town. Nor was that all. Friend Perotti still had to lay the contents of the tray on the cane table specially prepared for it at the

* A kind of Jewish pastry filled with mince or almond paste.

side entrance to the court, under a big umbrella with red and blue segments, and one of his daughters would come and join him, either Dirce or Gina, both about the same age as Micòl, and both maids "in the house", Dirce as housemaid, Gina as cook (the two boys, Titta and Bepi, the first about thirty, the second eighteen, looked after the park, doing double duty in the flower and kitchen gardens. We had never managed to catch more than occasional glimpses of them in the distance, bending over their work, and as we shot past them on our bikes their ironical blue eyes turned on us, flashing). The daughter would come pulling a rubber-wheeled trolley loaded with carafes, jugs, glasses and cups, behind her along the path that led from the *magna domus* to the tennis court. In the jugs made of china and pewter there was tea, milk, and coffee; in the steamy carafes of Bohemian glass, lemonade, fruit juice, and *Skiwasser*: this last a thirst-quenching drink made of equal parts water and raspberry juice, with a slice of lemon and a few grapes thrown in, which Micòl liked better than anything, and of which she was particularly proud.

Oh, that *Skiwasser*! In the pauses between games, Micòl would bite into a roll that she always, not without a show of religious nonconformity, picked out among the ham ones and pour down a whole glass of her "dear old drink" at a go, urging us all the time to help ourselves, "in honour of the defunct Austro-Hungarian empire", she laughed. The recipe, she told us, "had actually been given to her in Austria, at Offgastein, in the winter of '34, the only winter in which she and Alberto, "in coalition", had managed to get away for a fortnight's skiing on their own. And although the *Skiwasser*, as the name showed, was a

winter drink, and so should really be served boiling
hot, even in Austria some people still took it this
way in summer, in an iced "version", and without
lemon; in which case they called it *Himbeerwasser* instead.

But we should really note, she added, raising a finger
with comical emphasis; the bits of grape–"terribly
important"!–she herself, on her own initiative, had
introduced into the classic Tyrolean recipe. It had been
all her own idea: and she was really attached to it, it
was no laughing matter. The grape represented Italy's
special contribution to the high, holy cause of *Skiwasser*, or more precisely, the special "Italian variant,
not to say Ferrarese, not to say . . . etc. etc.".

Chapter Four

The other members of the household took a little
longer to be seen.

As far as they were concerned, in fact, an
odd thing happened on the first day, which, when I
remembered it about the middle of the following week,
when neither professór Ermanno nor signora Olga had
yet appeared, made me suspect that those Adriana
Trentini lumped together as the "old guard" had
unanimously decided to steer clear of the tennis court:

perhaps so as not to embarrass us, so as not to change
the nature of parties that were not really parties at all,
but just a matter of youngsters getting together in the
garden.

This odd thing happened right at the beginning,
shortly after we were greeted by Perotti and Yor, who
stayed there gazing after us as we cycled away along
the drive. Having crossed the Panfilio canal by a peculiar, hefty black girder bridge, our cycling patrol got
to within a hundred yards of the solitary neo-Gothic
pile of the *magna domus*, or rather of a gloomy,
gravelled open space entirely in shadow that opened
up in front of it, and everyone's attention was drawn
to two people right in the middle of this space: an
old lady sitting in an armchair, propped up by a pile
of cushions, and a buxom young blonde, who looked
like a maid, standing behind her. As soon as she had
seen us approaching, the old lady was seized by a kind
of trembling, after which she immediately began
making terrific signals with her arms, which meant
no, we mustn't come any farther, we mustn't come
across towards the gravel where she was, as there was
nothing but the house behind her; we must turn left,
along the path covered by an archway of climbing
roses which she showed us, at the end of which (Micòl
and Alberto were already playing: couldn't we hear,
from where we were, the regular thud of their rackets
as they hit the ball?) we would automatically find the
tennis court. It was signora Regina Herrera, signora
Olga's mother. I recognized her at once from the peculiar intense whiteness of her thick hair gathered round
a pad at the back, hair I had always admired every time
I happened to catch a glimpse of it through the grating
of the woman's part at the synagogue. She waved her

arms and hands with petulant energy, at the same time making a sign to the girl, who turned out to be Dirce, to help her up: she was tired of being there, and wanted to go indoors. And the maid obeyed zealously, at once.

One evening, all the same, against all our expectations, professór Ermanno and signora Olga did turn up. They looked as if they were passing the tennis court just by chance, after a long walk in the park. They were arm in arm. He, shorter than his wife, and very much more bent than he had been ten years before, at the time of our whispered talks from bench to bench in the Italian synagogue, was wearing one of his usual pale, light-weight linen suits, with a black ribboned panama hat pulled down over his thick pince-nez, and, as he walked, leaning on a bamboo cane. She, all in black, was carrying a large bunch of chrysanthemums obviously picked in some remote part of the garden, during their walk. She held them clasped sidelong to her bosom, holding them in her right arm in a tenderly possessive, almost maternal way. Although she was still straight, and a full head taller than her husband, she too seemed to have aged a great deal. Her hair had become completely grey, an ugly, dismal grey; under her bony, jutting forehead, her intensely black eyes still glittered with the same fanatical, sickly glow as before.

Those of us sitting round the umbrella rose and those who were playing stopped.

"Don't get up," said professór Ermanno, in his pleasant, musical voice. "Please don't disturb yourselves. Do go on playing."

Of course he wasn't obeyed. Micòl and Alberto introduced us at once: Micòl did most of it. Apart from giving our full names, she stopped to say what she supposed would arouse her father's interest in each one of us: what we were studying and doing, in the first place. She started with me and Bruno Lattes, speaking of us both in a remote, noticeably objective tone: as if to stop her father, in those special circumstances, from showing the least sign of special friendships and preferences. We were the two "literary ones in the gang", two "really bright ones". Then she went on to Malnate, joking about his "rare" passion for chemistry which had made him leave a town as full of resources as Milan ("*Milàn l'è on gran Milàn!**") to come and bury himself in a "poky hole" like Ferrara.

"He works in the industrial zone," explained Alberto, simply and seriously. "In one of the Montecatini factories."

"They're meant to produce synthetic rubber," Micòl went on, "but it seems they've not managed it yet."

Possibly afraid her ironic tones might hurt the stranger, her father hastened to speak.

"You were at the university with Alberto, weren't you?" he said, speaking directly to Malnate.

"Well, in a way we were," said Malnate. "But actually I was three years ahead of him, and in a different faculty too. But we were the best of friends all the same."

"I know, I know. My son's often spoken about you. He's told us he was often at your home, and that your parents were extremely kind to him on several occasions. Will you thank them for us, when you see them again? In the meantime we're delighted to have you here, in our house. And do come back, won't you? . . . Come back whenever you like."

* "What a big city Milan is!": Milanese dialect.

He turned to Micòl and asked her, indicating
Adriana:

"And this young lady, who is she? If I'm not mistaken she's a Zanardi. Or am I wrong?"

The conversation dragged on like that, until all the
introductions were completed, including those of Carletto Sani and Tonino Collevatti, whom Micòl defined
as the two "white hopes" of tennis in Ferrara. In the
end, professór Ermanno and signora Olga, who had
stayed by her husband the whole time without saying
a word, just smiling benevolently at times, walked
away towards the house still arm in arm.

Although professór Ermanno had said good-bye
with a cordial: "See you again soon," no one would
have dreamt of taking this very seriously.

But the following Sunday, while Adriana Trentini
and Bruno Lattes on one side, and Désirée Baggioli and
Claudio Montemezzo on the other, were playing a
tremendously keen match in which, according to
Adriana, who had got it up, they would repay her and
Bruno, "morally at least", for the ugly trick played on
them by marchese Barbicinti (but things didn't seem
to be going quite the same way this time: Adriana
and Bruno were losing, and pretty definitely so): suddenly, towards the end of the match, the entire "old
guard" appeared along the path of climbing roses, one
behind the other. They made quite a procession. At the
head of it, professór Ermanno and his wife. There followed, shortly afterwards, the Herrera uncles from
Venice: one, with a cigarette between his thick protu-
berant lips, hands clasped behind his back, looking
around with the faintly embarrassed air of a townsman
landed reluctantly in the country; the other a few yards
behind him, with signora Regina on his arm, regula-

ting his pace to his mother's very slow one. If the T.B. specialist and the engineer were in Ferrara–I said to myself–they must be here for some religious celebration. But which? After Roshashanà, which fell in October, I couldn't remember any other feasts in the autumn. Could it be Succoth? Very likely. Unless Federico, the engineer, had equally probably been expelled from the State Railways, which suggested a special family council had been called. . . .

They sat down tidily, making hardly any noise. The only exception was signora Regina. As she was being settled into a deck-chair, she said two or three words in the family slang in her loud, deaf-woman's voice; complaining, I think, of the garden's dampness (*"mucha umidità"*) at that hour. But her son Federico, the railway engineer, was still beside her, looking after her, and, no less loudly (but his tone was neutral: the tone of voice my father also used occasionally, in *mixed* company, when he wanted to communicate with a member of the family, and no one else), quickly quietened her, telling her to be *callàda*, quiet. Couldn't she see the *musafir*?

I leant down to Micòl's ear.

"Instead of saying 'be *callàda*', we say 'be *sciadok*'. But what does *musafir* mean?"

"Guest," she whispered back to me. "*Goi*, though."

And she laughed, childishly covering her mouth with one hand and winking: Micòl-1929-style.

Later, at the end of the match, and after the "new arrivals", Désirée Baggioli and Claudio Montemezzo had been introduced in their turn, I happened to find myself a little apart with professór Ermanno. In the park, the day was as usual snuffing out in diffused, milky shadows. I had moved away about ten steps.

Behind me I heard Micòl's sharp voice dominating the others. Heaven knows who she was grumbling at now, and why.

I looked towards the Wall of the Angels, still lit by the sun.

*"Era già l'ora che volge il disìo,"** a soft ironical voice declaimed beside me.

I turned, surprised. It was professór Ermanno, smiling good-naturedly at me, pleased to have made me start. He took me delicately by the arm, and then very slowly, pausing occasionally, we took a turn right round the tennis court, making a very wide circle well away from the wire-netting around it. In the end, though, so as not to risk ending up where we started, among the friends and relations, we turned back. Backwards and forwards: we repeated the manœuvre several times, in the gathering darkness. Meantime we talked: or rather he talked most of the time, professór Ermanno.

He began asking me what I thought of the tennis court, whether it really seemed to me so frightful. Micòl had quite made up her mind: she said it needed remaking completely, up to modern standards. But he doubted it: maybe his "darling earthquake" was exaggerating, as usual, maybe they wouldn't have to make a clean sweep of the whole thing, the way she wanted to.

"Whichever way it is," he went on, "it'll start raining in a few days, there's no point in deluding ourselves. We'd better put off everything until next year, don't you agree?"

Then he went on to ask me what I was doing, what

* "Now in the hour that melts with homesick yearning": Dante, *Purgatory* (translated by D. Sayers).

I meant to do in the immediate future. And how my parents were.

While he asked me about "Papa", I noticed two things: first of all, that he found it hard to use the "*tu*" in addressing me, in fact, shortly afterwards he stopped suddenly and told me so explicitly, and immediately I asked him, very warmly and sincerely, to do so please, and told him he simply mustn't call me "*lei*" or I'd be hurt. Secondly: that the interest and respect in his voice and face as I told him about my father's health (in his eyes, chiefly: the glasses of his spectacles, enlarging them, accentuated the seriousness and mildness of their expression), was not at all forced, not in the least hypocritical. He urged me to remember him to my father. And to congratulate him, too: on the many trees planted in our cemetery, since the community had entrusted him with the task of seeing to it. In fact: would pines be any use? Cedars of Lebanon? Firs? Weeping willows? I was to ask my father. If by any chance they were of use (and in this day and age, with the methods of modern agriculture, transplanting even large-trunked trees was no trouble at all), he'd be very happy to put whatever number we wanted at our disposal. Why, it was a marvellous idea! Filled with large beautiful plants, our cemetery in time would rival the one of San Niccolò del Lido, in Venice.

"Don't you know it?"

I said I didn't.

"Oh, but you must, you really *must* try and visit it as soon as possible!" he said, with great liveliness. "It's a national monument! Besides, you who are a literary man will obviously remember how Giovanni Prati's *Edmenegarda* begins."

Once more I was forced to admit my ignorance.

"Well," he went on, "Prati starts his *Edmenegarda*
right there, in the Jewish cemetery of the Lido, which
in the nineteenth century was considered one of the
most romantic spots in Italy. Mind, though: if and
when you go there don't forget to tell the caretaker–
he's the one who's got the keys of the gate–that you
mean to visit the old cemetery, mind you say the old
cemetery, where no one's been buried since the eigh-
teenth century, and not the other one, the modern one,
which is beside it but separate. I discovered it in 1905,
just think. Although I was twice your age, I was still a
bachelor. I was living in Venice (I'd been settled there
for two years) and the time I didn't spend at the Record
Office, at campo dei Frari, rummaging through the
manuscripts concerned with the various so-called
nations the Jewish community in Venice was divided
into in the sixteenth and seventeenth centuries–the
Levantine nation, the western, the German, the Italian
–I spent there: sometimes even in winter. The fact is
I hardly ever went there alone"–here he smiled–"and
in a way, deciphering the stones in the cemetery one by
one, many of which go back to the beginning of the
sixteenth century, and are written in Spanish and Portuguese, I was carrying on my archives work out of
doors. Oh, those were exquisite afternoons . . . such
peace, such serenity . . . with the little gate, facing the
lagoon, which opened only for us. We actually became
engaged there, Olga and I."

He was silent for a while. I took advantage of it to
ask him what was the exact object of his researches in
the Record Office.

"At first I started off with the idea of writing a history of the Jews in Venice," he answered. "A subject
suggested to me by Olga herself, which Roth, the

(Jewish) Englishman Cecil Roth, dealt with so brilliantly ten years later. Then as so often happens to historians who are too much . . . enamoured of their work, some seventeenth-century documents that happened to fall into my hands absorbed my interest completely, and ended up by carrying me away from the idea. I'll tell you about it, I'll tell you about it if you come back . . . it's really like a novel, in every way . . . In any case, instead of a fat historical volume, in two years all I managed to put together—apart from a wife, of course—were two pamphlets: one, which I think is still useful, where I collected all the inscriptions in the cemetery, and one where I wrote about those seventeenth-century papers I mentioned, but just like that, putting down the facts and not trying to interpret them in any way. Would you be interested in seeing them? You would? Then one of these days I'll give myself the pleasure of presenting you with copies of them, then. But, forgetting that for the moment: do please go along to the Jewish cemetery at the Lido! It's well worth it, you'll see. You'll find it exactly the same as it was thirty-five years ago: identically the same."

We went slowly back towards the tennis court. By the look of it, there was nobody left there. And yet, in almost complete darkness, Micòl and Carletto Sani were still playing. Micòl was groaning: that the boy was making her run too much, that he was not being "a gentleman", and that the darkness was, quite frankly, "a bit much".

"Micòl tells me you aren't sure whether to take your degree in the history of art or in Italian," professór Ermanno was saying to me, in the meantime. "Or have you now made up your mind?"

I answered that I had, that I'd finally decided on a

thesis in Italian. My uncertainty, I explained, was due simply to the fact that until a few days ago I had hoped to be able to take my degree under Longhi, professor of the History of Art, and instead, at the last minute, professór Longhi had asked for and obtained leave of absence from teaching for two years. The thesis I had in mind to undertake under his guidance was on a group of Ferrarese painters in the second half of the sixteenth century and the beginning of the seventeenth: Scarsellino, Bastianino, Bastarolo, Bonone, Galetti, Calzolaretto. Only under Longhi would I have been able to do anything worth while on such a subject. And as Longhi had got the ministry's permission to take two years off, I would rather do any old thesis, in Italian.

He listened to me, thoughtfully.

"Longhi?" he asked in the end, looking doubtful. "Who's he? Have they *already* appointed the new professor to the chair of the History of Art?"

I didn't understand.

"Why, yes," he insisted. "I've always heard the Professor of the History of Art at Bologna is Igino Benvenuto Supino, one of the shining lights of Italian Jewry. So . . ."

So he had been – I interrupted – so he had been: until 1933. After which, Roberto Longhi took over in '34, when Supino retired on account of his age. Didn't he know – I went on, pleased to catch him slipping up over his facts as well – didn't he know Roberto Longhi's fundamental essay on Piero della Francesca? And his others on Caravaggio and his school? And the *Officina ferrarese*, a work which had aroused so much interest in '33, at the time of the Renaissance exhibition held here in the same year, at the Diamanti palace?

If I'd written the thesis, I'd have based myself on the final pages of the *Officina*, which just touched on the theme: in a masterly way, certainly, but without going deeply into it.

I talked, and professor Ermanno, more bent than ever, listened to me in silence. What was he thinking of? Of the number of "shining lights" Italian Jewry had given the universities since the unification of Italy? Very likely.

But suddenly I saw him grow animated.

Looking round and lowering his voice to a stifled whisper, neither more nor less than as if he were going to share a state secret with me, he told me the great news; that he owned a group of unpublished letters from Carducci, letters written by the poet to his mother in 1875. Would I be interested to see them?–he asked me. If by any chance I thought they would make a suitable subject for a thesis for my degree in Italian, he would be very happy to put them at my disposal.

Thinking of Meldolesi, I couldn't help smiling. What about the essay to send to the *Nuova Antologia*? After all his talk, hadn't he cooked up anything? Poor Meldolesi: a few years ago he had been transferred to the Minghetti school at Bologna–delighted, of course! Some day or other I must really go along and see him. . . .

In spite of the darkness, professór Ermanno realized I was smiling.

"Oh, I know, I know," he said, "you youngsters haven't taken Giosue Carducci very seriously for some time now. I know perfectly well you even prefer Pascoli or D'Annunzio."

It was easy to persuade him that I had smiled for

quite another reason – that is, from disappointment. If only I'd known there were some unpublished letters of Carducci's in Ferrara! Instead of suggesting a thesis on Panzacchi to Professor Calcaterra, as unfortunately I'd already done, I could perfectly well have suggested a "Ferrarese Carducci", of undoubtedly greater interest. But maybe, if I spoke frankly to professor Calcaterra, who was extremely nice, maybe I could still manage to change over from Panzacchi to Carducci without losing too much face.

"When will you be getting your degree?" professór Ermanno asked me at last.

"Well, in June next year, I hope. But don't forget I'm *fuori corso** myself."

He nodded several times, in silence.

"Are you?" he sighed, at last. "Well, nothing wrong with that."

And he made a vague gesture with his hand, as if to say that, with what was happening, we had plenty of time before us, his children and I; too much, in fact.

But my father was right: basically he didn't seem to mind very much about it at all. On the contrary.

* See note on page 66.

Chapter Five

Micòl wanted to be the one to show me the garden. She was quite determined. "I think I've a right to!" she grinned, looking at me. Not the first day. I had played tennis until late, and it was Alberto, when he had stopped playing with his sister, who took me to a kind of miniature Alpine hut half-hidden in the middle of a copse of fir trees and about a hundred yards from the tennis court (*Hütte*, he and Micòl called it), in which hut or *Hütte*, which was used as a changing room, I was able to change, and then, in the gathering darkness, take a warm shower and dress.

But the following day things went differently. We played doubles, with Adriani Trentini and Bruno Lattes against the two youngest boys (Malnate, sitting up high on the umpire's chair, playing the patient score-keeper), and it soon started to look like one of those matches that never come to an end.

"What shall we do?" Micòl said to me suddenly, jumping up. "I've got a feeling that before taking over from these four you and I and Alberto and our friend from Milan will have to wait a good hour. Listen: why don't we take the chance of a first look round the garden?" As soon as the court was free–she went on–Alberto would obviously remember us and give us a call. He'd pop three fingers in his mouth and produce one of his famous whistles.

She turned to Alberto, who was dozing there beside us on a third deck-chair in the sun, his face hidden under a countryman's straw hat.

"Hey, you old pasha, that's true, isn't it?"

Without disarranging himself, Alberto nodded.

We went off. Yes, her brother was terrific–Micòl went on to explain. When they were needed, he could bring out such powerful whistles that the kind shepherds made were just footling, by comparison. Wasn't it odd?–someone like him. You'd never think so, to look at him. And yet. . . . The mystery was where he got all that breath from!

Thus, nearly always to avoid waiting between games, we started our long excursions together.

At first we used to take our bicycles. A bike was indispensable–Micòl decided straight away–if I wanted to get a clear enough idea of the whole place. The garden was about ten hectares, and the roads through it, large and small, added up to six kilometres all together. But apart from that, without bikes it would have been out of the question to get far enough west, for instance, to see where she and Alberto as children used to go and watch the trains shunting in the station! If we walked as far as that we might hear Alberto's "fog-horn" and not be able to get back fast enough.

So that first day we went to watch the trains shunting in the station. And then? Then we went back. We went round the tennis court, crossed the open space in front of the *magna domus* (deserted, as usual, and sadder than ever), and, beyond the black girder bridge over the Panfilio canal, went back along the drive as far as the tunnel of rattan canes and the gate on to Corso

Ercole I. There, Micòl insisted on our turning left,
along a path that followed the entire garden wall; at
first on the side of the Wall of the Angels, so that in a
quarter of an hour we came back to the side of the park
from which you could see the station; and then on the
opposite side, which was much more wooded, and
rather glum and melancholy, running along the whole
length of the deserted via Arianuova. We were there,
in fact, toiling through clumps of ferns, stinging
nettles, and thorn bushes, when suddenly, across the
thick barrier of tree-trunks, came Alberto's shepherd
whistle, enormously far away, calling us quickly back
to "hard labour".

With a few variations of the route, we explored ex-
tensively again, three or four times, in the afternoons
that followed.

When the roads and paths were wide enough to
allow it we pedalled along side by side. I often rode
holding on with one hand, resting the other on her
handlebars. In the meantime we talked: about trees,
mostly, at least at the beginning.

I knew nothing about them, or practically nothing,
which never ceased to astonish Micòl. She looked at
me as if I were a monster.

"How can you possibly be so ignorant?" she kept
exclaiming. "Why, you must have done a bit of botany
at school, even!"

"Now, sir," she would ask, already preparing to
raise her eyebrows in the face of some new enormity,
"let's hear just what sort of tree you'd say that one
over there was?"

She could name them all: from honest elms and
home-grown limes to the rarest exotic plants, African,
Asian, American, that only a specialist could have

identified; since there was everything at Barchetto del Duca, simply everything. I always answered at random, in any case: partly because I was really quite unable to tell an elm from a lime, and partly because I realized there was nothing she enjoyed so much as hearing me make these howlers.

It seemed absurd to her that someone like me should exist in the world, someone who wholly lacked her own feeling of passionate admiration for trees, "great, strong, and thoughtful trees". How could I fail to *understand*? How could I go on living without *feeling*? At the end of the tennis court clearing, for instance, west of the court, there was a group of seven very tall slim *Washingtoniae graciles*, or desert palms, isolated from the rest of the growth behind them (dark trees with thick trunks, European forest trees: oaks, holm oaks, plane trees, horse-chestnuts), with a fine stretch of grass around them. Well, every time we passed in that direction on our bicycles, Micòl always had some new loving thing to say about the *Washingtoniae*.

"There they are, my seven old darlings," she might say. "Look at those impressive old beards of theirs!"

Seriously—she insisted—didn't they seem to me, even to me, like the seven hermits of the Thebaid, dried by the sun and by fasting? What elegance, what "holiness", in their dark, dry, bent, scaly trunks! Honestly, they looked like the legs of so many John the Baptists, fed on nothing but locusts.

But it wasn't only the exotic trees she liked: the palms of various species, the *Howaeniae dulces*, which produced deformed tubers full of a honey-flavoured pulp, the American aloe shaped like the candelabra of the *menoràh*, which—she told me—flowered only once every twenty or twenty-five years, and then died; the eucalyptus, the *Zelkoviae sinicae*, with their small green trunks flecked with gold (she never told me why, but she felt curiously uneasy about the eucalyptus, as if through the years something not at all pleasant had happened between them and her, something that mustn't be brought up again).

For an enormous plane tree, with a whitish, blotchy trunk thicker than that of almost any other tree in the garden, and, I think, the whole province, her admiration overflowed into reverence. Of course, it wasn't "grandmother Josette" who had planted it; but Ercole I d'Este himself, maybe, or Lucretia Borgia.

"D'you realize? It's nearly five hundred years old!" she murmured, her eyes widening. "Just imagine all the things it must have seen, since it came into the world!"

And it seemed as if it had eyes like ours, the great ugly beast, that gigantic old plane tree: eyes to see us as well as ears to hear us.

For the fruit trees, too, that grew on a wide strip of land right below the Wall of the Angels, sheltered from the north winds and open to the sun, Micòl felt an affection—I had noticed—very much like hers for Perotti and all the members of his family. She talked to me about those humble domestic trees with the same kindliness and the same patience; and very often bringing out a bit of dialect, the dialect which, in dealing with people, she used only with Perotti, or Titta and Bepi, when we happened to meet them and stopped to exchange a few words. Her custom, every time, was to pause at a large plum tree, with foliage as thick and trunk as powerful as an oak: her favourite. The sour plums, *i brógn sèrbi*, it produced—she told me—

had seemed to her extraordinary as a child. In those days she preferred them to any Lindt chocolates. Then, when she was about sixteen she suddenly stopped wanting them, and didn't like them any more, and now she preferred chocolate, Lindt or non-Lindt (but bitter chocolate, only the bitter stuff!). She called apples *i pum*, figs *i figh*, apricots *i mugnàgh*, and peaches *i pèrsagh*. Only dialect was suitable when she spoke of these things. Only dialect words allowed her, when she spoke of trees and fruit, to twist her lips in the half tender, half scornful expression prompted by the heart.

Later, when the trips of inspection were done, we started on our "pious pilgrimages". And since all pilgrimages, according to Micòl, must be made on foot (else whatever sort of pilgrimages were they?), we stopped using bicycles, and went on foot, almost always accompanied, step by step, by Yor.

To start with I was taken to see a small solitary landing-stage on the Panfilio canal, hidden among a thick growth of willows, white poplars, and arum lilies. From that minute wharf, with a mossy red-brick bench running all round it, you could very likely, in the old days, sail along to the River Po and the Castle Moat. And she and Alberto used to sail off from there when they were children – Micòl told me – and row away for ages in a canoe with two paddles. They'd never actually got to the foot of the Castle towers, in the middle of town, in their boat (as I knew, nowadays the Panfilio canal reached the Castle Moat underground). But they'd got to the River Po, right opposite the Isola Bianca! Did I like the place? she asked finally. Actually they couldn't think of using the canoe any longer: it had fallen to bits, and was reduced to a kind of dust-

covered "ghost ship"; some day, if she remembered to
take me, I could see its carcass in the coach-house. But
she'd always gone on using the harbour bench: always,
always. It was her secret refuge. It was an ideal place,
apart from everything else, to come and work peacefully for exams, when it started getting hot.

Another time we ended up at the Perottis'. They
lived in a real tenant farmer's house, with hayloft and
cowshed, half-way between the big house and the fruit
trees dominated by the Wall of the Angels.

We were received by old Perotti's wife, Vittorina,
a faded *arzdóra** of indefinable age, sad and cadaver-
ously thin, and by Italia, the wife of the eldest son,
Titta, a strong fat woman of thirty from Codigoro
with watery blue eyes and red hair. She sat at the front
door on a straw chair, surrounded by chickens, giving
suck, and Micòl bent down to caress the baby.

"Well now, when are you going to ask me to eat your
bean soup again?" she asked Vittorina, in dialect.

"Whenever you like, *sgnurina*. So long as you're
happy . . ."

"We really must, one of these days. Vittorina makes
the most *terrific* bean soup," she said, turning to me.
"With bacon, of course. . . ."

She laughed, and then:

"Like to have a look at the cowshed? We've got six
cows, no less."

Vittorina went ahead, and we followed her to the
cowshed. The *arzdóra* opened the door with a large
key she kept in the pocket of her black apron, then
stood aside to let us in. As we went into the cowshed, I
realized she was looking furtively at us: worried, I felt,
and secretly satisfied.

* "Housewife": Ferrarese dialect.

A third pilgrimage was given over to the place
sacred to the *"vert paradis des amours enfantines"*.

We had gone past it repeatedly in the last few days
on our bikes, but without ever stopping. There was the
exact point of the garden wall – Micòl now said, showing
it to me with her finger – where she used to prop up the
ladder; and there were the notches ("yes, sir, notches!")
which she used when, as sometimes happened, the
ladder wasn't available.

"Don't you think we ought to put up a small com-
memorative plaque here?" she asked me.

"I expect you've already got the inscription worked
out."

"More or less: 'Here – escaping the vigilance of two
enormous ugly dogs. . . .' "

"Hey, stop. You were talking about a small plaque,
but I've got a feeling this inscription would need a
stone the size of the Victory Bulletin one. The second
line's too long."

So we quarrelled over it. I played the part of the pig-
headed interrupter, and Micòl, raising her voice and behaving babyishly, accused me of my "usual pedantry".
It was obvious – she cried – that I *must* have suspected
her intention of not even mentioning me in her inscription, and so, out of pure jealousy, I was refusing to
listen to her.

Then we calmed down. Once more she began talking to me about when she and Alberto were children.
If I really wanted to know the truth, both she and
Alberto had always felt enormously envious of people
like me who were lucky enough to go to state schools.
Did I believe her? They even got to the point of waiting impatiently for exam time each year, just for the
fun of going to school themselves.

"But why, if you liked going to school so much, were you always taught at home?" I asked.

"Papa and Mama, Mama above all, just wouldn't hear of school. Mama's always had an obsession about germs. She said schools were made just to spread the most frightful diseases, and it was never the slightest use Uncle Giulio trying to make her see it wasn't true, every time he came here. Uncle Giulio used to tease her; but although he's a doctor, he believes in medicine only in a very relative sort of way, in fact he believes in the inevitability and usefulness of illness. As you can imagine he didn't get much of a hearing. from Mama, who has practically never put her nose outside the door since poor Guido, our older brother who died before Alberto and I were born, in 1914. Later on we rebelled a bit, of course; we both managed to go to the university, and even skiing in Austria one winter, as I think I've already told you. But when we were children what could we do? I often escaped (Alberto didn't; he's always been very much quieter than me, very much more obedient). But one day I stayed away rather too long, wandering around on the city walls with a gang of boys I'd made friends with, who gave me rides on the bars of their bikes, and when I got home I found Mama and Papa in such despair that ever since (because Micòl's a good sort really, she's got a heart of gold!), ever since then I decided to be good, and never escaped again. The only relapse was in June 1929, in honour of you, kind sir!"

"And to think I imagined I was the only one!" I sighed.

"Well, if you weren't the only one you were certainly the last. And besides: I never asked anyone else to come into the garden!"

"Honestly?"

"Quite honestly. I always looked in your direction in the synagogue. . . . When you turned round to talk to Papa and Alberto your eyes were so blue! In my heart I'd even given you a nickname."

"A nickname? What was it?"

"Celestino."

"*Che fece per viltade il gran rifiuto . . .*"* I stammered.

"Exactly!" she exclaimed, laughing. "In any case, I think that for a while I actually had just the least little thing about you!"

"And then?"

"Then life came between us."

"But what a notion, fixing up a synagogue all for yourselves. Why was it: still scared of germs?"

"Well . . . sort of . . ." she said.

"What d'you mean, sort of?"

But I couldn't get her to confess the truth. I knew perfectly well why professór Ermanno had asked permission to do up the Spanish synagogue for himself and his family, in 1933: it was the shameful, shameful and grotesque occasion when the Party was opened to all comers, that decided him. But she kept saying that once again the determining factor had been her mother's wishes. The Herreras in Venice belonged to the Spanish school. Her mother, her grandmother Regina and her uncles Giulio and Federico had always been terribly keen on the family traditions. So Papa, to please Mama . . .

"But why have you now come back to the Italian synagogue?" I objected. "I wasn't there on the evening

* "The coward spirit of the man who made/The great refusal": Dante, *Hell* (translated by Dorothy Sayers). The reference is to Pope Celestine V.

of Roshashanà: it's three years since I set foot in the synagogue. But my father, who was there, described the scene in the minutest detail."

"Oh, don't worry, your absence has been very much observed, Mr. Freethinker!" she replied. "By me, too."

Then she grew serious again:

"Well, why not . . . we're all in the same boat now. I think myself that at this point, staying there on our own and making all those distinctions still would be pretty ridiculous."

Another day, the last day, it started to rain, and while the others went to the *Hütte*, playing cards and ping-pong, the pair of us, careless of a soaking, ran half-way across the park to shelter in the coach-house. The coach-house was at present functioning only as a coach-house, Micòl had told me. At one time, though, half of it had been made into a gym, with poles, ropes, balancing boards, rings, wall bars, etc.: all with the sole object of allowing her and Alberto to be well prepared for the yearly physical education exam as well. Certainly the lessons professór Anacleto Zaccarini, who'd been pensioned off for some time and was over eighty (imagine!), gave them twice a week weren't terribly serious. But they were fun anyway, possibly more fun than any of the others. Micòl never forgot to take a bottle of Bosco wine into the gym. And old Zaccarini, his red nose and cheeks growing gradually more and more purple, drank it slowly to the very last drop. Sometimes, when he left on winter evenings, he actually seemed to send out a glow of his own.

It was a long low building of dark brick, with two side windows, strongly barred, an overhanging tile roof, and its walls almost completely hidden by ivy. Not far from Perotti's barn and the squarish glass of a greenhouse, you approached it through a wide, carefully painted green gate that faced in the direction of the big house, away from the Wall of the Angels.

We stopped for a while outside it, leaning against the gate. The rain was pouring down in long oblique lines on the lawns, on the great green clumps of trees, on everything. It was cold. Teeth chattering, we looked around. The spell in which the season had so far been strung was irreparably broken.

"Shall we go in?" I asked at last. "It'll be warmer inside."

Inside the enormous room, at the end of which, in the half light, there gleamed the top of two pale polished gymnasium poles that reached the ceiling, an odd smell hung about: a mixture of petrol and lubricating oil, old dust and citrus fruits. It was a gorgeous smell, Micòl said at once, noticing me sniffing it curiously. She liked it a lot as well. And she showed me, up against one of the side walls, a tall set of shelves in dark wood, loaded with large round yellow fruit I had never seen before, bigger than oranges and lemons. Grapefruit, put there to ripen, she explained to me: grown in the greenhouse. Hadn't I ever eaten them?– she asked me, taking one and offering it to me to smell. What a shame she hadn't got a knife to cut it in two "hemispheres". Its juice had a hybrid flavour, like that of oranges and lemons. With just a touch of bitterness, besides, that was all its own.

The middle of the coach-house was taken up with two vehicles, side by side: a long grey Dilambda* and a blue carriage, the shafts of which, standing on end, were only slightly lower than the gym poles behind it.

"We don't use the carriage any more now," said

* A type of Lancia car.

Micòl. "The few times Papa has to go into the country
he goes by car. And so do Alberto and I, when we have
to go away: he to Milan and me to Venice. It's that
everlasting Perotti who takes us to the station. He's the
only one here who can drive (and he's a ghastly
driver), apart from Alberto. I can't, I haven't got my
licence yet. But I'm going to get it, I really must make
up my mind to get it next spring, provided they don't
get it into their heads to make difficulties about that
as well. . . . The trouble is it simply gulps down petrol,
the huge old thing!"

Then, going up to the carriage, which looked hardly
less shining and efficient than the car:

"Recognize it?" she asked.

She opened a door, got in, sat down: and then, tapping the cloth of the seat beside her, invited me to do
the same.

I climbed up and sat down on her left. And no sooner
had I sat down than, rolling slowly on its hinges by
pure force of inertia, the door slammed shut on its own
with a dry, precise click, like a trap.

The rain beating on the roof of the coach-house was
no longer audible. We really seemed to be in a little
parlour: a small, stifling parlour.

"How beautifully you keep it," I said, without managing to control a sudden emotion that was reflected
by a slight tremor in my voice. "It still seems new. The
only thing missing are the flowers in the vase."

"Oh, Perotti still puts those in, when he goes out
with my grandmother."

"So you do still use it!"

"Not more than two or three times a year, and then
only to take a few turns round the garden."

"And what about the horse? Still the same one?"

"Yes, the same old Star. He's twenty-two. Didn't you see him at the end of the stable the other day? He's half blind now, but harnessed in here he still looks pretty . . . frightful."

She burst out laughing, shaking her head.

"Perotti's got a real mania about this carriage," she went on harshly, "and it's mostly to please him (he hates and despises cars: you can't imagine how much!) that we occasionally let him drive my grandmother around a bit. Every ten days or a fortnight he comes in here with buckets of water, sponges, doeskin, and rug-beaters; and that explains the miracle, that's why the carriage, especially when you see it in the half light, still doesn't look too bad."

"Too bad?" I protested. "Why, it looks brand new!"

She snorted crossly.

"Don't talk nonsense, for heaven's sake!"

Moved by some unforeseeable impulse, she had shifted abruptly away from me, and was crouched up in her corner, gazing frowningly ahead, her features pinched by an expression of curious spleen.

For a few minutes we stayed like that, in silence. Then, without changing her position, clasped round her sun-burnt knees as if she were feeling very cold (she was wearing shorts and a cotton jersey, with a pullover knotted round her neck by the sleeves), Micòl went on talking.

"Perotti spends so much time and elbow grease on this wretched old ruin," she said. "No, believe me: here, where it's practically dark, you might think it's a miracle, but outside, in daylight, there's no getting away from it, you can see any number of flaws straight away: the varnish has gone in places, the spokes and hubs of the wheels are worm-eaten, and the cloth on this seat (you can't see it now, but I guarantee it) is worn out, in places it's just like a spider's web. And so I wonder what's the point of all Perotti's *struma**? Is it worth it? The poor old fellow keeps trying to get Papa to let him re-varnish the whole thing, restoring it in the way he wants it; but Papa keeps putting it off as usual, and won't make up his mind. . . ."

She was silent; and moved slightly.

"But look at the canoe," she went on, and, through the glass of the windows our breath was just beginning to fog up, pointed to a dim, skeletal, oblong outline up against the wall opposite the one taken up by the grapefruit shelves. "Just look at that little canoe instead, and please admire the honesty, dignity, and moral courage with which it's managed to draw all the right conclusions from its own complete loss of function. Things die, too, you know. And so, if they too have to die, well there it is, it's so much better to let them go. That has much more style about it, apart from everything else, don't you agree?"

* "Effort": Ferrarese dialect.

PART
THREE

Chapter One

Endlessly, during the winter, spring and summer that followed, I turned back to what had happened (or rather hadn't happened) between Micòl and me in old Perotti's beloved carriage. If, that rainy afternoon on which the luminous Indian summer of 1938 suddenly ended, I had at least managed to speak – I told myself bitterly – things might have gone differently for us. If I'd talked to her, kissed her: it was then, when everything was still possible – I never stopped telling myself – that I ought to have done it! And I forgot to ask myself the essential question: whether, in that supreme, single, irrevocable moment – a moment that perhaps had decided my life and hers – I was really capable of trying to do or say anything at all. Did I, for instance, already know that I was *really* in love? No, the fact was I didn't yet know it. Neither then, nor later, not for at least another two weeks; that is, some time after the bad weather, which had now settled down on us, had scattered our group.

I remember it well: an uninterrupted downpour for days on end – and then it would be winter, the gloomy relentless winter of the northern plain – that made any further time spent in the garden seem unlikely. And yet, in spite of the change in the weather, everything went on in much the same way, and I managed to delude myself that nothing, substantially, had changed.

At half-past two on the day after our last visit to the Finzi-Continis', in fact–about the time we had usually been seen emerging, one after the other, from the arcade of climbing roses with cries of "hello!" or "Hi" or "your servant"–the telephone rang for me at home, and, across the squalls of rain pouring down over the entire city, I was again in touch, just the same, with Micòl's voice. That same evening I rang her; and she rang up again the following afternoon. We managed to carry on talking exactly the way we had been doing those last few days, thankful now, as we had been thankful then, to be left alone by Bruno Lattes, Adriani Trentini, Giampiero Malnate and all the others, to be given no sign of being remembered by them. And anyway, when had we even thought of them, Micòl and I, in our long meanderings about the park, first on bicycles and then on foot: meanderings so long that sometimes, when we got back, we found not a living soul either on the tennis court or in the *Hütte*?

Followed, as a rule, by anxious glances from my parents, I would shut myself in the tiny telephone room, and dial the number: and often it was Micòl who answered at once; so quickly, too, that I thought she must have the receiver continually by her.

"Where are you speaking from?" I tried asking.

She burst out laughing.

"Well . . . from home, I suppose."

"Thanks for telling me. But what I really wanted to know was how you manage to answer so quickly: tick-tock, just like that. How d'you do it? D'you have your 'phone on the desk like a tycoon? Or d'you prowl round the telephone from morning till night, like the caged tiger in Machaty's *Nocturne*?"

I sensed a slight hesitation on the other end of the line. If she got to the telephone before the others – she answered – it was only because of the legendary efficiency of her muscular reflexes, that's all; and her natural intuition, of course, which meant that every time I got the notion of ringing her she happened to be passing the telephone. Then she changed the subject. How was my thesis on Panzacchi going? And what about Bologna, when was I going to start my old trips back and forth, if only for a change of air?

But sometimes it was the others who answered: Alberto, or professór Ermanno, or one of the two maids, and once even signora Regina, who had surprisingly sharp ears on the telephone. In these cases I could hardly avoid giving my name, of course, and saying I wanted to speak to "signorina" Micòl. But after a few days (at first the whole business embarrassed me dreadfully, but gradually I got used to it), after a few days all I had to say was "Hello" into the receiver and whoever was on the other end passed me on quickly, without even asking whom I wanted to speak to. Even when Alberto came on the line, he did this; and Micòl was always there at once, ready to grab the receiver from whoever had it: just as if the whole lot of them were gathered together in a single room, living-room, drawing-room, library, or whatever it was, each of them deep in a big leather armchair, with the telephone just a few yards away. Really, I came to suspect that. And to warn Micòl, who suddenly looked up when the telephone rang (I seemed to see her), all they did, very likely, was hold out the receiver from a distance, Alberto adding a wink of his own, perhaps, half affectionate and half sardonic.

One day I ventured to ask her to confirm whether I was right, and she listened to me in silence.

"Isn't that the way it is?" I asked.

But it wasn't. Seeing I was determined to get at the truth—she said—well, here it was: each of them had a line to his own room (after she'd got one for herself, the rest of the family had ended up getting one as well): it was terrifically useful, and really she recommended it, because you could ring anyone up at any hour of the day or night without bothering anyone else or being bothered, and—just think!—without moving a step out of bed at night. What an amazing idea!—she then exclaimed, laughing. What on earth had put it into my head that they all sat around together the whole time, like people in an hotel lounge? Why ever should they? Anyway it was odd I hadn't noticed the click of the extension switch when she didn't answer me first go.

"No," she said firmly. "To protect your own freedom, there's nothing like a good private line. Honestly, you ought to get one for yourself, in your own bedroom. Imagine the chats I'd have with you, especially at night!"

"So you're ringing from your bedroom now."

"Certainly. And in bed, at that."

It was eleven o'clock in the morning. "You're not exactly an early bird," I said.

"Oh heavens, you, too!" she moaned. "It's all very well for Papa, aged seventy, and with all he's got on his plate, to get up at half-past six because, so he says, he wants to set us a good example and stop the rot of all this soft living; but when one's best friends start wagging reproving fingers that really seems a bit much. D'you know I've been on my feet since seven o'clock this morning? And you dare to be surprised at catching me back in bed at eleven! Besides, I don't sleep, you know; I read, scribble a few lines of the old thesis, look outside. I've always got masses to do when I'm in bed. Being snug under the blankets makes me madly busy."

"Describe your room," I said.

She clicked her tongue against her teeth several times, meaning no.

"No, never. *Verboten. Privat.* If you like I can describe what I'm looking at through the window."

From her first-floor window she could see the feathery tops of her *Washingtoniae graciles*, which the wind and the rain were lashing "shamelessly", and you couldn't tell if Titta and Bepi's efforts–they'd already started binding up their trunks with their usual winter petticoats of straw–you couldn't tell, anyway, whether these efforts would stop them freezing to death during the next few months, which seemed likely enough every winter, but so far they'd managed to avoid, praise be. Then farther on, hidden in places by tufts of drifting fog, she saw the four Castle towers, which the pouring rain had turned the colour of charcoal. And behind the towers, a kind of spooky whiteness occasionally hidden by the fog, the distant marble front and campanile of the cathedral. . . . Oh, the fog! When it looked like that, like dirty rags, she didn't like it a bit. But the rain would stop sooner or later: and then the morning mist pierced by the feeble rays of sunlight would turn into something precious, and delicately opalescent, with shifting reflections like all those of the *làttimi** she had the room full of. Winter was a bore, of course, because it stopped you playing tennis,

---

* Objects made of milk-coloured glass are called *làttimi*, but the word makes the narrator think of milk foods: hence his question a few lines later.

among other things, but it had its compensations.
"And there's no situation, however sad and dreary it
is," she concluded, "that hasn't got some underlying
compensations, and often very big ones."

"*Làttimi?*" I asked. "What's that? Something to
eat?"

"Oh no, no," she moaned, horrified by my ignorance, as usual. "It's glass: drinking glasses, chalices,
bottles, tiny bottles, small boxes: little things, usually
chucked out by dealers. In Venice they call them
làttimi: outside Venice they're called *opalines*, or *flutes*.
You can't imagine how I *adore* this stuff. I know *every*
single thing there is to know about them. Ask me and
you'll see."

It was at Venice–she went on–perhaps inspired by
their local mists, which were so different from our
gloomy Po Valley fogs, infinitely vaguer and more
luminous (only one painter on earth had managed to
"get" them: "our own" De Pisis, far more than the
later Monet), it was at Venice that she had begun being
keen on *làttimi*. She spent hours and hours going round
the antique shops; and there were some, especially in
the direction of San Samuele, around campo Santo
Stefano, or else in the ghetto, down there towards the
station, which sold practically nothing else. Uncle
Giulio and Uncle Federico lived in the calle del Cristo,
near San Moisè. Towards evening, having nothing else
to do, and of course with signorina Blumenfeld the
housekeeper in tow (a lady-like *jodè* in her sixties from
Frankfurt-on-Main, who'd been in Italy for over thirty
years: and a real old drear!), she would pop out on a
làttimi-hunt in calle XXII March. Campo Santo
Stefano's only a few steps from San Moisè. But not
San Geremia, where the ghetto is; if you go through

San Bartolomío and the Lista di Spagna, it's at least
half an hour's walk from San Moisè, but it's just round
the corner if you cross the Grand Canal at palazzo
Grassi, and then carry on along the Frari. . . . But to go
back to the *làttimi*. What a "rhabdoromantic "shiver
she had every time she managed to dig out something
new and rare! How many pieces did I think she'd
managed to collect? Nearly two hundred. I was careful
not to point out how this hardly tallied with her
avowed dislike of trying to save things, objects, from
the inevitable death that awaited "them as well", and
in particular of Perotti's mania for preserving them.
What I wanted was to make her talk about her room;
I wanted her to forget she had said: *verboten, privat*, a
short while ago.

And I got my way. She went on talking about her
làttimi (she had set them out on three high sets of dark
mahogany shelves that covered almost the entire wall
opposite the one her bed stood against); and as she
spoke the room, whether with or without her realizing
it, started taking shape, and gradually all its details became clear as well.

Well then, to get things straight: there were two
windows. Both faced south, and were so high above
the floor that when you looked out over the sill, with
the park spread below, and the roofs spreading beyond
the park as far as you could see, it felt like looking out
from the deck of an ocean liner. Between the two
windows stood a fourth set of shelves: for French and
English books. Up against the left-hand window was a
desk with a green baize top and a lamp, and beside it a
small table with a typewriter on it and a fifth bookcase, the one where she kept her books of Italian literature, classics and modern works, and her translations,

mostly from the Russian, Pushkin, Gogol, Tolstoy,
Dostoievsky, Chekhov. On the floor was a large Per-
sian carpet, and in the middle of the room, which was
long but rather narrow, three armchairs and a Récamier sofa, to lie on and read. There were two doors:
one the entrance, at the end of the room beside the
left-hand window, giving directly on to the staircase
and the lift, and another just by the opposite corner of
the room, leading into the bathroom. At night she
slept without ever closing the shutters completely, and
a little lamp always alight above the bedside table, and
the trolley with the thermos of *Skiwasser*–and the
telephone–so near as well that all she had to do was
stretch out an arm if she wanted it. If she awoke at
night all she did was take a sip of *Skiwasser* (it was *so*
useful to have something "nice and hot" always there:
why didn't I get a thermos for myself as well?) and
then, when she lay down again, she gazed around at
the gleaming mistiness of her beloved *làttimi*, and
sleep, as unobtrusive as high tide in Venice, came gently
back to submerge and "exterminate" her.

But these weren't our only topics of conversation.

As if she too wanted to delude me into thinking that
nothing had changed, that everything between us was
just as it had been "before", when we could see each
other every afternoon, Micòl lost no opportunity of
taking me back to that series of stupendous, "incredible" days.

We had talked of so many things, then, as we wandered about the park: about trees, and plants, about our
childhood, our families. And meantime Bruno Lattes,
Adriana Trentini, "that" Malnate, Carletto Sani,
Tonino Collevatti, and the others who had come along

later, were mentioned only very briefly and occasionally, and even referred to now and then in a hasty and rather scornful way as "that lot".

But now, on the telephone, our talk kept going back to them, especially to Bruno Lattes and Adriana Trentini, between whom, according to Micòl, there was definitely *something*. Oh, come now!—she kept saying to me: could I possibly not have realized that they were going steady? Why, it was perfectly obvious! He never took his eyes off her for a moment, and she too, although she treated him like a slave, and flirted a bit with everyone, with me, and that bear Malnate, and even with Alberto, even she went along with him, when you got down to it. *Dear* Bruno! With his sensitivity (faintly morbid, you must admit: all you need do to see that was watch the way he worshipped, quite literally, two nice little morons like Sani and Collevatti, heaven help us!), with his sensibility he had some pretty uneasy months ahead of him, given the present situation. There was no doubt Adriana felt the same (one evening in the *Hütte*, in fact, she had seen them half lying on the sofa, kissing away for all they were worth), but whether she was the type to carry on with anything so difficult, in the face of the racial laws and his family and hers, was another matter. No, Bruno hadn't an easy winter ahead of him. Not that Adriana was a bad girl, of course not! Nearly as tall as Bruno, blonde, with that marvellous Carole Lombard skin of hers, at any other time she might have been just the girl for Bruno, who obviously liked "real Arians". But there was no denying she was a bit flighty and emptyheaded, and unconsciously cruel as well. Didn't I remember the way she glared at poor wretched Bruno that time they lost the famous return match against

Désirée Baggioli and Claudio Montemezzo? It was really she who'd lost the match, with those endless double faults of hers–at least three in every game–far more than Bruno! And yet she was so completely thoughtless that throughout the whole match she did nothing but yelp at him, as if he, "poor soul", wasn't already depressed and cast-down enough on his own account. It would really have been funny, if it hadn't turned out so sour! But there, it was always the way: moralists like Bruno never failed to fall for geese like Adriana: which meant jealous scenes, snoopings, surprises, tears, promises, even blows and . . . horns, quite honestly, that's what it came to. No, no: after all, Bruno ought to thank his stars for the racial laws. He was going to have a difficult winter, it was true. But the racial laws, which weren't always such a bad thing, as it turned out, would prevent him doing the stupidest thing of all: getting engaged.

"Don't you think so?" she added, once. "And then, like you, he's a literary man, he wants to write. I think I saw some of his poems, two or three years ago, on the third page of the *Corriere ferrarese*, under the comprehensive title 'Poems of an *avanguardista*'*."

"Good God!" I said. "But what d'you mean? I don't follow."

She laughed silently, I could hear perfectly well.

"Well, what I mean is, a bit of heartache won't do him any harm," she said. " '*Non mi lasciare ancora, sofferenza*,'† as Ungaretti says. He wants to write, doesn't he? Well, let him stew in his own juice a bit, and then we'll see. Anyway, all you have to do is look at him:

---

* A member of the *Avanguardia Giovanile*, the fascist organization which boys who went to the *liceo* were obliged to join.

† "Do not yet leave me, suffering."

you can see quite plainly that at heart all he wants is suffering."

"You're disgustingly cynical: quite a pair with Adriana."

"Now that's where you're wrong. In fact I'm hurt. Adriana's an innocent angel. Capricious, maybe, but innocent like–'*tutte–le femmine di tutti–i sereni animali –che avvicinno a Dio.*'* Whereas Micòl's good, I've told you so already and I'm telling you again, and *always* knows what she's up to, don't forget."

Rather more rarely she mentioned Giampiero Malnate, towards whom her attitude was always curious, fundamentally critical and sarcastic: as if she was jealous of the friendship between him and Alberto–a rather exclusive friendship, to tell the truth–but at the same time disliked admitting it, admitting being jealous, that is, and for that very reason was trying to "knock down the idol".

According to her, "that" Malnate wasn't even "physically attractive": too big, too fat, too "fatherly" to be taken seriously from that point of view. He was one of those excessively hairy men who, however often they shave during the day, always look a bit dirty and unwashed: and, quite frankly, that just wasn't pretty. Maybe, from what she could see of them through those enormously thick glasses that everlastingly camouflaged him (they seemed to make him sweat: it made you want to take them off for him), maybe his eyes weren't too bad: grey eyes, *steel grey*, strong man's eyes. But far too solemn and severe. Too constitutionally matrimonial. In spite of his scornful misogynism on the surface, such eternal feelings lurked

* Umberto Saba: "all the females of all gentle animals that bring us near to God".

underneath that they'd make any girl shiver, even the quietest and best-conducted.

He was a sulky old fellow, though: and not even as quaint as he seemed to think. She was willing to bet that if you questioned him carefully he'd tell you at some point that he felt uncomfortable in town clothes, and of course preferred the windcheaters, knicker-bockers, and ski boots he wore on his everlasting week-ends on Mottarone or Monte Rosa! That faithful old pipe of his, when you came to think of it, was pretty revealing: it meant an entire programme of masculine Lombard austerity, it was like flying a flag.

He and Alberto were great friends, although Alberto, whose character was more passive than a punching ball, was basically everyone's friend and no one's. They had spent whole years together in Milan: and this mattered, of course. But those endless confabulations they went in for, weren't they really a bit much? Clackety-clack, on and on and on: the minute they met, nothing and no one could keep them apart and stop them nattering away. And heaven knows what it was all about! Women? Of course not! Knowing Alberto, who'd always been pretty reserved, not to say mysterious, on the subject, she wouldn't bet tuppence on it, quite honestly.

"D'you still see him?" I got round to asking her one day, slipping in the question in the most indifferent tone I could muster.

"Well, yes . . . I think he sometimes comes along to see his old Alberto," she answered calmly. "They shut themselves up in his room, have tea, smoke their pipes (Alberto's been puffing away at one too, just lately), and talk and talk, blissfully happy doing nothing but talk."

She was too intelligent, too sensitive not to have guessed what I was hiding under my indifference: and that was a sudden piercing – and symptomatic – longing to see her again. But she behaved as if she hadn't understood, without even indirectly mentioning the possibility that sooner or later I, too, might be invited to her house as well.

Chapter Two

I spent the next night in great agitation. I slept, woke up, and slept again. And every time I dreamt of her again.

I dreamt for instance that I was watching her play tennis with Alberto, just as I had done the first day I set foot in the garden. Again, in my dream, I couldn't take my eyes off her. Again I kept telling myself that she was splendid, that I liked her all rosy and sweating like that, with a line down the middle of her forehead of almost ferocious keenness and determination, all strung up as she was in the effort of beating her smiling, rather slack and bored elder brother. But now I felt oppressed by a feeling of uneasiness, bitterness, almost unbearable pain. What was left of the child of ten years ago – I wondered desperately – in this twenty-two-year-old Micòl, in shorts and a cotton shirt, in this Micòl who seemed so free, so sporty, so modern (free above

all), that you'd think she had spent the last years exclusively at the famous tennis centres of the world: London, Paris, the Côte d'Azur, Forest Hills? Yes–I
thought, comparing them–there was still the child's
fair, floating hair with streaks that were almost white,
and blue Scandinavian eyes, and honey-coloured skin,
and on her breast, occasionally bouncing out of the
neck of her shirt, the small gold disc of the *schiaddai*.
But otherwise?

Then we found ourselves shut up inside the carriage,
in that grey, stuffy twilight: with Perotti outside, sitting up on his box, motionless, silent, beetling. If
Perotti was up there–I reasoned to myself–with his
back turned obstinately to us, obviously it was to
avoid seeing what was happening or might happen inside the carriage, in fact out of servile discretion. But
he knew just *everything* there was to know, the old
lout, of course he did! His wife, that washed-out Vittorina, spying through the half-shut coach-house door
(occasionally I caught a glimpse of her small reptilian
head, its smooth raven-black hair gleaming as it poked
gingerly round the edge of the door: and one of her
eyes, just the same colour, looking worried and dis-
satisfied), his wife was there on the watch, half in and
half outside the door, stealthily making the sort of
faces and gestures they had agreed on.

And we were even in her bedroom, Micòl and I, but
even this time we were not alone, but "bothered"–it
was she who murmured it–by the "inevitable" outsider's presence: this time it was Yor, crouched in the
middle of the room like an enormous unbreakable idol,
Yor staring at us with his two icy eyes, one black and
one blue. The room was long and narrow, just like the
coach-house; and like the coach-house full of things to

eat: grapefruit, oranges, mandarins: and *làttimi*, above all, *làttimi* in rows like books on the shelves of big, austere, churchy-looking black bookcases, right up to the ceiling: and these *làttimi* weren't objects made of glass, as Micòl herself had tried to make me believe, but on the contrary, just as I had imagined, cheeses, yes, small, dripping, round, whitish cheeses, shaped like bottles. Laughingly, she pressed me to try one of her cheeses; and heavens, then she stood on tiptoe, and was just going to touch one of the ones placed on the top shelf (the ones at the top were best and freshest, she explained), but I said no, I simply wouldn't accept it, I was in agony because, apart from the dog being there, I knew that while we were arguing, the water of the lagoon was rising fast outside. If I delayed even a little, the high tide would shut me in there quite definitely, and prevent my leaving her room without being seen. Actually I had gone there secretly, and at night, into Micòl's bedroom: without Alberto, or professór Ermanno, or signora Olga, or signora Regina, or Uncle Giulio or Uncle Federico, or the pure-minded signorina Blumenfeld knowing I was there. And Yor, the only one who knew, the only witness of the *thing* there was *also* between us, Yor couldn't talk about it.

I dreamt too that we talked, and at last without pretences, at last our cards on the table.

As usual, we quarrelled a bit: Micòl saying that the *thing* between us had started the first day on which she and I, still full of the surprise of finding and recognizing one another, had slipped off to look round the park, and I was saying it wasn't so, that I thought the *thing* had begun even earlier, on the telephone, from the moment she had told me she'd grown "ugly", a "red-nosed old maid". Deep down in me I'd never believed it, of course. And yet she couldn't begin to imagine–I said, with a lump in my throat–how much her words made me suffer. In the days that followed, before I saw her again, I thought of them continually, unable to feel at peace.

"Oh well, maybe you're right," Micòl agreed at this point, pityingly, laying her hand on mine. "If the idea that I'd grown red-nosed and ugly immediately bothered you, then I give in, it means you're right. But, anyway, what are we to do now? Tennis is no excuse any more, and it's not seemly or suitable to ask you to the house with the danger of being trapped by the high tide (you see what Venice is like?)."

"What's the need for that?" I retorted. "You could come outside, after all."

"Me come out?!" she exclaimed, opening her eyes wide. "Well, dear friend,* let's hear: where could I go?"

"Well . . . I don't know. . . ." I stammered. "On the Montagnone, say, or in piazza d'Armi, on the Aqueduct side, or else, if you'd hate to be compromised, in piazza della Certosa on the via Borso side. It's there that everyone goes walking out, as you know perfectly well. I don't know if yours did, but my parents did in their day. And what's wrong with walking out, after all, when you get down to it? It's not like making love! You're on the first step, on the edge of the abyss. But before you get down to the bottom of the abyss, there's quite a slope, you know!"

And I was on the point of adding that if, as it appeared, even piazza della Certosa wasn't what she wanted, we might eventually take separate trains and meet in Bologna. But I was silent, unable to dare this

* In English in the original.

even in a dream. And besides, shaking her head and smiling, she was already telling me it was pointless, impossible, *verboten*: she'd never come outside the house and garden with me. What was it? she said, winking amusedly. After she'd let me cart her round and round the usual "outdoor" places, in keeping with "the gentle erotic muse of the countryside", was it Bologna I was already scheming to take her to? Yes, Bologna, and maybe one of the "big" hotels her grandmother Josette had patronized, like the *Brun*, or the *Baglioni*—but did I realize we'd have to comply with the request to give our precious rubber-stamped particulars at the reception desk?

The evening of the following day, as soon as I got back from a sudden trip to Bologna, to the university, I got on to the telephone.

Alberto answered it.

"How are things?" he drawled ironically, for once showing that he recognized my voice. "It's ages since we met. How are you? What are you doing?"

Disconcerted, my heart thudding, I started talking at random: muddling up all kinds of things: my degree thesis which (this was true) loomed up ahead of me like an unscalable wall; the weather, which after that fortnight of rain had seemed to offer a glimmer of hope since morning (but you couldn't trust it: the sharp air clearly showed that winter was upon us and those fine October days must now be forgotten), and adding an extremely detailed account of my quick "excursion to via Zamboni"—just as if he, Alberto, who was studying in Milan, should know Bologna as well as I did.

In the morning, I said, I had been to the university, where I had some things to fix up with the bursar, then I went up to the library to check a number of items for

the Panzacchi bibliography I was preparing. At one
o'clock I had lunch at the *Pappagallo*: not the one at
the foot of the Asinelli, the so-called "dry" one*;
which, apart from being terribly expensive, didn't
really seem to me to live up to its reputation, but the
other, the *Pappagallo in brodo*, which was in a little side
street off via Galliera, and was known for its stews and
soups, and for its cheapness, too, its really good value.
In the afternoon I had seen a few friends, gone round
the bookshops, had tea at the Zanarini, the one in
piazza Galvani, at the end of the Pavaglione: in fact, I
concluded, I hadn't had a bad day, "pretty much as it
was when I went there regularly".

"And just think, before I went back to the station,"
I went on at this point, quite out of the blue, and
prompted by heaven knows what sudden desire to
make up such a tale, "I even had time for a peep at via
dell'Oca."

"Via dell'Oca?" said Alberto, suddenly livening up,
yet sounding alarmed.

This was all I needed to discover in myself my
father's sour wish to appear much cruder and more
goi than he really was, compared with the Finzi-
Continis.

"What!" I exclaimed. "Never heard of via dell'Oca?
Why, that's where you find one of the most famous
. . . little family hotels in Italy."

He coughed, embarrassed.

"No, I didn't know it."

Then, abruptly changing the tone and subject, he
said that in a few days he too would have to leave for
Milan, staying there at least a week. June wasn't as
far ahead as it seemed, and he hadn't yet found a don

* The "dry" one because it specialized in *pasta*.

who'd give him the chance of "stringing some old thesis together": in fact, to be quite honest, he hadn't even tried to.

Then he jumped to another subject (his voice, meantime, had recovered its usual bored, mocking tone), and asked me if I'd happened to be riding my bicycle along the Wall of the Angels just lately. He'd been out in the garden, seeing what sort of state the rain had reduced the tennis court to. But partly because of the distance, and partly because the light was going, he couldn't be sure if it really was me sitting up on the saddle, leaning one hand against a tree trunk up there, and gazing down, perfectly still. Oh, so it was? he went on, after I had admitted, not without hesitation, that I had in fact gone along the Wall of the Angels on the way home from the station: because, I explained, it made me shudder every time, deep down inside me, to pass some of those ugly mugs that collected opposite the Caffé della Borsa, in Corso Roma, or lined up along Giovecca. Ah, so it was me? he repeated. He thought it was! Well then, if it was, why hadn't I answered his shouts and whistles? Hadn't I heard him?

No, I hadn't, I lied once again; in fact I hadn't even noticed he was in the garden. And now we really had nothing else to say, nothing with which to fill the sudden silence that had opened up between us.

"But . . . you wanted to talk to Micòl, didn't you?" he said at last, as if remembering.

"Yes," I answered. "D'you mind putting me through?"

He'd have been happy to, he replied: but – and it was very odd that, as far as he could see, the "dear girl" hadn't warned me – Micòl had left for Venice early that afternoon, meaning to "get a move on" with her thesis,

too. She had come down to lunch all dressed up for the
journey, with her suitcase and all, and "to the family's
dismay" announced what she meant to do. She was
fed up, she said, with trailing the work along behind
her. Instead of taking her degree in June she'd take it in
February, and with the *Marciana* and the *Querini-
Stampalia* available in Venice, it would be perfectly
easy, whereas in Ferrara she couldn't get on, her thesis
on Emily Dickinson, for all sorts of reasons, would
never get ahead as fast as it should (this was what she
said, at least). Heaven knows how Micòl would put up
with the depressing atmosphere of Venice, and of a
house, her uncles', which she disliked. It was highly
likely that in a week or two we'd see her back to base
again, with damn all done. He'd think he was dreaming
if Micòl ever managed to stay away from Ferrara for
more than three weeks or a month on end. . . .

"Ah well, we shall see," he concluded. "In any case,
what would you say (this week's impossible and so's
next, but the one after that I think really I could),
what would you say to driving up to Venice together?
It would be fun to land on my little sister: you and I
and Giampi Malnate, say!"

"It's an idea," I said. "Why not? We might talk it
over."

"In the meantime," he went on, with an effort in
which I sensed a sincere wish to compensate me, at least
a little, for what he'd just told me, "in the meantime,
if you've nothing better to do, why don't you come
and see me here at home? Say tomorrow, about five in
the afternoon? That Malnate'll be here, too, I think.
We can have tea . . . listen to some records . . . talk. I
don't know if you, being a literary man, would want
to spend time with an engineer (that's poor me) and an

industrial chemist. But if you'll *deign* to, let's not be formal: come along, and we'll be delighted."

We went on for a bit longer, Alberto growing more and more excited and enthusiastic at his idea, which seemed to have come to him quite suddenly, of having me to his home, and I attracted by it but at the same time repelled. Yes, it was perfectly true–I remembered –that a little earlier I'd gazed down at the garden for nearly half an hour from the top of the Wall of the Angels, and above all at the house, which, from where I was, and through the almost leafless branches of the trees, I saw cut out against the evening sky from base to pinnacled roof, frail and elongated as an heraldic emblem. Two windows on the mezzanine floor, at the level of the terrace leading down into the garden, were already lit up, and the electric light shone above, as well, from the single, very high window that opened just under the top of the end tower. For a long time, my eyes aching in their sockets, I had stayed there, staring at the little light in the upper window–a calm, tremulus glimmer that hung in the gradually darkening air like a star–and only Alberto's distant whistles and Tyrolean yells, that made me afraid of being recognized, and my longing to hear Micòl's voice at once on the telephone, managed to chase me away. . . .

But what now?–I asked myself gloomily. What did I care about going to *their* house, if Micòl was no longer there?

But when I came out of the telephone room and my mother told me that Micòl Finzi-Contini had rung up and asked for me about midday ("she asked me to tell you she'd got to leave for Venice, she said good-bye and that she'd write," my mother went on, looking away), it was enough to make me suddenly change my

mind. In fact from that moment the time separating
me from five o'clock next day started crawling.

Chapter Three

So it was then that I began being a daily guest in
Alberto's own room (he called it his studio; and
so it was, with a bedroom and an adjoining bathroom), in that famous room behind double doors, from
which, as she went by it in the passage, Micòl heard
nothing but the jumbled voices of her brother and his
friend Malnate, and where, apart from the maids
coming with the tea trolley, I never met a single other
member of the family during the entire winter. Oh,
that winter of '38–'39! I remember those long motionless months, that seemed strung above time and despair (in February it snowed, and Micòl still wasn't
back from Venice), and even now, more than twenty
years later, the four walls of Alberto Finzi-Contini's
room go back to being my vice, the drug that, without my realizing it, I needed every day, at that
time. . . .

I was not at all in despair that first December evening
when I crossed Barchetto del Duca on my bicycle
again. Micòl had left: yet I pedalled along the drive in
the darkness and the fog, as if expecting to see her, and
only her, a little later. I was excited and gay: almost

happy. I looked round me, my bicycle lamp searching out places from a past that seemed to me distant, admittedly, but still recoverable, not yet lost. Here was the little wood of rattan canes; there, but farther ahead, on the right, the vague outline of Perotti's house, from a first-floor window of which came a yellowish glow; there, still farther on, loomed the eerie framework of the bridge over the Panfilio canal: and here at last, forecast a bit ahead by the crunch of my tyres on the gravel of the open space in front, the gigantic bulk of the *magna domus*, inaccessible as an isolated rock, and entirely dark except for the very bright white light coming through the cracks of a small side door, obviously left open to welcome me.

I got off my bicycle and stood a moment looking through the deserted doorway; and saw, cut obliquely across by the black left-hand side of the door, which had stayed shut, a steep staircase carpeted in red: a vivid scarlet, the colour of blood, with polished brass stair-rods that gleamed like gold.

I leant the bicycle against the wall, bending over to padlock it. And I was still there in the shadows, down beside the door through which, apart from the light, came a fine warmth from the central heating (in the darkness I couldn't manage to work the padlock, and was just thinking of lighting a match to get a better look), when professór Ermanno's familiar voice suddenly came from beside me.

"What are you doing? Locking it up?" he said, standing at the doorway. "That's good idea. You never know, you can never be too careful."

Without knowing, as usual, whether his faintly querulous kindness was secretly mocking me, I got up at once.

"Good evening," I said, taking off my hat and holding out my hand.

"Good evening, dear boy," he replied. "But keep on your hat, do keep it on!"

I felt his small fat hand slide almost sluggishly into mine, and then draw away at once. He wore no coat, but an old sports cap was rammed down over his spectacles and a woollen scarf wound round his neck.

He looked mistrustfully sidelong, in the direction of the bicycle.

"You have locked it, haven't you?"

I said I hadn't. And then, put out, he insisted on my going back and locking it up as he asked me to, because, he repeated, you never knew. It wasn't likely to get stolen – he kept saying from the doorway, as I tried to get the padlock and chain round the spokes of the back wheel again – but you couldn't really trust the garden wall. Along it, and especially on the Wall of the Angels side, there were at least ten places where any moderately agile boy would have no trouble at all in getting over. And getting out afterwards, even burdened with a bike across his shoulders, would be nearly as easy.

At last I managed to fix the padlock; then looked up, but the doorway was empty.

Professór Ermanno was waiting for me in the little hall at the foot of the stairs. I went in, careful to shut the door behind me, and only then did I realize that he was looking at me in a worried, regretful way.

"I wonder," he said, "whether you wouldn't have done better to bring the bike right inside. . . . In fact, do that next time you come, bring it right in. If you leave it there under the stairs it won't be in anyone's way."

He turned and started going up the stairs ahead of me. He went slowly, hobbling more than ever and holding on to the banister with one hand, with his cap still on and the scarf round his neck. Meantime he talked, or rather muttered: as if talking to himself rather than to me.

Alberto had told him I was coming to see him today. And as Perotti had been in bed all day with a slight temperature (just a touch of bronchitis: but he was being looked after, to avoid any possible infection, apart from everything else . . .) for once in a while he'd taken on the job of watchman. You couldn't rely on Alberto, who was always so absent-minded, so distracted, so much in the clouds, as we all knew. If Micòl were at home, now, he wouldn't worry in the least, because Micòl, heaven knows how, always managed to see to everything, not just her own studies, but the running of the house in general, and even of the kitchen, for which in fact–and a very good thing too, in a woman!–she had a passion only slightly less intense than her passion for literature. (It was she who made up accounts at the end of the week with Gina and Vittorina, she who saw personally to cutting the throats of the poultry, when necessary: in spite of the fact that she loved animals so much, poor pet!). But Micòl wasn't at home that day (had Alberto told me she wasn't there?), as she'd had to leave for Venice yesterday afternoon, alas; which explained why he, in the absence of their "guardian angel" and of Perotti, had, for the moment, to act as porter.

He talked of other things, too, which I cannot remember. But at last he returned to Micòl again, not to take pleasure in her this time, but to regret her "recent uneasiness"–these were his actual words, and he sighed

–an uneasiness which, according to him, obviously depended on "so many factors", of course, but above all . . . here he was suddenly silent, and said no more about it. And during all this time we had not only reached the top of the stairs but had gone down two passages and through several rooms, professór Ermanno still in the vanguard and not letting me catch up with him except when he switched off the lights.

Absorbed as I was in what he was saying about Micòl (the detail that it was she, with her own hands, who killed the chickens in the kitchen fascinated me strangely), I looked about, but almost without seeing. In any case we were passing through rooms not unlike those in other houses of Ferrarese good society, Jewish and non-Jewish, filled with the usual sorts of furniture: monumental cupboards, hefty seventeenth-century locker-seats, with lion's feet, refectory-type tables, folding leather chairs with bronze buttons, upholstered armchairs, complicated glass or wrought-iron lamps hanging from the centre of beamed wooden ceilings and thick carpets spread everywhere on dark shining wooden floors, tobacco-coloured, carrot, ox-blood red. Here, perhaps, there were more nineteenth-century paintings, landscapes and portraits, and more books, most of them bound volumes in rows behind the glass of large, dark mahogany bookcases. Big radiators centrally heated the house to such a pitch that, if it had been at home, my father would have called it crazy (I seemed to hear him!): it was the warmth of a large hotel rather than a private house, and in fact enough to make me start sweating almost at once, and needing to take off my overcoat.

He ahead and I behind, we crossed at least a dozen rooms of varying sizes, some as large as real stately drawing-rooms, some tiny and linked, at times, by passages which were not always straight or on the same level. At last, when we were half-way down one of these passages, professór Ermanno stopped outside a door.

"Here we are," he said, gestured at the door with his thumb, and winked.

He apologized for not coming in, because–he explained–he had to look through some accounts from the country; he promised to "send one of the maids up with something hot right away"; after which, having shaken my hand, and had my assurance that I would come again (he still had the copies of his little historical works on Venice waiting for me, I mustn't forget!; and besides, he did *so* much enjoy spending a little time now and then "with intelligent young people"), he turned away, walked down the passage, and vanished quickly at the end of it.

"Ah, here you are," said Alberto, when he saw me come in.

He was deep in an armchair. He stood up by pushing with both hands on the arms, laid the book he was reading open and face downwards on a low table beside him, and then came over to me.

He was wearing grey vicuna trousers, one of his beautiful pullovers, a kind of dry-leaf colour, brown English shoes (real Dawsons, he told me afterwards: he found them in Milan, in a small shop near San Babila), and an open-necked flannel shirt without a tie; and had his pipe between his teeth. He shook hands, not looking noticeably friendly, and stared at a point behind me in the meantime. What was attracting his attention? I didn't understand.

"Excuse me," he murmured.

Leaning out sideways, willowy as he was, he pushed

past me, and in that same moment I realized I had left the double door half open. But Alberto was already there, seeing to it himself. He took the handle of the outside door, but before drawing it towards him poked his head out into the passage, for a look.

"What about Malnate?" I asked. "Hasn't he come yet?"

"No, not yet," he said, coming back towards me.

He got me to hand over my hat, scarf and overcoat, and disappeared into the little room next door. And so I was able to see something of it through the door: part of the bed, with a red-and-blue-checked woollen counterpane on it, a leather pouffe at the foot of the bed, and, on the wall beside a small door opening into the bathroom, half open as well, a small male nude by De Pisis in a simple light-wood frame.

"Sit down," Alberto said, meantime. "I'll be back in a minute."

And in fact he reappeared at once, and now, sitting in front of me, in the armchair I had seen him pull himself out of a little earlier with a very faint show of weariness, perhaps of boredom, he considered me with the curious expression of detached friendliness, an objective look I knew meant he was as interested as he possibly could be in somebody else. He smiled at me, showing the large incisors inherited from his mother's family, which were too big and strong for his long pale face and for the gums above them, which were no less bloodless than his face.

"Would you like to hear some music?" he suggested, indicating a radiogram that stood in a corner by the door. "It's a Philips, and really first class."

He made a movement to get up from the armchair again, but I stopped him.

"No, wait," I said. "Later perhaps."

I gazed about, taking in the room.

"What records have you got?"

"Oh, a bit of everything: Monteverdi, Scarlatti, Bach, Mozart, Beethoven. I've got quite a lot of jazz too, don't worry: Armstrong, Duke Ellington, Fats Waller, Benny Goodman, Charlie Kunz. . . ."

He went on mentioning names and titles, polite and equable as ever, but indifferently: neither more nor less than if he were asking me to choose from a list of dishes, which he personally would be very careful not to taste. He came alive–moderately so–only to describe the virtues of *his* Philips. It was, he told me, a "pretty exceptional" machine, because of various changes he'd worked out and got going with the help of a really good mechanic in Milan, to do with the quality of the sound, above all. There wasn't just a single amplifier, but four distinct ones: one for the bass sounds, one for the middle sounds, one for the high sounds, and one for the very high, so that anything coming through this very high one, even whistles, say –and he giggled–"came through" perfectly. But I mustn't imagine they were all four of them stuck there together–oh, no! *Inside* the radiogram there were only two: middle sounds and high. The very high amplifier he'd thought of hiding over there by the window, and the fourth, the bass one, was right under the sofa I was sitting on: all this so as to give a certain stereophonic effect.

At that moment Dirce came in, wearing a blue linen dress and a white apron tight at the waist, and pulling the tea trolley along behind her.

I saw Alberto look faintly annoyed. The girl must have noticed it too.

"It was the master," she justified herself, "who told me to bring it right away."

"It's all right. It just means we'll have a cup, *in the meantime*."

Fair and curly-haired, with the rosy cheeks you find in Venetians from the foothills of the Alps, and downcast eyes, Perotti's daughter silently arranged the cups on the small table and left. A pleasant smell of soap and talcum powder hung about the room. Even the tea, it seemed to me, tasted faintly of it.

As I sipped, I kept looking about me. I admired the way the room was furnished in such a rational, functional, and modern way, so radically unlike the rest of the house, but I couldn't understand why a gradually growing feeling of uneasiness, of oppression, was creeping over me.

"D'you like the way I've fixed up the studio?" Alberto asked.

He seemed suddenly anxious for my approval: which I didn't stint, of course, praising the simplicity of the furniture, getting up from the sofa to look more closely at the large drawing-board that stood at an angle by the window surmounted by a perfectly articulated metal lamp, and finally saying how especially I approved of the indirect lighting, which I thought very restful and at the same time extremely good for working in.

He let me carry on and seemed pleased.

"Did you design the furniture?" I asked.

"Well, no: I copied it–a bit from *Domus* and from *Casabella*, and a bit from the *Studio*, you know, that English magazine. . . . Then I had them made here at Ferrara, by a little man in via Coperta."

He was delighted, he went on, to hear I approved of

his furniture. What point was there in living or working surrounded with hideous objects or simply with
junk? Giampi Malnate (he blushed faintly, as he named
him), Giampi Malnate kept insinuating that the studio,
fixed up like this, was more like a *garconnière* than a
studio, and, as a good communist, he thought that anyway *things*, in themselves, were at the most just palliatives, temporary ersatz substitutes, and he was on
principle against palliatives and substitutes of every
kind, and even against technique, whenever it seemed
to be saying that a drawer that shut perfectly, just to
give an example, solved all a man's problems, moral
and political included. Whereas he–and he indicated
his own chest–he thought otherwise. Though he
respected Giampi's opinions (yes, he was a communist:
didn't I know?), he felt that life was already so muddled
and dreary that there was no reason why furniture and
fittings, those silent, faithful indoor companions,
should be muddled and dreary as well.

It was the first and last time I saw him get excited,
and wave the flag for certain ideas instead of certain
others. We drank a second cup of tea, but the conversation now languished, so much so that we had to turn
to music.

We listened to a couple of records. Dirce came back,
bringing a tray of small cakes, and at last, at about
seven, the telephone on the desk opposite the drawing-
board rang.

"What d'you bet that's Giampi?" muttered Alberto,
dashing over to it.

Before he picked up the receiver he hesitated a
moment: like a player who, having got his cards, puts
off the moment when he looks squarely at his luck.

It was in fact Malnate, as I realized at once.

"Well then, what are you up to? Aren't you coming?" said Alberto regretfully, his voice almost childishly disappointed.

Malnate talked on for some time. From the sofa, though I couldn't quite grasp what he was saying, I heard the instrument vibrating under his thick, placid, Lombard voice. Finally I heard a *"ciao"* and he rang off.

"He's not coming," said Alberto.

He went slowly back to his armchair, dropped into it, stretched, yawned.

"It seems he's been held up at the factory," he went on, "and he'll be there for another two or three hours. He apologized, and asked me to say hello to you as well."

Chapter Four

Rather more than the generic "see you soon" which I exchanged with Alberto when I left him, it was a letter from Micòl I got a few days later that persuaded me to return.

It was a gay little letter, not too long and not too short, written on both sides of two sheets of blue paper which her dashing but light handwriting had filled quickly, without hesitations or corrections. She began by apologizing: she had left suddenly, and hadn't even said good-bye, which wasn't exactly the thing, she was quite ready to admit. Before leaving she had tried to ring me up, without finding me at home, though, alas; and so she had told Alberto he was to chase me up if I happened never to turn up again. If I'd really vanished, had Alberto done what he'd solemnly sworn, and got hold of me at the peril of his life? He always ended up by dropping everyone, with that famous old phlegm of his, but I couldn't imagine how much he needed people, poor soul! The letter went on for another two and a half pages, talking about the thesis, which was now "getting near the winning post", saying that Venice in winter "just made one cry", and ending up surprisingly with a verse translation of a poem by Emily Dickinson.

It was this:

> *Morii per la Bellezza; e da poco ero*
> *discesa nell'avello,*
> *che, caduto pel Vero, uno fu messo*
> *nell'attiguo sacello.*
>
> *"Perché sei morta?" mi chiese sommesso.*
> *Dissi: "Morii pel Bello."*
> *Io per la Verita: dunque è lo stesso,*
> *–disse,–son tuo fratello"*
>
> *Da tomba a tomba, come due congiunti*
> *incontratisi a notte,*
> *parlavamo così; finché raggiunti*
> *l'erba ebbe nomi e bocche.**

> * *I died for beauty, but was scarce*
> *Adjusted in the tomb,*
> *When one who died for truth was lain*
> *In an adjoining room.*

He questioned softly why I failed?
"For beauty," I replied.
"And I for truth,—the two are one;
We brethren are," he said.

And so, as kinsmen met a night,
We talked between the rooms,
Until the moss had reached our lips,
And covered up our names.

A postscript followed, saying: *"Alas, poor Emily.**
See what compensations poor wretched spinsterhood
is forced to!"

I liked the translation, but it was the postscript that
struck me above all. Whom should I refer it to? To
"poor Emily" herself, or to Micòl feeling depressed
and self-pitying?

In my reply I was careful once again to hide myself
in a thick smokescreen. After mentioning my first visit
to her house, with no mention of how disappointing I
had found it and promising I would soon return, I
stuck prudently to literature. Emily Dickinson's poem
was superb, I wrote, but her translation was really good
too. What interested me about it was the fact that it
was in a rather dated, Carduccian style. Then, diction-
ary in hand, I compared it with the English text, with
the result that I found only one thing to quarrel with,
and that was her translation of the word "moss" as
"*erba*". She mustn't misunderstand me, though: her
translation was perfectly fine as it was, and in this kind
of thing pleasing inaccuracy was always preferable to
pedantic ugliness. In any case the defect I had pointed
out was easily remedied. All it needed was a change in
the last verse—something like this:

* In English in the original.

*Da tomba a tomba, come due congiunti
incontratisi a notte,
parlavamo: finché il mucchio raggiunti
ebbe i nomi, le bocche.*

Micòl replied two days later, by telegram, thanking
me very effusively for my literary advice, and then,
the following day, she sent me a note by post with two
new typewritten versions of the translation. I answered
with a ten-page letter that dealt with hers point by
point. All in all, we were far clumsier and more lifeless
by letter than we were on the telephone, and so quite
soon we stopped corresponding. But in the meantime
I had continued visiting Alberto's studio, regularly
now, more or less every day.

Giampi Malnate came too, almost as eager and punctual as myself. Talking, arguing, often quarrelling–
loving and hating at once, in fact, right from the very
first minute–we quickly came to know each other
well, and got on familiar terms.

I remembered what Micòl had said about him
"physically". I too found "that" Malnate stout and
oppressive; I too, like her, often felt real impatience at
the sincerity, the loyalty, the eternal and obtrusive air
of manly frankness, the placid trust in a communist
Lombard future, that gleamed in his all too human
grey eyes. In spite of this, from the first time I sat
facing him in Alberto's studio, I had only one wish:
that he should think well of me, that he shouldn't think
I came between him and Alberto, in fact that he
shouldn't consider the three of us, who now met every
day, and certainly not through his initiative, an ill-
assorted group. I think it was then that I too started
smoking a pipe.

We talked of a great many things, the two of us (Alberto preferred to listen), but, quite obviously, of politics most of all.

Those were the months immediately after the Munich agreement, and this, Munich and its results, was in fact the subject we most often talked about. What would Hitler do, now that the Sudeten territories were happily incorporated into the Reich? Where would he strike now? I wasn't too pessimistic, and just for once Malnate agreed with me. According to me, the agreement France and England had been forced into at the end of the crisis last September wouldn't last very long. Yes, Hitler and Mussolini had made Chamberlain and Daladier abandon Benes's Czechoslovakia to its fate. But what next? If Chamberlain and Daladier were swapped for younger, tougher characters (see the advantage of the parliamentary system!—I exclaimed), France and England would soon be ready to show their teeth. Time was on their side, I said.

But all we had to do was talk about the war in Spain, which was now at its last gasp, or mention the U.S.S.R. in any way, for Malnate's attitude to the western democracies, and so to me, considered ironically as their representative and champion, to become far less accommodating right away. I can still see his large dark head poking forward, his forehead gleaming with sweat, his eyes fixed on me in the everlasting unbearable effort at half moral and half mawkish blackmail he so easily slipped into, while his voice took on a low, warm, persuasive, patient tone. Would I please tell him—he asked—who'd really been responsible for Franco's revolt? Wasn't it the French and English right wing who'd not only tolerated it at the start, but had

actually bolstered and applauded it later? Just as the
way the French and English had behaved, quite cor-
rectly but in fact ambiguously, allowed Mussolini to
gobble up Ethiopia in '35, so in Spain it was above all
the wicked wavering of Baldwin, and Halifax, and of
Blum himself, that turned the balance in Franco's
favour. No good blaming the U.S.S.R. and the International Brigade – he said, growing gentler – no good
saying it was the fault of Russia, who'd become every
idiot's whipping-boy, that things had got into such a
state. The truth was quite different: only Russia had
realized right from the start what the Duce and the
Führer were like, only Russia had foreseen clearly that
the pair of them would inevitably get together, and so
in good time had acted accordingly. Whereas the
French and English right wings, who undermined
democracy as every right wing in every country and
at any time had always done, had always regarded
Fascist Italy and Nazi Germany with ill-concealed
friendliness. The reactionaries of France and England
might find the Duce and the Führer rather uncomfortable, perhaps, a bit rough and a bit much; but in every
way preferable to Stalin, who, as everyone knew, had
always been the devil himself. After grabbing and an-
nexing Austria and Czechoslovakia, Germany was
starting to weigh in on Poland. Now if France and
England had been reduced to the point where all they
could do was watch what was happening and lump it,
it was perfectly plain: the full responsibility for their
present impotence fell on those fine, upstanding,
decorative gents in tails and top-hats – whose way of
dressing, at least, responded to the nostalgia for the
nineteenth century so many literary decadents went in
for – who now governed them.

But what really stirred Malnate into argument was what had been happening in Italy during the past few decades.

It was obvious, he said, that to me, and basically even to Alberto, fascism was nothing but a sudden inexplicable disease that had crept up on a healthy organism, or rather, to use a favourite expression of Benedetto Croce's, "your common master" (at this point Alberto glumly shook his head, but Malnate took no notice), an invasion by the Hyksos. To us the liberal Italy of Giolitti, Nitti, Orlando, and even that of Sonnino, Salandra and Facta, had been perfectly fine and holy; a kind of golden age, to which we should return, if we could, with everything exactly as it had been. But we were wrong, as wrong as could be! Evil hadn't crept up on us suddenly. On the contrary, it went back a very long way, right back to the early years of the Risorgimento, which was in fact achieved, practically speaking, without the people, the real people, having a hand in it at all. Giolitti? It was *our* Giolitti, and Benedetto Croce too, both of them ready to swallow the bitterest pills so long as it stopped the advance of the working classes, it was they we must thank for the fact that Mussolini managed to survive the crisis after the Matteotti affair, when everything around him seemed to be crumbling and even the king actually wavered; yes, it was they, our dream liberals, who gave Mussolini time to draw breath. Less than six months later he repaid them by suppressing the freedom of the press and dissolving the parties. Giovanni Giolitti retired from political life and slunk off to his estates in Piedmont; Benedetto Croce went back to his beloved philosophical and literary studies. But there were people who, though very much less guilty, in fact not

guilty at all, had paid far more dearly. Amendola and
Gobetti were beaten to death; Filippo Turati died in
exile, far from his home in Milan where, a few years
earlier, he'd buried poor signora Anna; Antonio
Gramsci had ended up in gaol (he'd died last year in
prison, didn't we know?); Italian workers and peasants,
together with their natural leaders, had lost every
effective hope of social redemption and human dignity,
and, for nearly twenty years now, had been vegetating
and dying in silence.

It wasn't easy for me to stand up to these ideas, for
several reasons: first of all because Malnate, who had
breathed in socialism and anti-fascism from his earliest
years at home, had a political culture that far surpassed
mine; secondly because the role he tried to press me
into – that of the decadent or "hermetic" literary man,
as he put it, whose politics were based on Croce's books
– seemed to me inadequate, didn't correspond to my
real personality, and so had to be rejected before we
even started any discussion. As a result I preferred to
keep silent, smiling vaguely and ironically. I bore it,
and smiled.

As for Alberto, he was silent as well, of course:
partly because, as usual, he had nothing to put forward, but mainly to allow his friend to be cruel to me,
which, it was only too obvious, he liked best of all. If
you shut three people up in a room to argue for days
on end, two of them will almost inevitably gang up on
the third. However that may be, Alberto seemed ready
to take anything from Giampi, even being classed with
me, very often, just to show he was on Giampi's side,
and sticking by him. It was true: Mussolini and his
chums were working up to some frightful outrages and
insults against the Jews – Malnate would say, for in-

stance; you couldn't say whether last July's notorious
Racial Manifesto, drawn up by ten so-called "fascist
scholars", was more shameful or ridiculous. But admitting that–he went on–could we tell him how many
"Israelite" anti-fascists there had been in Italy before
1938? Pretty few, he was afraid, a tiny minority, since
even in Ferrara, as Alberto had told him several times,
a very high percentage of them had been fascist party
members. I myself had taken part in the Littoriali della
Cultura* in '36. Was I already reading Croce's *History
of Europe* at that time? Or did I wait for my revelations
till the following year, the year of the *Anschluss* and the
first brushes with Italian racialism?

I bore it and smiled, sometimes protesting, but more
often not; in spite of myself overcome by his frankness
and sincerity, which were a little too rough and pitiless,
admittedly, a little too *goi*–this was how I put it to myself–but underneath really compassionate because really
concerned with equality, with brotherliness. And when
Malnate, leaving me alone for a moment, turned on
Alberto, and good-naturedly accused him and his
family of being, "after all", dirty landowners, the evil
exploiters of undercultivated estates, and aristocrats,
what's more, harking back nostalgically to medieval
feudalism, so that it wasn't, after all, so unfair for them
to pay the penalty a bit for the privileges they'd so long
enjoyed (under Malnate's abuse Alberto laughed till he
cried, and kept nodding, to say he was perfectly ready
to pay), it was not without secret pleasure that I listened
to him thundering against his friend. The child of the
years before 1929, who, walking beside his mother
along the cemetery paths, had heard her call the Finzi-
Continis' immense solitary tomb a "perfect horror",

* Fascist cultural competitions for university students.

rose all of a sudden from the depths of me and applauded nastily.

At times, though, Malnate seemed almost to forget my presence. This was when he recalled the years in Milan with Alberto, the friends they had then had in common, male and female, the restaurants they had been to together, evenings at the Scala, football matches at the Arena or at San Siro, winter trips to the mountains or the Riviera. They had both belonged to a "group", membership of which, it appeared, required only one thing: intelligence, and scorn for every kind of provincialism and affectation. Those were the days, the days of their youth, of Gladys, a music-hall dancer who appeared at the Lirico now and then, and for a time was Giampi's mistress; and then took a fancy to Alberto, who simply refused to hear of it, and ended up by dropping them both. Oh, Gladys wasn't at all bad, Malnate said: gay, a good mixer, not really out for what she could get, and appropriately, just as she should be, a tart.

"I never understood why Alberto pushed her off, poor Gladys," he said one evening, suddenly winking at me. And then, turning to Alberto:

"Be brave now! It's more than three years ago and we're nearly three hundred kilometres from the scene of the crime: so why not put your cards on the table at last?"

But Alberto parried him, blushing; and as far as Gladys was concerned the cards never got on the table, either then or later.

He liked the work he'd come to do in Ferrara – Malnate often said – he liked Ferrara, too, as a town, and couldn't understand how Alberto and I could consider it a kind of tomb or prison. Of course, our situation was quite special. But our mistake, as usual, was to think we belonged to the only persecuted minority in Italy, without realizing there were plenty of others, lots of other minorities who suffered as much as we did, or more. What about the workmen in the factory where he worked, for instance, what did we think they were: unfeeling brutes? He knew some who'd not only never joined the fascist party, but, being socialists or communists, had been beaten up and given the "castor oil treatment" several times, and still they had carried on undaunted, sticking to their ideas. He'd gone to some of their secret meetings, and been slightly surprised to find there, apart from workmen and peasants who'd come specially all the way from Mésola or Goro, three or four of the best-known lawyers in town: which proved that even in Ferrara the entire middle class hadn't supported fascism, and not every part of it was guilty. Had we ever heard of Clelia Trotti? We hadn't? Well, she was an ex-primary school teacher, a little old woman who, as far as he'd heard, had been the guiding spirit of local socialism, and still was, because although she was over seventy there wasn't a single meeting she didn't take part in. In fact, that was how he'd met her and got to know her. Of course you couldn't expect much from her sort of socialism; humanitarian, Andrea-Costa type, it was. But what ardour, what faith, what hope she had! Even physically, especially her blue eyes, those of a one-time blonde, reminded him of signora Anna, Filippo Turati's companion, whom he'd known very well as a boy in Milan, in about 1922. His father, a lawyer, had spent nearly a year in prison with the Turatis, in '98. He was an intimate friend of them both, and was one of the few people who dared visit them in their modest flat in the Galleria on Sunday afternoons. And he, Giampi, had often gone along there with him.

No, for heaven's sake: Ferrara wasn't at all the kind of prison you'd think it, from hearing us. Of course if you looked at it from the industrial zone, shut up, as it appeared, within the circle of its old walls, you might easily get an impression of isolation, especially in bad weather. But around Ferrara there was the country-side, rich, alive, and busy; and at the end of that, only forty kilometres east, was the sea, with empty beaches fringed with marvellous forests of holm oaks and pines: the sea, yes, which is always a great thing to have near. But apart from that, the town itself, if you got right inside it as he had decided to do, if you looked at it closely, without prejudice, had, like any other place, such treasures of honesty, intelligence and goodness, that only those who were blind and deaf, or else shrivelled, could fail to know or refuse to acknowledge them.

Chapter Five

At first Alberto kept saying he would soon be off to Milan. Then gradually he stopped talking about it, and the question of his degree thesis imperceptibly became, to me and possibly to Malnate as well, something embarrassing we must skirt cautiously.

He didn't talk about it; and we realized he wanted us to drop it too.

As I have said, he took part in our talks very rarely, and when he did, it was always off the point. He was on Malnate's side, there was no doubt at all about that. But as a stooge, without ever taking the smallest initiative. He never took his eyes off Malnate for an instant, happy if he triumphed, worried if I seemed to win. Apart from that he was silent; all he did was make the odd exclamation, giggle a bit, clear his throat. "Oh, that's rich! . . ."; "Ah, but you know, in a way . . ."; "Just a minute—let's look at this calmly . . .".

Even physically he tended to take cover, to vanish, to fade out. As a rule, Malnate and I sat facing each other in the middle of the room, one on the sofa and the other in one of the two armchairs, with the table between us, and both of us well in the light; and once we had sat down, we never got up except to go to the bathroom, or else to look at the state of the weather through the big horizontal window facing the park. Alberto, quite unlike us, preferred to tuck himself away, and sheltered behind the double barricade of the desk and the drawing-board. More often, though, we saw him tiptoeing about the room, his elbows close to his sides. He changed the records, always careful that the volume of sound didn't drown our voices; saw to the ashtrays, emptying them in the bathroom when they were full; regulated the indirect lighting; asked us softly if we wanted more tea; put things in their proper place. He had the busy, unobtrusive air of a host with only one thing on his mind: that his guests' important brains should do their job in the most favourable conditions and surroundings.

Yet I am sure it was his meticulous tidiness and

relentless, obsessive efforts on our behalf that gave his room the vaguely oppressive air I noticed at once when I first came into it. When, for instance, in a pause in the conversation he began to illustrate say, the virtues of the armchair I was sitting in, the back of which, he said, had been "studied" to give the backbone the most "anatomically" correct and favourable position; or when, say, in offering me the box of pipe tobacco for me to help myself, he reminded me of the various qualities of cut which, according to him, were indispensable if our respective Dunhills and G.B.D.s were to give the best results (mild: so much; strong: so much; Maryland: so much); or finally when, for reasons that were never very clear, and known only to him, he smilingly announced that one or two of the radiogram's amplifiers had been temporarily suspended: in every such case there was a nervous outburst, an uncontrolled protest just below the surface in me, ready to break out.

One evening, in fact, I could no longer control myself. Of course–I shouted at Malnate–his dilettante's attitude, which was basically a tourist's one, could allow him to be mild and indulgent towards Ferrara to an extent I envied. But how would he, who carried on about treasures of honesty, intelligence and goodness, judge what had happened to me, yes, to me, just a few mornings before?

I had had the bright idea–I started telling them–of moving over with my books and papers to the reading room of the city library in via Scienze: a place I'd used a great deal in the last few years, but where they'd known me, please note, since my schooldays, as it was there I used to go whenever the fear of being questioned at maths made me play truant. It was a second home to me, where everyone, especially since I'd taken up literature, had always gone out of the way to be kind. Ever since then the director, Dr. Ballola, had started considering me a kind of colleague, and he never saw me there without coming to sit beside me, and telling me about the progress of his ten-year-old researches into some biographical material of Ariosto which he kept in his own private study, researches that would allow him (he said so himself) to go a great deal further than the important work already achieved in this field by the famous Catalano. And as for the various employees: they treated me in such a trusting friendly way that they generally excused me the chore of filling in a special form for every volume I wanted, and when there weren't many people around they even let me smoke the odd cigarette.

Well then, as I was saying, I had the bright idea of spending the morning at the library. But I'd hardly had time to sit down at a table in the reading room and take what I needed out of my brief-case, before one of the employees, a fat jolly fellow of about sixty, called Poledrelli, famous for the amount of pasta he could put away and unable to string two words together except in dialect, came up to tell me to leave at once. Strutting along with his great belly tucked in and his chest stuck out, and actually managing to express himself in proper Italian, the dear good soul explained in a loud official voice that the director had given precise orders on the subject: and so–he repeated–would I kindly get up and clear out, at the double. The reading room was particularly crowded with secondary schoolboys that morning, and the scene was followed in sepulchral silence by no less than fifty pairs of eyes and as many pairs of ears. Well this alone–I went on

–made it hardly pleasant for me to get up, collect my books and papers from the table, shove the lot away in my brief-case, and then, step by step, reach the glass door. All right, then: that creep Poledrelli had done nothing but carry out orders! But if Malnate happened to meet him (and it wasn't outside the bounds of possibility that Poledrelli might belong to the school-mistress Trotti's little gang), he should be very careful not to let himself be taken in by the phony air of good nature on that great plebeian mug of his. Inside that chest as huge as a cupboard there lurked a heart just as tiny as this: pumping his working-class blood round all right, but not the least bit to be trusted.

So!–I said. So then!–Wasn't it to say the least out of place for him, to come along and preach–well, I wouldn't say to Alberto, whose family had always steered clear of communal life in Ferrara, but to me, who was born and had grown up in a circle that was perhaps rather too ready to open up trustfully, to join in with others in everything and for everything? My father had volunteered in the war and joined the fascist party in 1919; I myself had belonged to the G.U.F.* until just now. In fact, we'd always been the most normal people you could think of, so normal we were downright banal, in fact, and for this reason it seemed to me really ridiculous that now he should sud-denly expect us to behave in an exceptional way, just like that, out of the blue. Summoned to the Federation to hear himself expelled from the party, and so kicked out of the Circolo dei Commercianti as undesirable: it would have been most peculiar if my father, poor man, had looked less agonized and bewildered than he did in the face of such treatment. And what about my

* See note on page 82.

brother Ernesto, who'd had to leave Italy if he wanted
to go to the university, and take a course at the Polytechnic at Grenoble? And my sister Fanny, who was
just thirteen, and had to carry on her schooling at the
Jewish school in via Vignatagliata? Did he expect
them, wrenched suddenly away from all their friends
at school and at home, to behave in any remarkable
way? Well, not to worry: one of the hatefullest forms
of anti-semitism was this very thing: complaining that
the Jews weren't enough like other people, and then,
admitting they'd been pretty well assimilated into their
background, complaining of the opposite: that they
were exactly the same as everyone else, that is, and not
the least bit out of the common run.

I had let myself be carried away by anger, and had
gone rather beyond the limits of what we were discussing; which Malnate, who had been listening carefully, didn't fail to point out to me at the end. He, anti-
semitic?–he muttered; quite frankly this was the very
first time he'd ever been accused of such a thing! Still
excited, I was just going to say more, and really rub it
in, when I saw Alberto, flitting confusedly behind my
opponent with the speed of a frightened bird, fling me
an imploring look. "That's enough, I beseech you!"
his look said. The fact that, without his bosom friend
realizing it, he made such an appeal to what was most
secret between the two of us, struck me as quite extraordinary. I didn't answer, I said no more. And at once
the first notes of a Beethoven quartet played by the
Busches rose in the smoky atmosphere of the room to
seal my victory.

This was not the only important thing that evening,
though. Around eight o'clock it started raining so
violently that Alberto, after a quick telephone talk in

the family jargon, probably with his mother, suggested we should stay to supper.

Malnate said he accepted with pleasure. As a rule he had supper at *Giovanni's*, he told us, "as lonely as a dog": he just couldn't believe he was going to spend an evening "with friends". I accepted too, but asked if I could ring home.

"Why, of course!" exclaimed Alberto.

I sat down where he usually sat, behind the desk, and dialled the number. As I waited, I looked out sideways through the windows streaked with rain. The clumps of trees were scarcely visible through the thick darkness. Beyond the blackness of the park, heaven knows where, a small light glimmered.

My father's doleful voice answered at last.

"Oh, is that you?" he said. "We were beginning to be anxious. Where are you ringing from?"

"I'm staying out to supper," I answered.

"In this rain!"

"That's just why."

"Are you still at the Finzi-Continis'?"

"Yes."

"Come in and see me a minute, will you, whatever time you get home. As you know, I can't get to sleep. . . ."

I put down the receiver and looked up. Alberto was watching me.

"Done?" he said.

"Done."

The three of us went out into the passage, crossed various rooms, large and small, went down a big staircase at the foot of which Perotti was waiting, in a jacket and white gloves, and then went straight into the dining-room.

The rest of the family was already there: professór Ermanno, signora Olga, signora Regina, and one of the uncles from Venice, the T.B. specialist, who got up when he saw Alberto come in, and went up and kissed him on both cheeks, after which, as he absent-mindedly lowered the rim of Alberto's eye with his finger, he started explaining why he was there: he'd had to go to Bologna for a consultation–he said–and then, on the way back, it seemed a good idea to stop and have dinner between one train and the next. When we went in professór Ermanno, his wife, and his brother-in-law were sitting in front of the fire, with Yor stretched full length at their feet. But signora Regina was sitting at the table, right under the central lamp.

Inevitably the memory of my first dinner at the *magna domus* (we were still in January, I think) tends to become confused a little with memories of many other dinners I had at the Finzi-Continis' house that same winter. But I remember, with odd exactness, what we ate that evening: a *minestra di riso in brodo e fegatini*, a *polpettone* of turkey in jelly, tongue *salmis-trata** with black olives and spinach stalks in oil, choco-late cake, fresh fruit and dried fruit: walnuts, hazelnuts, raisins, pine seeds. I remember, besides, that almost at once, as soon as we sat down at the table, Alberto started telling the family how I had recently been thrown out of the city library, and once again I was surprised at the old people's lack of surprise at such a thing. The com-ments that followed on the general situation, and on Ballola and Poledrelli, which kept coming up all through dinner, were not even particularly bitter, but

* Soup with rice and chicken livers, a kind of terrine of turkey in jelly, a salami of tongue served cold and in thin slices.

elegantly sarcastic as usual, you might almost say gay. And gay, decidedly gay and pleased, was professór Ermanno's tone when he took my arm, much later, and suggested I should in future make full, free use whenever I wished of the twenty thousand odd books they had at home, an important part of which, he told me, were concerned with Italian literature of the middle and late nineteenth century.

But what struck me most, from that first evening on, was definitely the dining-room itself: with its *art nouveau* furniture in reddish wood, its huge fireplace with a sinuous, curved, almost human mouth, its walls covered in leather, except for one entirely of glass that opened on to the dark storm in the park like the port-hole of the *Nautilus*: so cosy, so sheltered, so–I would almost say–buried; so well suited to me as I was in those days, above all–I can see it now!–so well fitted to protect the kind of slow-burning coal that the heart of the young so often is.

When we went in, both Malnate and I were wel-comed with great friendliness, not just by professór Ermanno, who was as kind and jolly and lively as ever, but even by signora Olga. It was she who showed us where to sit at the table. Malnate sat on her right, and I, at the other end of the table, was on her husband's right; her brother Giulio sat on her left, between her and their old mother. And she, too, looking very hand-some with her rosy cheeks, and her silky white hair thicker and more shining than ever, looked about her in an amiable, amused sort of way.

The table, with its plates, glasses and cutlery, seemed laid for a seventh guest. As Perotti went round with the tureen of soup and rice, I quietly asked professór Ermanno for whom the chair on his left was kept. And he answered, quietly too, that it was nothing, the place was "presumably" not laid for anyone (he checked the time with his large Omega wrist-watch, shook his head, sighed), being just the chair usually used by his Micòl: "*Micòl mia*"–as he put it, exactly.

Chapter Six

Professór Ermanno had not deceived me. It was quite true that among the twenty thousand odd books in the house, many of them scientific, or historical, or on various learned subjects–most of these in German–there were several hundred on Italian literature of the second half of the nineteenth century. As far as Carducci's circle at the end of the century was concerned, in the many years he taught at Bologna, there was pretty well everything: verse and prose not just by the Master himself, but by Panzacchi, Severino Ferrari, Lorenzo Stecchetti, Ugo Brilli, Guido Mazzoni, the young Pascoli, the young Panzini, and the very young Valgimigli: first editions, mostly, almost all of them signed copies presented to baroness Josette Artom di Susegana. Collected in three glass-fronted bookshelves that stood on their own, taking up the entire wall of an enormous first-floor room next to professór Ermanno's own study, and carefully catalogued, there was not the smallest doubt that any public library, including the *Archiginnasio* at Bologna, would have coveted such a prize. Even the almost unobtainable little volumes of Acri's lyrical prose were there: Acri, the famous translator of Plato I had known till then only as a translator: not quite as "pi", then, as Meldolesi would have had us believe in the fifth form – he'd been a pupil of Acri's, too – since his inscriptions to Alberto and Micòl's grandmother showed altogether more gallantry than the others, more masculine awareness of the haughty beauty to whom they were addressed.

With a complete specialized library at my disposal, and every convenience in using it, and, apart from that, strangely eager to be there each morning, in the large, warm, silent room lit by three tall windows with red and white striped pelmets, and a billiard table in the middle covered with a grey cloth, I completed my thesis on Panzacchi in the two and a half months that followed. Had I really wanted to, I could probably have finished it sooner. But did I really want to? Or was I not trying to hang on as long as possible to the right to turn up at the Finzi-Continis' in the mornings *as well*? The fact is, anyway, that about the middle of March (Micòl had got her degree, meantime, we heard: with top marks), I still clung numbly to my poor morning privilege of using the house she insisted on steering clear of, heaven only knew why. We were only a few days from the Christian Easter, which that year almost coincided with *Pesach*, the Jewish paschal feast. Although spring was pretty well upon us, a week before it had snowed amazingly heavily, and then had grown intensely cold again. It looked almost as if winter were reluctant to go; and I too, my heart a dark, mysterious pool of fear, clung to the small desk professór Ermanno had had brought into the billiard room in January, and put under the middle window for me, as if by doing so I could stop the inexorable march of time. I would get up, go to the window, and look down into the park. Buried under a thick blanket of snow, Barchetto del Duca stretched before me like an ice landscape in a Nordic saga. Sometimes I surprised myself hoping for just that: that the snow and ice would never melt, that they would last for ever.

For two and a half months my days had been almost exactly the same. Punctual as a clerk, I left home in the biting cold at half-past eight, nearly always on my bicycle but sometimes on foot; after twenty minutes at the most I was ringing at the gate at the end of Corso Ercole I d'Este; then I crossed the park, over which, around February, hung the delicate scent of the yellow calicanthus; at nine I was already at work in the billiard room, where I stayed until one o'clock, and to which I returned in the afternoon about three; later, about six, I went on to Alberto's, sure of finding Malnate there as well: and often, as I have said, we were both asked to dinner. In fact it soon became so normal for me to stay out for dinner that I didn't even ring up home to warn them not to wait for me. I might say to my mother as I left the house: "I think I'll be staying there for dinner." There: and I had no need to say anything more precise.

For hours and hours I worked away, without a soul turning up, except Perotti at about eleven o'clock, carrying a cup of coffee on a silver tray. This coffee at eleven became a daily rite almost at once, a habit we had picked up which it wasn't worth wasting words on. What Perotti talked about as he waited for me to finish sipping the coffee was the "running" of the

house, which he felt had seriously deteriorated in the
overlong absence of the "signorina", who of course
had to become a teacher, although . . . (and his "although", accompanied by a dubious grimace, might
allude to all sorts of things: to the fact that his bosses,
lucky people, had absolutely no need to earn their
living; or to the racial laws, which in any case would
make our degrees worth only the paper they were
written on, without the smallest practical use) . . . but
this didn't exempt her from coming home on, say,
alternate weeks, as without her the house was quickly
going *"a remengo"**. With me, Perotti always found a
way of complaining about the family. He bit his lips,
and winked, and shook his head as signs of mistrust and
disapproval. When he mentioned signora Olga he
went so far as to tap his forehead with his blunt first
finger. I took no notice, of course, and firmly rejected
his repeated invitations to a low kind of complicity
that not only disgusted but offended me; so that soon,
in the face of my silences and cold smiles, Perotti could
do nothing but go, and leave me alone again.

One day his younger daughter Dirce turned up instead of him. She too waited beside the desk for me to
finish drinking the coffee. I drank it and glanced furtively at her.

"What's your name?" I asked her, when I gave back
the empty cup; my heart had started beating fast,
meantime.

"Dirce," she smiled, and coloured violently.

She was wearing her usual thick blue linen overall,
that smelt oddly of the nursery. Avoiding my eyes,
that were trying to meet hers, she made off. And a
moment later I was already ashamed of what had hap-

* "To rack and ruin": Venetian dialect.

pened (but what had happened, anyway?), as if it had been the vilest, the most sordid betrayal.

Of the family, the only one who appeared now and then was professór Ermanno. He would open his study door at the end of the room so cautiously, and then tiptoe across the room, that generally I noticed him only when he was right beside me, bending respectfully over the papers and books I had before me.

"How's it going?" he would ask, looking pleased. "You look as if you're getting on at a spanking pace!"

I would make a move to get up.

"No, no, carry on with your work," he would say. "I'm just going."

And, in fact, he usually never stayed more than five minutes, during which time he always found a way of showing me how much he liked and admired the tenacity with which I worked. He looked at me with glowing, shining eyes: as if expecting heaven knows what from me, and from my future as a man of letters; as if he were counting on me to fulfil some secret plan of his, that transcended not only him but me as well. . . . And I remember that this attitude of his towards me, although it flattered me, saddened me a little too. Why on earth didn't he expect as much from Alberto –I wondered–who was his own son, after all? Why had he accepted without protest or regret–in fact he never complained of it–that Alberto had given up taking his degree? And what about Micòl? In Venice, Micòl was doing exactly the same as I was: finishing a thesis. And yet he never mentioned Micòl without sighing; as if saying: "She's a girl, and women ought to stick to the house, not to literature!" But was I really to believe him?

One morning, though, he lingered on and talked for

rather longer than usual. Gradually he got round to Carducci's letters again and to his own "little works" on the Venetian subjects: all stuff–he said, indicating his study behind me–which he kept "in there". He smiled mysteriously, as he did so, looking at me slyly, invitingly. It was clear that he wanted to take me "in there", and at the same time wanted me to be the one to suggest being taken.

As soon as I realized what he wanted, I hastened to do it. So we went into his study, which was not much smaller than the billiard room, but looked smaller, in fact seemed actually cramped by an incredible collection of the most dissimilar things.

Books, to start off with: there were a very great many in the study as well: literary and scientific works –mathematics, physics, economics, agriculture, medicine, astronomy–all jumbled up; and books on the history of the country, of Ferrara or Venice, mixed up with others on "Jewish antiquities". They were crowded any old how into the usual glass-fronted bookcases, quite at random, taking up most of the large walnut table over which very likely only the top of professór Ermanno's cap emerged when he sat down; they were piled perilously on the chairs, and even scattered about the floor in heaps. Then there was a large globe, a lectern, a microscope, half a dozen barometers, a steel strong-box painted dark red, a small white bed, of the kind you find in a doctor's surgery, several hourglasses of various sizes, a brass kettledrum, a small upright German piano with two metronomes on it shut up in their pyramid-shaped cases, and all kinds of other objects mysterious to me, which I cannot remember, giving the place an air of Dr. Faustus that professór Ermanno was the first to smile at and apologize for, as if it were a completely personal and private weakness, a remnant of his youthful crazes. I forgot to say, though, that, unlike almost every other room in the house, which was overloaded with pictures, here I saw only a single one; an enormous life-size portrait by Lenbach, hanging like an altar-piece on the wall opposite his table. The magnificent standing figure, blonde and bare shouldered, with a fan in her gloved hand, and the silk train of her white dress brought forward to emphasize the length of her legs and the fullness of her figure, was obviously none other than baroness Josette Artom di Susegana. With that marble brow, those eyes, those scornful lips, that bosom, she really looked a queen. His mother's portrait was the one thing, out of everything in his study, that professór Ermanno never smiled at: either that morning, or later,

That same morning, anyway, I was at last presented with the two Venetian pamphlets. In one of them, professór Ermanno explained to me, all the inscriptions from the Jewish cemetery at the Lido were collected and translated. The other dealt with a Jewish poetess who lived in Venice in the first half of the seventeenth century, and was as well known in her own day as now, "alas", she was forgotten. She was called Sarah Enriquez (or Enriques) Avigdòr. For many years she had held an important literary salon in her house in Ghetto Vecchio, and her visitors included not only Leone da Modena, the learned rabbi who was half-Ferrarese and half-Venetian, but many of the most important men of letters of the time, and not only Italians, either. She wrote a great many "excellent" sonnets, which still awaited the person capable of championing their beauty; for over four years she corresponded brilliantly with the celebrated Ansaldo Cebà, a Genoese patrician who wrote an epic poem on Queen Esther, and had the notion of converting her to Catholicism, though in the end, seeing his efforts were hopeless, he had to give up the idea. A great woman, in fact: a credit and an honour to Italian Jewry in the full spate of the Counter Reformation, and in a way part of "the family"–professór Ermanno went on, as he sat down to write a short inscription to me–as it seemed that his wife, on her mother's side, was descended from her.

He got up, came round the table, took my arm, and led me over to the window.

But there was just one thing–he went on, lowering his voice as if afraid someone might hear–which he felt he should warn me about. If, in the future, I happened to have anything to do with this Sarah Enriquez (or Enriques) Avigdòr myself–a subject that deserved far more profound and careful study than he had managed to give it in his youth–at a certain point, quite fatally, I would have to come up against certain dissident . . . discordant . . . voices, in fact with the writings of various third-rate literary men, mostly contemporaries of the poetess (libellous writers fairly bursting with envy and anti-semitism), who tried to insinuate that not all the sonnets signed by her, and not even all the letters she wrote to Cebà, were . . . how could he put it? . . . all her own work. Well now, when he wrote his essay, he hadn't, of course, been able to help knowing of the existence of these rumours, and in fact, as I'd see, he had faithfully set them down; all the same. . . .

He stopped, to stare into my face, doubtful of my reactions.

All the same–he went on–if I, "at some later date", thought . . . uhm . . . decided to attempt a revaluation

. . . a revision . . . he would advise me straight away
not to take these malicious suggestions too seriously.
Picturesque and even amusing they might be, but they
were quite beside the point. What, after all, was the
business of a good historian? His ideal, certainly, was
to get at the truth, but in doing so he must never lose
his sense of what was suitable and just. Didn't I agree?
I nodded in agreement, and, relieved, he patted me
lightly on the back with the palm of his hand.

Having done this he drew away from me, crossed
the room, round-shoulderedly as ever, and bent
over to fiddle with a strong-box, which he opened,
finally bringing out a trinket-box covered in blue
velvet.

He turned and came back to the window, all smiles,
and even before he opened the casket he said yes, he'd
guessed that I'd guessed: inside it were the famous
letters from Carducci. There were fifteen of them:
and perhaps–he went on–I shouldn't find all of them
of very great interest, since a good five dealt with the
single subject of a certain *salama da suge* "from our own
property", which the poet had been given as a present,
and seemed to have highly appreciated. All the same I
would find one among them that would certainly
strike me: a letter written in the autumn of '75, that is
when the crisis of the Italian Right was already beginning to appear on the horizon. In the autumn of '75
Carducci's political position was as follows: as a demo-
crat, as a republican, and a revolutionary, he declared
he could line himself up only with the left of Agostino
Depretis. On the other hand the man he called a
"rough wine-merchant from Stradello" and the
"rabble" that were his friends seemed to him vulgar
people, "nobodies". They'd never be in a position to

restore Italy to her true mission, to make her a great Nation, worthy of its ancient Fathers. . . .

We stayed talking together until lunch time. With the result that from then on the door between the billiard room and the study, which until then had always been shut, often stayed open. Most of the time we both carried on in our respective rooms, of course. But we met much more often than before: professór Ermanno coming to see me, and I going in to see him. When the door was open we even exchanged a few words: "What's the time?", "How's the work going?" and so on. Some years later, in the winter of 1944, in prison, these were the phrases, the kind of questions, I was to exchange with an unknown neighbour in the next cell, shouting up through the cell window: spoken like that, above all for the need to hear one's own voice, to feel alive.

Chapter Seven

At home, that year, *Pésach* was celebrated with a single supper instead of two.

It was my father who wanted it so. With Ernesto studying in France – he said – it wasn't really suitable for us to have a *Pésach* like those in previous years. And then, apart from that, how could we possibly manage it? *My* Finzi-Continis had been marvellously clever, as usual: with their garden as an excuse, they'd managed to keep on all the servants they wanted, passing them off as outdoor workers. But what about us? Since we'd been forced to get rid of Elisa and Mariuccia, and instead get that hopeless old Cohèn creature, we'd been to all intents and purposes without servants. In the circumstances you couldn't expect even Mother to do miracles.

"Isn't that so, my love?"

His love's feeling for the sixty-year-old signorina Ricca Cohèn, a distinguished pensioner of our community, were not really much warmer than my father's. Apart from rejoicing, as always, when she heard some of us running down the poor old thing, mother agreed gratefully to the idea of a subdued Pascal feast. That was fine—she said approvingly: just one supper, the one on the first evening, and with ten guests at the most, there'd been nothing in that, would there? She and Fanny could manage practically on their own, without "her"—and she waved in the direction of signorina Cohèn, who had bolted into the kitchen, quite off her own bat—making trouble with one of her usual sulks. What's more, just to avoid her having to go back and forth with plates and dishes, at the risk of tumbling around on those poor old legs of hers, what about doing something else: instead of having it in the drawing-room, which was so far from the kitchen, and this year, what with the snow and things, just about like Siberia, lay it all here, in the small dining-room instead. . . .

It was not a gay meal. The wicker basket holding, besides the ritual "morsels", the earthenware dish of *haròset*, the bunch of bitter herbs, the unleavened bread, and the hard-boiled egg reserved for me, the first-born, stood grandly but pointlessly in the centre of the table under the blue and white silk handkerchief embroidered forty years before by grandmother Ester. Although it was carefully laid, in fact just because of that, the table in the small dining-room looked rather as it did on the evening of Yom Kippur, when it was prepared only for Them, the family dead, whose bones lay down in the cemetery at the end of via Montebello, and yet were still very much present here, in spirit and in effigy. Here, instead of them, we, the living, sat that evening; but fewer than we had been before, and instead of being gay, all laughter and shouting, we were as sad and thoughtful as the dead. I looked at my father and mother, who had both aged so much in a few months; I looked at Fanny, who was now fifteen, but who, as if a secret fear had stopped her development, looked no more than twelve: I looked at them all, one by one, uncles and aunts and cousins, most of whom were to be swallowed up in the German crematoria within the next few years; not that they dreamed, of course, of ending up that way, and neither did I imagine it, but none the less even then, that evening, their poor faces looked to me so dingy under their respectable little hats, framed in their respectable permanent waves, and I knew their minds to be so obtuse, so utterly unable to see what the present really meant and to read into the future, that they already appeared to me wrapped round in the same aura that now enfolds them in my memory – mysterious, statuesque, predestined; I looked at old signorina Cohèn the few times she dared peep out from the kitchen door: Ricca Cohèn, the lady-like spinster of sixty let loose from the home in via Vittoria to act as maid to her comfortably off co-religionists, but who wanted

nothing more than to go back to the home, and die
there before things got any worse; finally I looked
at myself, reflected in the opaque water of the large
looking-glass opposite, no different from the others,
already slightly grey-haired, caught up in the same
mechanism as they were, and yet reluctant, still un-
resigned. I wasn't dead, I said to myself. I was still
very much alive! But then, if I was still alive, what was
my object, how could I hang around here, with all
these others? Why didn't I get away at once from this
desperate and grotesque gathering of ghosts, or why
at least didn't I plug my ears so as to hear no more
about favoured categories, patriotic merits, certificate
of Aryanness, quarters and eighths of blood, so as to
stop hearing the petty complaints, the grey, monoton-
ous, pointless dirge the family was intoning softly
around me? The dinner would drag on like that, and
it was anyone's guess how many hours it would last,
with the same old talk, with my father every now and
then recalling, with bitter glee, the various "affronts"
he had suffered during the past months, starting from
when the Federal secretary Consul Bolognesi had told
him, in the Federation office, looking pained and
guilty, that he was forced to "cross him off" the list of
party members, and ending with the time when, looking no less sad, the President of the Circolo dei Commercianti had sent for him to tell him he must accept
his resignation. Oh, the tales he'd have to tell! Till
one o'clock, till two! And after that? After that,
there'd be the last scene of all, the farewell scene. I
could see it already. We had gone down the dark staircase in a group, like a flock of sheep worried along.
When we reached the portico, someone (me, perhaps)
went ahead to open the street door a little, and now,

for the last time before we parted, the good nights, good wishes, handshakes, hugs, and kisses on the cheek started up all over again, from everyone, including me. But suddenly, through the front door half-opened on to the darkness, comes a violent gust of wind, a hurricane, out of the night. It hurtles into the portico, crosses it, goes whistling out through the gates that separate the portico from the garden, forcibly scattering anyone who wants to stay, and, with its wild roar, suddenly silencing anyone who still lingers to talk. Thin voices, faint shouts, are immediately overwhelmed, blown away like light leaves, like bits of paper, like the hair on a head turned white with the years or with terror. . . . Oh, Ernesto was lucky, really, not to have been able to go to the university in Italy. He wrote from Grenoble that he went hungry, that with the little French he knew he could understand practically nothing of the Polytechnic lectures. But he was lucky to suffer from hunger and be scared of failing exams – maths, especially! I had stayed here and, having stayed, had once again, out of pride and barrenness, chosen solitude, nursing vague, nebulous, impotent hopes; but for me there was no hope, simply no hope at all.

But who can ever see ahead? What can we know about ourselves, and about what we are going to meet?

As it turned out, at about eleven, when my father, obviously hoping to dissipate the general gloom, had just begun singing the *Pésach* rigmarole of *Caprét ch' avea comperà il signor Padre** (it was his favourite: his hobby-horse, as he called it), I happened to glance up into the large looking-glass opposite and noticed the

* The little goat that Father bought: Jewish Ferrarese jargon.

door of the telephone room very gently opening behind me. And through the opening, cautiously, poked
old Cohèn's face. She was looking at me, right at me;
and seemed to be asking for help.

I got up and went over to her.

"What is it?"

She pointed at the receiver dangling on its cord, and
vanished in the opposite direction, through the door
into the hall.

Left alone, in complete darkness, even before I put
the instrument to my ear I recognized Alberto's voice.

"I can hear singing," he cried, strangely gay.
"Where've you got to?"

"To *Capret ch' avea comperà il signor Padre*," I replied.

"Oh, good. We've already finished. Why don't you
come over?"

"Now!" I exclaimed, astonished.

"Why not. Conversation's beginning to droop, and
with your well-known talents you can perk it up for
us." He giggled. "And besides," he went on, "we've
got a surprise for you."

"A surprise? What sort of a one?"

"Come and see."

"You *are* being mysterious." My heart was thudding
furiously. "Come on, tell."

"No, don't hold off. Come along and you'll see."

I went straight into the hall, took my overcoat, scarf
and hat, poked my head into the kitchen and asked old
Cohèn softly to say, if anyone wanted me, that I'd had
to go out for a moment, and two minutes later was
down in the street.

It was a splendid moonlight night, freezing, dead
clear. There was practically no one about in the streets,
and corso Giovecca and corso Ercole I d'Este, so white

they looked almost salty, opened out ahead of me as smooth and uncluttered as two great race-tracks. I pedalled along the brightly lit middle of the street, ears aching with the cold; but I had drunk a good deal of wine at dinner and didn't feel the cold, in fact I was sweating. The bicycle tyres swished faintly on the hardened snow, and the dry dust they raised filled me with carefree joy, as if I were skiing. I rode fast, not afraid of slithering; and as I rode I thought of the surprise Alberto had said was waiting for me at the house. What was it: could Micòl be back? It was odd, though. Why hadn't she come to the telephone herself? And why, before supper, hadn't she turned up at the synagogue? If she'd been there I'd have known it already. My father, at the table, enumerating those present at the ceremony, as usual (it was partly for my benefit: an indirect reproach for not having gone), obviously wouldn't have forgotten to mention her. He'd mentioned all of them, Finzi-Continis and Herreras, but not her. Could she possibly have arrived on her own at the very last minute, on the quarter-past nine express?

With the snow and the moon gleaming together even more intensely, I set off across Barchetto del Duca in the direction of the *magna domus*. Half-way across, I remember, a little before I got on to the bridge over the Panfilio canal, a gigantic shadow suddenly loomed up in front of me. It was Yor. I recognized him after a second's hesitation, when I was just going to cry out. And the moment I recognized him fear changed into almost equally paralysing premonition. So it was true –I said to myself–Micòl was back. Warned by the bell from the street, she'd got up from the table and come down, and now, sending Yor ahead to meet me, was waiting at the little side door used only by members of the household and close friends. A few more turns of the pedals and then Micòl, Micòl herself: a small dark figure outlined against a glaringly white background, like a power station, and haloed by the protective breath of the central heating. In a few seconds I would hear her *"ciao"*.

"*Ciao*," said Micòl, standing there. "This is fine, your coming."

I had foreseen everything exactly: everything except that I would kiss her. I got off the saddle, answered: "*Ciao*. How long have you been here?" and she still had time to say: "Since this afternoon, I came with my uncles," and then ... then I kissed her. It happened all of a sudden. But how? My face was still hidden in her warm scented neck (it was a strange scent: a smell of childish skin and talcum powder together) when I started wondering. How could it have happened? I had taken her in my arms, she had made a faint effort at resistance, and then had let me. Was this how it happened? Maybe it was. But what about now?

I drew away slowly. Now she was there, her face just ahead of mine. I stared at her without speaking or moving, incredulous, already incredulous. Leaning back against the doorpost, a black woollen shawl round her shoulders, she was staring back at me in silence. She was looking into my eyes, and her look went straight inside me, sure and hard: clear and inexorable as a sword.

I was the first to look away.

"Sorry," I murmured.

"Why sorry? Maybe it was me, I was wrong to come and meet you. It's my fault."

She shook her head. Then she sketched a smile, nice, affectionate.

"All this gorgeous snow!" she said, motioning to-

wards the park with her chin. "Just think: none at all
in Venice, not an inch. If I'd known there was such a
lot here . . ."

She finished with a movement of her hand: her right
hand. She had pulled it out from under her shawl, and
I noticed a ring at once.

I took her wrist.

"What's that?" I asked, touching the ring with the
tip of my first finger.

She made a face, which looked scornful.

"I'm *engaged*, don't you know?"

Straight afterwards, she broke into a hearty laugh:
"Oh, no, cheer up . . . can't you see I'm joking? It's
not much of a ring. Look."

She took it off, moving her elbows a lot, and handed
it to me, and it was really not much of a ring: just
a circle of gold with a small turquoise. Her grandmother Regina had given it to her years before – she
explained – hidden inside an Easter egg.

When she got the ring back, she put it on again, and
then took my hand.

"Come on now," she whispered, "otherwise they're
quite likely" – and she laughed – "to be worried, up
there."

As we went up, she was still holding my hand (she
stopped on the stairs, looked carefully at my lips in the
light, and concluded the examination with a casual
"That's fine!"), and never stopped talking for a
moment, very volubly.

Yes – she said – the thesis business had gone better
than she'd dared to hope. When she sat for the oral
exam for her degree, she'd kept going for a good hour,
haranguing away for all she was worth. At the end of
it they'd sent her outside, and she'd been able to listen

comfortably to all the examiners said about her, through the stained glass door in the main hall. Most of them wanted her to get the highest marks, but one, the professor of German (a real dyed-in-the-wool Nazi!) wouldn't hear of it. This charming fellow was quite definite. They couldn't, he said, give her high marks without provoking the most serious scandal. Whatever were they thinking of!-he cried.-Why, the girl was Jewish, and what was more not even in the favoured category, and here they were actually considering giving her honours! Shame on them! She was lucky she'd been allowed to take her degree at all. . . . The chairman, though, whose subject was English, retorted sharply that work was work, and that intelligence and being well prepared (heavens alive!) had nothing to do with blood groups, etc. etc. But when it came to the point, the Nazi won, as you might have guessed. And all the satisfaction she had-apart from the English don's apologies later, when he dashed down the stairs at Ca' Foscari (poor soul: his chin was trembling, he had tears in his eyes)-all the satisfaction she had was to receive the verdict with the most impeccable of Roman salutes. The dean of the faculty, in the act of calling her doctor, raised his arm. So what could she do? Give a sulky little nod? Certainly not!

She laughed gaily, and I laughed too, excitedly, and told her about my expulsion from the city library, with a wealth of comic detail. But when I asked her why she had stayed on in Venice for another month after getting her degree-in Venice, I added, where she said she not only disliked the place but had no friends at all, male or female-at this point she grew serious, withdrew her hand from mine, and gave me a quick sidelong glance as her only answer.

A foretaste of the gay welcome we were to receive
in the dining-room was given us by Perotti, who was
waiting in the hall. As soon as he saw us come down the
main staircase, followed by Yor, he gave us an extraordinarily delighted smile, with a kind of complicity
about it. At any other time his behaviour would have
shocked me, I would have felt insulted by it. But for
the last few minutes I had been feeling in a quite
special state of mind. Stifling every reason for uneasiness, I went ahead feeling strangely light, as if borne on
invisible wings. Perotti was a good soul, when you got
down to it, I thought. He too was pleased to have the
"signorina" back at home. And what was wrong with
that in the poor old fellow? From now on he'd obviously stop his grousing.

We appeared side by side at the dining-room door,
and our arrival was greeted, as I say, with great excitement. All the faces round the table were lit up rosily,
all eyes were on us affectionately, benevolently. But
the room, too, as it appeared to me suddenly that
evening, seemed more welcoming and warmer than
usual, rosy as well in a way, with the polished light-
wood furniture, that gleamed a tender reddish brown
in the light of the long flames licking in the fireplace.
I'd never seen the room lit like this. Apart from the
glow from the fire, the big central light, shaped like
the corolla of a flower turned upside down, poured out
on to the table still covered in a rich dazzlingly white
linen cloth (plates and cutlery had obviously been
cleared away) a positive cataract of light.

"Come along in! Come in!"

"Nice to see you!"

"We were beginning to think you wouldn't want
the bother of coming."

This last remark was Alberto's, but I could feel that my coming really pleased him. They were all looking at me, in particular. Some, like professór Ermanno, had twisted round completely on their chairs; some were leaning forward, their chests on the edge of the table, or else were pushing away from it, stiff-armed; and some, like signora Olga, who was sitting at the head of the table, with the fire just behind her, were leaning forward, their eyes half shut. They watched me, examined me, stared at me from head to foot, and seemed pretty satisfied with me, with the figure I was cutting beside Micòl. Only Federico Herrera, the railway engineer, hesitated a moment before sharing in the general delight, no doubt because he couldn't remember who I was. But only for a moment. Having found out about me from his brother Giulio (I saw them discussing it briefly, their two bald heads together behind their old mother), he was all friendliness too, not only smiling to show his large top incisors, but even raising his arm in a gesture that was not so much a greeting as a movement of solidarity, rallying, sporty.

Professór Ermanno insisted on my sitting down at his right. It was my usual place, he explained to Micòl, who had sat down on his left opposite me; the one I usually took when I stayed to dinner. Giampiero Malnate, he went on, Alberto's friend, sat over there (he indicated where), on Mummy's right. And Micòl sat listening with a curious air, half nettled and half sardonic; as if she disliked seeing that the family's life while she was away had carried on in directions she hadn't completely foreseen, and at the same time was quite pleased that things had gone just that way.

I sat down, and at once, astonished to find I had been

mistaken, I realized the table wasn't cleared at all. A large flat silver tray stood in the centre, and in the middle of the tray, with a small space round it and then surrounded by a halo of pieces of white paper, with a letter of the alphabet in red pencil on each one, was a single glass of champagne.

"What's that?" I asked Alberto.

"Oh, that's the big surprise I told you about!" exclaimed Alberto. "It's simply fabulous; what happens is that three or four people in a ring put their fingers on the edge of this glass and it goes from one letter to another, answering."

"Answering?"

"Certainly! It *writes* the answers, very very slowly. And proper answers, you know, you just can't imagine what sensible ones!"

It was a long time since I had seen Alberto so euphoric, so excited.

"And where does it come from," I asked, "this brand new marvel?"

"It's only a game," said professór Ermanno, laying a hand on my arm and shaking his head. "Something Micòl brought from Venice."

"Ah, so it's your doing!" I said, turning to Micòl. "And does this glass of yours read the future, too?"

"Why of course!" she exclaimed, with a mischievous wink. "In fact, that's just its strong point, I'd say."

At that moment Dirce came in, a round dark wooden tray loaded with paschal sweets, balanced high on one hand. Dirce's cheeks were rosy, too, glowing with health and good humour. As the guest, and the latest arrival, I was served first. The sweets, called *zucarín*, made of sweet pastry mixed with raisins, were more or less the same as those I had tasted so reluctantly

a little earlier at home. But these at the Finzi-Continis'
at once seemed to me much better, quite remarkably
delicious; and I said so too, turning to signora Olga,
who, busy choosing a *zucarín* from the plate Dirce held
out to her, seemed not to notice my compliment.

Then Perotti came in, his big peasant hands clutching
the edge of a second tray (of pewter, this one) with a
flask of white wine on it and glasses for everyone. And
then, as we sat quietly round the table, slowly sipping
Albana and nibbling *zucarín*, Alberto told me, in particular, about the "divining powers" of the glass that
stood there in the middle of the table, as silent as any
plain honest "verre"* in the world, but which, until a
little time ago, had been quite exceptionally, quite
astoundingly chatty when they had put questions to it.

I asked what sort of questions.

"Oh, a bit of everything," Alberto said.

They had asked, for instance – he went on – whether
he, Alberto, would some day manage to get his degree
in engineering; and the glass had retorted at once with
the dryest of "noes". Then Micòl wanted to know if
she'd get married, and when; and to that the glass was
much less definite, in fact it was pretty confused, and
answered like a proper classic oracle, so that you could
interpret it in absolutely opposite ways. They'd even
asked it about the tennis court, poor wretched glass!;
trying to find out if Papa would stop his everlasting
game of putting off the work that needed doing from
year to year. And on this point the oracle, patient soul,
had gone back to being nice and explicit, and had
assured them that the improvements they longed for
would be made just as soon as possible during that
same year.

* In French in the original.

But it was on the question of politics, above all, that the glass had done marvels. Soon, in a few months–it had said–war would break out: a war that would be long, bloody, and painful to *everyone*, that would overturn the entire world, but which would end, after years of uncertain fighting, with the complete victory for the powers of good. "The powers of good?" Micòl, who had always been famous for putting her foot in it, asked at this point: "And which, pray, might the powers of good be?" At which the glass, dumbfounding everyone, replied with a single word: "Stalin."

"Can you imagine," exclaimed Alberto, while everyone roared with laughter, "can you imagine how thrilled old Giampi'd be if he were here? I must write and tell him."

"Isn't he in Ferrara?"

"No, he left yesterday. He's gone home for Easter."

Alberto went on rather long-windedly about what the glass had said, after which we took up the game again. I too was urged to put my first finger on the rim of the glass, I too asked questions and waited for replies. But now, heaven knows why, the oracle said nothing that made sense. Alberto hammered away, tougher and more obstinate than ever. No good.

In any case, I wasn't really too keen on it. I wasn't so much paying attention to him and the game with the glass as looking round the room, and outside, through the big round window that gave on to the park, and at Micòl, above all, who sat opposite me at the table: Micòl who, from time to time, feeling my eyes on her, stopped frowning, as she did when she played tennis, to give me a quick, thoughtful, reassuring smile.

I gazed at her lips, faintly coloured with lipstick.

Yes, I had actually kissed them myself, a short while ago. But hadn't it already been too late? Why hadn't I done so six months before when everthing was still possible, or at least during the winter? The time we'd wasted: I here in Ferrara, and she in Venice! I could perfectly well have taken the train one Sunday and gone to see her. There was an express that left Ferrara at eight in the morning and got to Venice at half-past ten. As soon as I arrived at the station I could have rung her up and suggested she take me to the Lido (that way, among other things – I'd say – I'd at last visit the famous Jewish cemetery of San Niccolò). Later we could have lunch together, still somewhere around there, and afterwards, having rung up her uncles' house to keep Fraulein quiet (oh, Micòl's face as she telephoned, the funny faces she'd pull!), we could go for a long walk along the empty beach. There had been all the time in the world for this as well. Then, when it came to leaving, I'd have had a choice of two trains, one at five and one at seven, on either of which I could have got home without the family noticing a thing. Yes, that was it: if I'd done it then, when I ought to have, it would have been perfectly easy. Nothing to it. Whereas now it was late, it was terribly late.

What was the time? Half-past one, or even two. I'd soon have to leave and probably Micòl would come downstairs with me, to the garden door.

Perhaps this was what she was thinking of, too; this was what was worrying her. Through room after room, passage after passage, we'd walk along side by side, not daring to look at each other or to exchange a word. We were both scared of the same thing, I could feel it: my leave-taking, the ever closer and less imaginable moment when we'd say good night, kiss good night. And yet, if by any chance Micòl didn't come with me, and left it to Alberto or (as indeed happened soon afterwards) actually to Perotti, how could I face the rest of the night, in what sort of state? And the next day?

But maybe not—I was already dreaming again, stubbornly, desperately—maybe there was no point, no need, to get up from the table. That night, in any case, would never end.

PART
FOUR

Chapter One

At once, next day, I began to realize it was going to be very hard for me to get back on the same footing with Micòl.

After much hesitation, I tried ringing up at about ten o'clock. I was told (by Dirce) that the young people were still in their rooms, and asked if I would be good enough to ring again about midday. To get over the waiting, I flung myself down on my bed. Haphazardly I picked up a book: *Le Rouge et le Noir;* but however hard I tried I couldn't concentrate. Supposing–I wondered–I didn't ring up at midday? But I soon changed my mind. Suddenly I felt I wanted only one thing from Micòl now: her friendship. It was very much better–I said to myself–to behave as if nothing had happened last night than to vanish. Micòl would understand. Struck by my tact, fully reassured, she'd very soon trust me completely, and give me her dear confidence, as she had before.

So, on the dot of midday, I plucked up courage and dialled the Finzi-Continis's number for the second time.

I had to wait a long time, longer than usual.

"Hullo," I said at last, my voice broken with feeling.

"Oh, is that you?"

It was actually Micòl's voice. She yawned: "What's up?"

Disconcerted, my mind a blank, for a minute I found nothing better to say than that I'd already rung up two hours before. It was Dirce–I stammered–who'd suggested I should ring up about midday.

Micòl heard me out. Then she started complaining about the day she had ahead of her, with so many things to see to after months and months away, suitcases to unpack, books and papers to tidy, etc. etc., and then the not exactly alluring prospect of a second "symposium". That was the trouble with going away –she grumbled–: afterwards, when you got back to the old routine and tried to pick up the threads again, it was even more of an effort than the pretty frightful effort of getting away in the first place. Was she coming to the synagogue later?–she said, in answer to a timid question of mine. Well, she might. She might and she might not. Just at this particular moment she didn't feel much like guaranteeing it.

She hung up without inviting me back that evening, or arranging when and where we should meet again.

I didn't ring again that day, and even stayed away from the synagogue, although she had said I might see her there. But about seven, as I went along via Mazzini, and noticed the Finzi-Continis' grey Dilambda parked behind the corner of via Scianze, on the side where the stones are, with Perotti, in chauffeur's cap and uniform, sitting at the wheel, I couldn't resist the temptation to stand at the angle of via Vittoria and wait.

For a long time I waited in the freezing cold. It was the busiest time of evening, when people were out before supper. Along both pavements of via Mazzini, slushy with half-melted, dirty snow, a crowd of people was hurrying in both directions. At last I had my reward: because at the end of the service, although from a distance, I saw her suddenly come out of the synagogue door and stop, alone, on the threshold. She was wearing a short leopard-skin coat drawn in at the waist with a leather belt, and, her blonde hair gleaming in the light of the shop windows, looked about as if in search of someone. Could I be the one she was looking for, taking no notice of the many who turned to gape and admire? I was just going to come out of the shadows and move forward, when the family, who had obviously followed at a distance down the stairs, appeared in a group behind her. They were all there, including grandmother Regina. Turning on my heels, I hurried off along via Vittoria.

Next day and the days that followed I kept on ringing up, but managed to talk to her only rather rarely. Someone else nearly always answered: Alberto, or professór Ermanno, or Dirce, or even Perotti, all of whom, with the exception of Dirce, who was as brief and impersonal as a switchboard operator, and for that very reason embarrassing and off-putting, involved me in long, pointless conversations. After a bit, admittedly, I could break in on Perotti. But with Alberto and professór Ermanno it wasn't so easy. I let them talk, always hoping they'd mention Micòl. No good. As if they were avoiding it deliberately, and in fact had agreed among themselves to do so, her father and brother left me the initiative of mentioning her; with the result that very often I hung up without having dared to ask them to put me through to her.

Then I started going there again: either in the mornings, with the excuse of my thesis, or in the afternoons, to see Alberto. I never made the smallest move to tell Micòl I was in the house. I was certain she must know, and that some day she would appear spontaneously.

The thesis, actually, although it was finished, still needed copying out again. So I brought my type-writer from home, and as soon as its tapping broke the silence of the billiard room, professór Ermanno came to his study door.

"What are you up to? The final copy already?" he cried gaily.

He came over and wanted to see the typewriter. It was a portable Italian one, a Littoria, which my father had given me a few years before, when I passed my school-leaving exams. Its make didn't make him smile, as I had feared it might. He seemed actually pleased, saying that "even" in Italy we could now produce typewriters that, like mine, seemed to work perfectly. They had three in the house—he said—one for Alberto, one for Micòl, and one for him: all three were Ameri-can, Underwoods. Those belonging to the children were portables: very strong, no doubt, but certainly not as light as this one (and he weighed it as he spoke, holding it by the handle). Whereas his was the ordinary kind: the sort you call an office typewriter, clumsy and old-fashioned, maybe, but solid, really comfortable. Did I know how many carbon copies you could make on it, if you wanted to? Anything up to seven.

He took me into his study and showed it to me, lift-ing a dreary metal cover, painted black, which I'd never noticed until then. It was really a museum piece, obviously used very little even when it was new. And it was hard to convince professór Ermanno that, although my Littoria couldn't manage more than three copies, two of them on very thin paper, I'd rather go on using that.

Chapter by chapter I tapped out on the keyboard, but my mind was elsewhere. And it was elsewhere in

the afternoons as well, when I was in Alberto's study.
Malnate had come back from Milan a good week after
Easter, full of indignation about the recent political
events (the fall of Madrid: ah, but it wasn't all over
yet!: the conquest of Albania: how shameful, what
buffoonery!). As far as Albania was concerned, he
mentioned sarcastically what he'd heard from some
friends he and Alberto had in common in Milan. The
campaign had been Ciano's special notion, he told us;
Ciano, jealous of von Ribbentrop, thought this revolt-
ing piece of baseness would show the world he could
go in for flash-diplomacy just as well as the Germans.
Could you believe it? It seemed even Cardinal Schuster
(which was just about saying everything!) had de-
plored the whole business and given a warning: and
although he'd spoken among the closest friends the
whole of Milan had heard of it afterwards. Giampi
talked about Milan as well: about a performance of
Mozart's *Don Giovanni* at the Scala, which luckily he
hadn't missed; and then about Gladys–yes, actually
Gladys–whom he'd met quite by chance in the Galleria, swathed in mink and arm in arm with a well-
known industrialist: and, friendly as ever, she'd turned
to him as she passed and made a tiny sign with her
finger, as if to say: "Ring me," or "I'll ring you."
What a bore he'd had to come straight back to the
grind! He'd have loved to stick a pair of horns on the
head of that famous steel tycoon, war-profiteer-to-
be. . . . He talked and he talked: turning mostly to me,
as usual, but, I had a feeling, rather less sharp and didac-
tic than he'd been the previous months: as if his trip
to Milan to see his family and friends had touched him
with a new feeling of indulgence towards others and
their opinions.

With Micòl, as I have said, I was only rarely in touch, and that only on the telephone; and when we spoke we both avoided mentioning anything very personal. All the same, a few days after I had waited for over an hour at the synagogue door, I couldn't resist the temptation of complaining of her coldness.

"D'you know," I said, "on the second Seder night I saw you again."

"Oh, did you? Were you at the synagogue too?"

"No, I wasn't. I was going along via Mazzini, noticed your car, and preferred to wait outside."

"What an idea."

"You were terribly smart. Shall I tell you what you were wearing?"

"Oh, I believe you, I'll take your word for it. Where were you?"

"On the opposite pavement, at the corner of via Vittoria. At one point you looked in my direction. Tell me honestly: did you recognize me?"

"No, why should I say something when I mean something else? But the thing is I just can't see why. . . . Couldn't you have waved, or something?"

"I was just going to, then when I realized you weren't alone I dropped the idea."

"Well, what a discovery, that I wasn't alone! You're a funny boy, aren't you. You could have come over and said hello to me all the same."

"Yes, I could, if I'd reasoned it out. The trouble is you can't always reason things out. And then: would you have wanted me to?"

"Oh heavens, what a fuss!" she sighed.

The second time I managed to talk to her, no less than a dozen days later, she told me that she was ill, with a "powerful" cold and a bit of a temperature.

What a bore it was! Why did I never come and see her? I'd really forgotten her!

"Are you . . . are you in bed?" I stammered, disconcerted, feeling the victim of an enormous injustice.

"I certainly am, and right under the bedclothes at that. I bet you won't come because you're scared of influenza."

"No, no, Micòl," I answered bitterly. "Don't make me out more of a coward than I am. I was just amazed to hear you accusing me of having forgotten you, when the fact is . . . Don't you remember," I went on, my voice thickening, "that before you went to Venice ringing you up was easy, whereas now, you must admit, it's become quite a feat. D'you know I've been to your house several times, these last few days? Did they tell you?"

"Yes."

"Well then! If you wanted to see me you knew perfectly well where to find me: in the mornings in the billiard room, in the afternoons down below at your brother's. The truth is you didn't want to in the least."

"What nonsense! I've never liked going to Alberto's, especially when he's got friends in to see him. And as for coming to see you in the mornings, aren't you working? If there's one thing I *loathe* it's bothering people when they're working. Anyway, if you really want me to, tomorrow or the day after I'll come along for a minute and say hello."

She didn't come next morning, but in the afternoon, while I was at Alberto's (it must have been about seven o'clock: Malnate had left abruptly a few minutes before), Perotti came in. The "signorina" asked me to go upstairs a moment–he announced stolidly, but he seemed to me in a bad mood. She apologized: she was

still in bed, else she'd have come down. What would I
rather do: go up right away, or else stay to supper and
go up afterwards? She'd rather I went up at once, as
she had a bit of a headache and wanted to put the light
out very early. But if I decided to stay . . .

"No, please," I said, looking at Alberto. "I'm coming right away."

I got up and made ready to follow Perotti.

"Look, don't stand on ceremony," Alberto said,
coming solicitously to the door with me. "I think that
there'll only be Papa and me at supper this evening.
My grandmother's in bed with 'flu as well, and
Mummy wouldn't think of leaving her room for a
minute. So if you'd like to have a bite with us, and then
go up to Micòl afterwards. . . . You know Papa's
always pleased to see you."

I declined the invitation, inventing a non-existent
engagement that evening, and ran after Perotti, who
had already reached the end of the passage.

Without exchanging a word we soon arrived at the
foot of the long spiral staircase that went up and up, as
far as the base of the tower-skylight. Micòl's set of
rooms, I knew, was the highest in the house, only half a
flight below the top landing.

I hadn't noticed the lift, and got ready to walk
up.

"You're young, of course," grinned Perotti, "but a
hundred and twenty-three steps is quite a climb.
Wouldn't you like to take the lift? It works, you
know."

And he opened the gate of the black outside cage,
then the sliding door of the lift inside, and stood aside
to let me in.

I walked into the lift, which was an antediluvian box

all of gleaming wine-coloured woods, and glittering stripes of glass adorned with an M, an F, and a C elaborately interwoven; it had a pungent, faintly suffocating smell, compounded of mould and turpentine, a smell that impregnated the stuffy air in that enclosed space; and felt an unmotivated sense of calm, of fatalistic tranquillity, of positively ironic detachment, all in the space of a moment. Where had I smelt a smell like that?—I wondered.—When?

The lift started moving slowly up through the well of the stairs. I sniffed the air and stared ahead of me at Perotti's striped linen back. The old man had left the seat upholstered in soft velvet entirely to me. Standing two feet away, absorbed, and alert, one hand on the brass handle of the sliding door, the other laid possessively and in its way tenderly on the highly-polished brass switches, that gleamed just as brightly, Perotti had shut himself up again in a silence that was pregnant with every possible meaning. But here I remembered and understood. Perotti was silent not because, as I had thought at one point, he disapproved of Micòl receiving me in her bedroom, but because the chance he had of working the lift—a fairly rare chance, perhaps—filled him with a satisfaction as intense as it was intimate and secret. The lift was no less dear to him than the carriage below in the coach-house. On these things, these venerable witnesses of a past which was now his own as well, he vented his hard-won love for the family he had served since he was a boy, his grudging, old domestic animal's fidelity.

"It goes up beautifully," I exclaimed. "What make is it?"

"It's American," he replied, half turning his head, and his mouth twisted into the curious grimace of scorn behind which peasants often hide admiration.

"*El gà** for over forty years, but it'd still pull up a regiment."

"It must be a Westinghouse," I hazarded, at random.

"Well, *sogio mi†* . . ." he muttered, ". . . one of those names."

Then he started telling me how and when it had been "fixed up". But the lift, stopping suddenly, made him break off almost at once, with obvious regret.

Chapter Two

I n my state of mind just then, one of temporary, undeluded calm, Micòl's welcome surprised me like an unexpected, undeserved present. I had been afraid she would be nasty to me, and treat me with the cruel indifference she had lately shown. But as soon as I entered her room (after bringing me there, Perotti closed the door discreetly behind me), I saw at once that she was smiling at me kindly, sweetly, like a friend. Even more than her explicit invitation to come forward, it was this luminous smile of hers, so full of tenderness and of forgiveness, that persuaded me to move away from the dark end of the room, closer to her.

* It's been going: Venetian dialect.
† *What do I know:* Venetian dialect.

So I went up to the bed, and stayed at the foot of it, my hands resting on the bar. Although she was tucked inside the bedclothes, the whole of Micòl's top half was outside. She was wearing a dark green pullover, with a high neck and long sleeves, the little gold medal of the *sciaddài* glittering on the wool, and two pillows propping her up behind. When I went in she was reading: a French novel, I noticed, recognizing the kind of cover, red and white, from a distance; and it was reading, probably, more than the cold that had sketched a line of tiredness under her eyes. No, she was still beautiful–I said to myself, as I looked at her–perhaps she had never been so beautiful and so attractive.

Beside the bed, at the height of the bolster, was a two-tiered wooden trolley, the top tier taken up by an articulated lamp, turned on, the telephone, a red china teapot, two white china cups with gold rims, and a white copper thermos flask. Micòl leant out to lay her book on the lower shelf, then turned, looking for the hanging electric light switch on the opposite side of the bedhead. Poor soul, she muttered away meantime–she shouldn't keep me in such a morgue! And as soon as the light went on she greeted it with a big "aah" of satisfaction.

Then she went on talking, more Finzi-Continian than ever: about the "squalid" cold that had kept her in bed for a good four days; about the aspirins with which, without Papa finding out, as he was no less bitterly opposed than uncle Giulio to things that made you sweat (bad for the heart, according to them, but this just wasn't true!), she'd vainly tried to ward it off; about what a bore it was to lie interminably in bed, without wanting to do a damn thing, without even

wanting to read. Ah, reading: at one time, when she
was constantly ill with 'flu and a high fever at thirteen,
she was quite capable of devouring, say, the whole of
War and Peace in a few days, or the whole cycle of
The Three Musketeers, whereas now, throughout an
entire wretched cold, although admittedly it was a cold
in the head, all she could manage to polish off was the
odd French novel, the kind with very large print. Did
I know Cocteau's *Les Enfants Terribles*?–she asked,
picking the book up from the trolley again and holding
it out to me. It wasn't bad, it was amusing and *chic*. But
could you compare it with *The Three Musketeers*,
Twenty Years After, and *The Vicomte de Bragelonne*? Ah,
now those were really novels! You'd got to admit it:
after all, even from the point of view of *chic** they were
"the very bestest".

Suddenly she broke in on herself.

"Well, but what are you stuck over there for?" she
exclaimed. "Heavens alive, you're worse than a child!
Take that armchair" (and she pointed it out) "and
come and sit down here beside me."

I hastened to obey, but it wasn't enough. Now I'd
got to drink something.

"What can I offer you?" she said. "Would you like
tea?"

"No, thanks," I answered, "I just don't feel like it
before supper. It rinses out the tum, and takes away
my appetite."

"A little *Skiwasser*, maybe?"

"The same thing goes for that as well."

"It's boiling, you know! If I'm not mistaken you've
only tried the summer version, the iced stuff that's
really *heretical: Himbeerwasser*."

* Note: in French in the original.

"No, no, thanks."

"Oh dear," she moaned. "Shall I ring and have you brought an aperitif? We never have them ourselves, but I expect there must be a bottle of Campari somewhere around. Perotti, *honni soit*, is bound to be able to find it. . . ."

I shook my head.

"Really not anything!" she exclaimed disappointedly. "What a fellow!"

"I prefer not."

I said "I prefer not" and she burst out laughing.

"Why are you laughing?" I asked, a bit hurt.

She was looking at me as if taking in my real appearance for the first time.

"You said 'I prefer not' like Bartleby. With the same face."

"Bartleby? And who might he be?"

"Well, obviously you haven't read Melville's stories."

All I'd read of Melville, I said, was *Moby Dick*, translated by Cesare Pavese. Then she asked me to get up and from the bookcase opposite, the one between the two windows, bring *Piazza Tales* over to her. As I searched the books she told me the plot of the story. Bartleby was a clerk–she said–a clerk employed by a well-known New York lawyer (a very good man at his job: active, capable, liberal, "one of those nineteenth-century Americans Spencer Tracy does so well") to copy out office papers, legal documents, and so on and so forth. Now so long as they kept him writing, this Bartleby was quite prepared to slave away conscientiously. But if Spencer Tracy got it into his head to give him some little extra job, like collating a copy with the original text, or popping down to the post office on the corner to buy a stamp, he wouldn't

hear of it: he just smiled evasively and answered,
politely but firmly: "I prefer not to."*

"But why?" I asked, coming back with the book.

"Because he wasn't going to be anything but a clerk.
A clerk, and that was all."

"But heavens," I objected, "I suppose Spencer Tracy
was paying him a regular wage?"

"Of course," said Micòl. "But what's that got to do
with it? Wages pay for work, but not for the *person*
who does it."

"I just don't understand," I said. "Spencer Tracy'd
taken Bartleby on as a clerk, it's true, but he'd also got
him to help keep the wheels turning in a general way
as well, I suppose. What was he really asking him? A
bit more that was really a *bit less*. A man who's got to sit
still all day should find a trip to the post office on the
corner just what he needs: a distraction, a pause, or in
any case a marvellous chance to stretch his legs a bit.
No, I'm sorry. I've got a feeling Spencer Tracy had
every reason to ask this Bartleby of yours to stop being
such a bore and get on with what he'd told him to."

We argued at some length about poor Bartleby and
Spencer Tracy. She reproached me for not *understanding*, for being so banal, the usual old inveterate conformist. Conformist? She carried on joking. The fact
remained that at the start, with a pitying air, she'd
compared me with Bartleby. Now she'd swapped
sides, seeing I was on the side of the "wretched em-
ployers", and had taken to exalting in Bartleby the "in-
alienable right of every human being to non-collabora-
tion", that is to freedom. In fact, strike high or strike
low she kept criticizing me, for completely opposite
reasons.

* Quotation from Herman Melville. In English in the original.

The telephone rang at one point. It was the kitchen ringing up to know if and when they should bring up her supper tray. Micòl said she wasn't hungry for the moment, and would ring them back later. Would she like some *minestra in brodo?*—she answered, with a grimace, to a definite question. Yes, she would. But they mustn't start getting it ready now, please: "long-term cooking" was something she couldn't bear.

She put down the telephone and turned back to me, staring at me with eyes that were at once sweet and serious, and for a few seconds said nothing.

"How's things?" she asked at last, in a low voice.

I swallowed.

"So-so."

I smiled and looked round.

"It's funny how every detail in this room is exactly the way I'd imagined it," I said. "There's the Récamier sofa, for instance. It's as if I'd already seen it. But in any case I *have* seen it."

I told her about the dream I'd had six months before, the night before she left for Venice. I pointed out the rows of *làttimi*, gleaming shadowy on their shelves: the only things in the room—I said—that had looked different in my dream from the way they were in fact. I explained the way I'd seen them, and she listened to me seriously, attentively, without interrupting.

When I had finished she stroked the sleeve of my jacket, caressing it lightly. Then I knelt down beside the bed, took her in my arms, kissed her on the neck, on the eyes, on the lips. And she let me do it, but staring at me all the time and all the time trying, with small movements of her head, to stop me kissing her on the mouth.

"No . . . no . . ." she kept saying. "Stop . . . please. . . .

Do be good. . . . No, no . . . someone might come in.
. . . No."

It was no good. Gradually, first one leg, then the
other, I got up on the bed. My full weight was now
pressed down on her, and blindly I went on kissing her
face, only very rarely able to touch her lips, and even
less able to make her lower her eyelids. At last I hid
my face in her neck. And while my body, as if quite
on its own, was moving convulsively on top of hers,
that lay still as a statue under the bedclothes, all at once,
with a sudden appalling wrench that shook my whole
self, I knew quite definitely that I was losing her, that
I had lost her.

She was the first to speak.

"Please get up," I heard her saying, very close to my
ear. "I can't breathe like this."

I was quite literally laid out. Getting off the bed
seemed beyond my strength. But I had no choice.

I pulled myself on to my feet. I swayed a few steps
about the room. At last I droppped into the armchair
beside the bed again, and hid my face in my hands. My
cheeks were burning.

"Why d'you behave like that?" asked Micòl. "In
any case, it's no use."

"Why's it no use?" I asked, looking up sharply.
"May I know why?"

She looked at me with the ghost of a smile.

"Won't you go in there a minute?" she said, waving
at the bathroom door. "You're all red, *impizà* red.*
Wash your face."

"Thanks, yes. Maybe I'd better."

I leapt up and went towards the bathroom. But just
at that moment, the door that gave on to the stairs was

* From *impizare*: "to inflame" in Ferrarese dialect.

shaken vigorously. Someone seemed to be heaving at
it with his shoulders.

"What is it?" I whispered.

"It's Yor," Micòl answered calmly. "Go and open it."

Chapter Three

I n the oval glass above the basin I saw my face
reflected.

I examined it carefully, as if it weren't mine, as if
it belonged to someone else. Although I had plunged
it repeatedly in cold water, it was still "red, *impizà*
red", as Micòl had said, with darker marks between
my nose and my upper lip, at the top and around
the cheekbones. Carefully objective, I looked at the
large well-lit face before me, gradually attracted by the
throbbing arteries under the skin of my forehead and
temples, or by the thick net of tiny scarlet veins that,
when I opened my eyes wide, seemed to squeeze the
blue discs of the irises tight, or by the beard, growing
thicker on the chin and along the jaw, or by some tiny,
scarcely visible pimple. . . . I wasn't really thinking of
anything. Through the thin dividing wall I could hear
Micòl talking on the telephone. With whom! With
the servants in the kitchen, presumably, telling them
to bring up her supper. That would certainly make our
farewells less embarrassing for both of us.

I went in as she was putting down the receiver, and again, not without surprise, I realized she had nothing against me.

She leant out of bed to pour out a cup of tea.

"Now please sit down," she said, "and have a drink."

In silence I obeyed. I drank in slow, unflustered sips, without looking up. Lying on the parquet floor behind me, Yor was asleep. His heavy, drunk tramp's snorting filled the room.

I put down the cup.

It was Micòl who started to talk. Without mentioning what had happened a while ago, she began by saying that for a long time, perhaps much longer than I imagined, she'd been meaning to talk to me frankly about the situation that had gradually grown up between us. Did I remember that time last October, she went on, when we'd sheltered from the rain in the coach-house, and sat in the carriage? Well, from then on she'd realized our relationship had taken a wrong turning, she'd realized right away that something false and mistaken and very dangerous had come between us, and it was mostly her fault, she was quite ready to admit, that things had gone from bad to worse ever since. What should she have done? Perfectly simple: she should have taken me aside and talked to me openly then, without any further delay. Whereas, like a real old coward, she'd done just what she shouldn't have and escaped. Oh, yes, it was easy to cut free: but where does it get you, especially in "delicate situations"? Ninety-nine per cent of the time the embers go on glowing away under the ashes: with the fine result that afterwards, when you meet again, talking quietly together like good friends has become fearfully difficult, in fact practically impossible.

I understood too–I broke in at this point–and was very grateful to her after all, for her sincerity.

But there was something I wished she'd explain. She'd run off quite suddenly, without even saying good-bye, and then, as soon as she got to Venice, she'd got only one idea in her head: to make sure I didn't stop seeing Alberto. "Why?" I asked. "If, as you say, you really wanted me to forget you (forgive the way I'm putting it, don't burst out laughing!) then couldn't you have dropped me altogether? It was hard: but it wasn't impossible that, if you didn't poke them at all, all the embers might have gradually gone out altogether, left on their own."

She looked at me without hiding her surprise: astonished perhaps that I was tough enough to counter-attack, however feebly.

I'd got something, she agreed, shaking her head thoughtfully: yes, I'd really got something there. But she begged me to believe her, all the same. When she'd done what she did, she hadn't meant to go looking for trouble in the least. She wanted my friendship, that was all, rather too possessively, even; and then, quite seriously, she was really worried about Alberto, who had absolutely nobody left to talk to except Giampiero Malnate. Poor Alberto!–she sighed.–Hadn't I realized, being with him in these past months, how much he *needed* company? I must agree that for a man like him, who was now used to spending the winter in Milan, with theatres, cinemas and all the rest of it to hand, the prospect of staying in Ferrara, shut up in the house for months on end and with pretty well nothing to do either, wasn't exactly very gay. Poor Alberto!–she repeated. Compared with him she was very much tougher, very much more *autonomous*: able to put up with the most frightful loneliness, if she had to. And besides, she thought she'd already told me: as far as gloominess went, Venice in winter was probably even worse than Ferrara, and her uncles' house was no less sad and "cut off" than this.

"This house isn't sad in the least," I said, suddenly stirred.

"D'you like it?" she asked, livening up. "Then I'll confess something: but you mustn't scold me, you mustn't accuse me of hypocrisy, now, or even of double-dealing! . . . I terribly much wanted you to see it."

"But why?"

"I don't know why. I honestly couldn't tell you why. I suppose the same way I'd have so liked to pull you in under Papa's *talèd*, when we were children in the synagogue. . . . Oh, if only I could have done it! I can still see you there, under your father's *talèd*, in the seat in front of ours. I felt so sorry for you! It's absurd, I know: but when I looked at you, I felt just as sorry as if you'd been an orphan, without father and mother."

Having said this, she was silent for a few minutes, her eyes fixed on the ceiling. Then, leaning her elbow on the pillow, she started talking to me again: but serious, now, grave.

She said she was sorry to hurt me, terribly sorry, but on the other hand she really must persuade me: we just mustn't spoil the happy memories of childhood we had in common, the way we were doing. To think of the pair of us making love! Did it really seem possible to me?

I asked why it seemed so impossible to her.

For any number of reasons—she replied, the first of

them being that the thought of making love with me was just as embarrassing as the thought of doing it with a brother, oh, with Alberto, say. It was true: as a child she'd had just a little bit of a *thing* about me: and maybe, who could tell, it was this very thing that now stood between us. I . . . I was *beside* her, did I see?, not in *front* of her: whereas love–at least so she imagined –love was for people who'd made up their minds to dominate, turn and turn about: a cruel, ferocious game, much crueller and more ferocious than tennis, played with no holds barred, where goodness of heart and honesty of purpose just never came into it, to alleviate things.

> *Maudit soit à jamais le rêveur inutile*
> *qui voulut le premier, dans sa stupidité,*
> *s'éprenant d'un problème insoluble et stérile,*
> *aux choses de l'amour mêler l'honnêteté*

we had been warned by Baudelaire, and he knew what he was talking about. And what about us? Both stupidly honest, as alike as two peas in everything and for everything ("and people who're alike don't fight, believe me!"), could we ever manage to dominate each other? Did we seriously want to rend one another? No, it wasn't possible. According to her, seeing the way the good Lord had made us, the whole business wasn't either desirable or possible.

But even supposing, quite hypothetically, we were unlike what we were, in fact that there was the faintest possibility of a cruel ferocious relationship between us, how on earth should we behave? *Get engaged*, say, with rings exchanged, and parents calling on each other, and so on and so forth? What an edifying idea! If he were still alive and told about it, she'd be ready

to bet Zangwill himself would draw a juicy little codi-
cil from it to add to his *Dreamers of the Ghetto.* And how
delighted, how devoutly delighted everyone would be
when we appeared together at the Italian synagogue
next Kippúr; a bit scraggy with fasting, but handsome
in spite of it, and a perfectly marvellous match!
There'd even be people who'd bless the racial laws
when they saw us, and say there was only one thing
to say in the face of such a wonderful union: it's an ill
wind that blows nobody any good. Maybe even the
Federal Secretary in viale Cavour might be moved by
it: wasn't he really a secret Jew-lover, dear old consul
Bolognesi? And she gave a sickened snort.

I kept silence, dejectedly. Micòl took advantage of
this to pick up the receiver and ask the kitchen to bring
up her supper, but in about half an hour, not before,
as–she said again–she wasn't the least bit hungry that
evening. It was only the following day, when I
thought it all over, that I remembered I had heard her
talking on the telephone while I was in the bathroom.
So I was wrong–I said to myself next day. She might
have been talking to someone else in the house (or
outside), but *not* to the kitchen.

But now I was deep in other thoughts. When Micòl
had put down the receiver I looked up.

"You said we were exactly alike," I said. "In what
way?"

Yes, yes, we were, she exclaimed: in the sense that I,
like her, hadn't the instinctive taste for things that *normal* people had. She could see it perfectly well: for me,
no less than for her, the memory of things was much
more important than the possession of them, and in
comparison with that memory all possession, in itself,
seemed just disappointing, delusive, flat, insufficient.

How well she understood me! The way I longed for
the present to become the past *at once*, so that I could
love it and gaze fondly at it any time; it was just exactly
the way she felt. It was *our* vice, this: looking backwards as we went ahead. Wasn't that so?

Yes, it was—I had to admit to myself—it really was
so. Only an hour before I had taken her in my arms.
And already, as always happened, everything had become unreal and fabulous again: it had become something I couldn't believe in, or of which I must be
afraid.

"You never can tell," I replied. "It may be much
simpler. Maybe you find me physically unattractive,
and that's all there is to it."

"What rubbish," she protested. "That's got nothing
to do with it!"

"Oh, hasn't it just!"

"*You are fishing for compliments,** and you know it
perfectly well. But I'm not going to give you the satisfaction: you don't deserve it, and then, suppose I did
try and tell you all the nice things I've ever thought
about those famous old glaucous eyes of yours (and not
only about your eyes, at that), what would be the
result? You'd be the first to think me a beastly hypo-
crite. You'd think: look at her: after the stick the
carrot, a sop to his . . ."

"Unless . . ."

"Unless what?"

I hesitated, then at last took the plunge.

"Unless," I said, "there's somebody else."

She shook her head, staring at me.

"There's not the faintest anybody else," she replied.
"Who might there be?"

* Note: in English in the original.

I believed her. But I was desperate, and wanted to hurt her.

"Are you asking me?" I said, pouting. "Anything might happen. Who's to say whether you met anyone this winter in Venice?"

She burst out laughing: a gay, fresh, crystalline laugh.

"What an idea," she exclaimed. "Why, I was slaving over my thesis the whole time!"

"You're not going to tell me that in all these five years at the university you've never made love with anyone! Come along, now: there must have been somebody after you, while you were there!"

I was sure she'd deny it. But I was wrong.

"Well, I have had some boy friends," she admitted.

It was as if a hand had suddenly gripped my stomach and was twisting it.

"Lots?" I managed to ask.

Lying flat as she was, her eyes staring at the ceiling, she raised an arm slightly.

"Well now . . . I wouldn't know," she said. "Let me think."

"So there've been such a lot?"

She glanced at me sidelong, with a sly, definitely bitchy expression, that I didn't know and that terrified me.

"Well . . . let's say three or four. In fact five, to be precise. . . . But just little *flirts*, of course, and perfectly harmless . . . and even rather dreary."

"*Flirts*, how d'you mean?"

"Oh, you know . . . long walks along the Lido . . . two or three Torcellos* . . . the odd kiss . . . lots of hand-holding . . . and *lots* of films. Orgies of films."

* Trips to Torcello, an island in the Venetian lagoon.

"All of them students?"

"More or less."

"Catholics, I suppose."

"Of course. But not on principle. You've got to make do with what there is, you see."

"Never with . . ."

"No. Never with *judím*, I must say. Not that there weren't any. But they were so solemn and ugly!"

She turned to look at me again, and smiled:

"But this winter there was nothing, I swear. All I did was work and smoke, so hard that signorina Blumenfeld actually urged me to go out."

From under the pillow she pulled out a packet of Lucky Strike, unopened.

"D'you want one? I've started with the tough stuff, as you see."

In silence I pointed to the pipe tucked into my jacket pocket.

"You as well!" she laughed, extraordinarily amused. "Why, that old Giampi of yours really has his followers!"

"And you were complaining you had no friends in Venice!" I said. "What lies. You're just like all the others, that's what you are."

She shook her head, whether pitying me or herself, I couldn't tell.

"Not even *flirts*, however small they are, can be mixed up with friendship," she said sadly; "and so, when I spoke to you about friendships, you must realize I was only half lying to you. But you're right. I *am* like other girls:—liar, traitress, *unfaithful*. . . . Not really any different from Adriana Trentini, when you get down to it."

When she said "unfaithful" she separated the syllables, with a kind of bitter pride. Then she went on to say that if I'd been wrong it was rating her rather too high. Not that she was trying to justify herself in the least–heavens, no! But it was a fact: she'd always seen such "idealism" in my eyes that she felt somehow forced to seem better than she actually was.

There wasn't much more to say. A little later, when Gina came in with her supper (it was now past nine), I got up.

"Well, I must go now," I said, holding out my hand.

"You know the way down, don't you? Or would you rather Gina took you?"

"No, it's quite all right. I can manage perfectly well on my own."

"Do take the lift, won't you?"

"Of course."

At the door I turned. She already had the spoon at her lips.

I said: "*Ciao.*"

"*Ciao,*" she smiled. "I'll ring you up tomorrow."

Chapter Four

But the worst started for me only three weeks later, when I got home from a trip I made to France during the second half of April.

I had gone to Grenoble for a very definite reason.

The few hundred lire a month we were legally allowed
to send my brother Ernesto was only enough, as he
kept telling us in his letters, to pay the rent of his room
in place Vaucanson. So it was urgent to get him more
money. And it was my father, one night when I got
home later than usual (he had waited up for me–he
said–on purpose to talk to me), who insisted on my
taking it to him myself. Why didn't I take the chance?
Breathing a bit of air unlike our own, seeing people,
having a change: all this would do me a world of good,
physically as well as morally.

So I left. I stopped a couple of hours in Turin, and
four at Chambéry, and reached Grenoble at last. There,
in the boarding-house where Ernesto went for meals,
I was at once introduced to a number of Italians his
own age, all in the same situation as himself and all of
them students at the Polytechnic: a Levi from Turin,
a Segre from Saluzzo, a Sorani from Trieste, a Cantoni
from Mantua, a Castelnuovo from Florence, a Pin-
cherle girl from Rome. But instead of joining up with
them, I spent most of my twelve days there in the
municipal library, looking at Stendhal manuscripts. It
was cold in Grenoble, and it rained. The mountains
looming over the town, only rarely showed their peaks,
hidden in fog and cloud, while in the evenings the exer-
cises with total blackout discouraged one from going
out. Ferrara seemed terribly far: as if I never had to go
back to it. And what about Micòl? Since I left, her
voice was always in my ears, the voice she used when
she said: "Why d'you behave like that? In any case,
it's no use." But one day something happened. I
chanced to read in one of Stendhal's notebooks the
words: *All lost, nothing lost*, and quite suddenly, as if by
a miracle, I felt freed, cured. I got a picture postcard,

wrote Stendhal's words on it, and sent it off to Micòl, just like that, without a greeting, without even a signature, for her to make what she liked of it. All lost, nothing lost. How true it was!–I said to myself. And I breathed again.

I was deluding myself, of course. When I went back to Italy at the beginning of May I found spring bursting out everywhere, the sprawling fields between Alessandria and Piacenza already yellow, the country lanes of Emilia full of girls out on bicycles, already bare-armed and bare-legged, the great trees along the walls of Ferrara already in leaf. I arrived on a Sunday about midday. As soon as I got home I had a bath, had lunch with the family, and answered a mass of questions pretty patiently. But the sudden frenzy that had seized me on the train the moment I saw the towers and belfries of Ferrara on the horizon, prevented me from delaying any longer. At half-past two, not daring to telephone, I was already dashing along the Wall of the Angels on my bike, staring at the luxuriant, motionless greenery of Barchetto del Duca coming gradually closer on the left. Everything had gone back to where it was before, as if I had spent the last fortnight asleep.

They were playing down there on the tennis court, Micòl against a young man in long white trousers, which it wasn't hard to make out as Malnate; and very soon I was seen and recognized, since the pair of them stopped playing and waved their rackets strenuously in wide swoops. They were not alone, though, Alberto was there as well. When I came out beyond the greenery, I saw him run into the middle of the court, look towards me and put his hand to his mouth. Then he whistled, two or three times. What was I doing up there on top of the wall?–they seemed to be asking me. Why didn't I come into the garden, old son of a gun that I was? I was already on my way down towards the opening on Corso Ercole I, already pedalling along by the garden wall, already in sight of the gate, and Alberto still kept sending out his foghorn sounds. "Hey, mind you don't sneak off!" his still deafening whistles were saying, but they now sounded cheerful rather than admonitory.

"Hi!" I cried, as I always did, when I came into the open from the arcade of climbing roses.

Micòl and Malnate had started playing again, and without stopping answered together with another "Hi." Alberto got up and came towards me.

"And just where, might I ask, have you been hiding yourself all this time?" he asked me. "I rang your home several times but you were never in."

"He's been in France," Micòl answered for me from the court.

"In France!" exclaimed Alberto, his eyes full of surprise that looked quite genuine. "Whatever for?"

"I've been to see my brother in Grenoble."

"Oh, of course, that's true, your brother's studying in Grenoble. And how is he? How's he getting on?"

We had sat down meantime on two deck-chairs placed side by side by the tennis court gate, in the best position to follow the game. Micòl was not wearing shorts as she had done the previous autumn, but a very old-fashioned woollen pleated skirt, a white blouse with the sleeves turned back and peculiar white stockings like a nurse's. Red-faced and sweating freely, she was doggedly sending shots into the farthest corners of the court; but Malnate, although he had grown fatter and was puffing hard, kept his end up against her pretty well, with tremendous keenness.

A ball rolled towards us and stopped a short distance
away. Micòl came across to pick it up, and for a
moment my eyes met hers. This visibly upset her.
Turning to Malnate, she shouted:

"Shall we play a set?"

"Right, let's," he replied. "How many games up can
I be to start with?"

"Not one," Micòl retorted drily, annoyed. "The
most I'll give you is the chance of first service. Come
on now, serve!"

She flung the ball over the net and took up her position to answer his service.

Alberto and I watched them playing for a few
minutes. I felt full of disquiet and unhappiness. The
way she used the familiar "*tu*" in speaking to Malnate,
the deliberate way she had ignored me, suddenly
showed me how long I had been away. As for Alberto,
he of course had eyes for no one but Giampi. But for
once, I noticed, instead of admiring and praising him,
he never stopped criticizing him for a moment.

He was the sort – he confided to me in a whisper: and
it was so surprising that however wretched I felt I
couldn't help paying attention – he was the sort who'd
never make a passable player, even if he was coached
every single day by a Nusslein or a Martin Plas. What
did he lack to stop him making progress? Let's see.
Legs? No, it couldn't be his legs, otherwise he wouldn't
be the pretty fair mountaineer he undoubtedly was.
Breathing? No, it couldn't be that either, for the same
reason. Muscular strength? He'd got plenty of that and
to spare, all you need do to see that was shake hands
with him. Well then? The fact was that tennis – he said,
giving careful emphatic judgment – was an art as well
as a sport, and like all the arts took special talent, a

certain "natural class", in fact, without it you were just no good. You'd be hopeless for the rest of your life.

"What's all this about?" Malnate called, at one point. "What are you grumbling at over there, the pair of you?"

"Get back to the game," Alberto retorted sarcastically, "and see to it you're not beaten by a girl!"

I could hardly believe my ears. Was it possible? Where had Alberto's mildness gone, his submissiveness towards his friend? I looked at him closely. His face looked suddenly peaked, emaciated, prematurely wrinkled with age. Was he ill? I was tempted to ask him, but didn't dare. Instead I asked if this was the first day they'd played tennis, and why Bruno Lattes, Adriana Trentini, and the rest of the *zozga** weren't there, like last year.

"So you really don't know a thing!" he exclaimed, laughing heartily and showing his pale gums.

About a week before – he went on to tell me – realizing that the fine weather had begun, he and Micòl decided to ring up about ten people, with the worthy object of starting up last year's tennis parties again. They telephoned Adriana Trentini, Bruno Lattes, the Sani and Collevatti boys, and various other perfectly splendid specimens of the younger generation he'd never even thought of last year, boys and girls. They all accepted with admirable promptness: so that the opening day, Saturday, May 1st (what a shame I couldn't have been there) was little less than a triumph. They had not only played tennis, chatted, flirted, and so on, but actually danced, there in the *Hütte*, to the music of the Philips "suitably installed".

* "Gang": Ferrarese dialect.

The second "session",* on Sunday afternoon, May
2nd, was an even greater success. But on Monday
morning, the 3rd, the trouble started. At about eleven,
announced by a sybilline visiting card, who should
turn up on a bike but the lawyer Tabet–yes, that's
right, Geremia Tabet, that thundering old fascist, in
person–who shut himself up with Papa in the study
and handed over definite orders from the Federal
Secretary that the scandal of these provocative daily
parties that had been taking place there for some time,
and apart from everything else weren't healthy sport-
ing events in the least, must stop at once. It was inconceivable–consul Bolognesi would have Papa know,
through their "common" friend Tabet–it was absolutely inconceivable, for obvious reasons, that the
Finzi-Continis' house should gradually be turned into
a kind of club competing with the *Elonora d'Este* tennis
club, an institution that had done so much for sport in
Ferrara. For which reason halt there!: in order to avoid
an official prohibition (and for anyone unwilling to do
so there was always deportation to the concentration
camp at Urbisaglia!), from now on no member of
the tennis club was to be drawn away from his natural
surroundings.

"And what did your father reply?" I asked.

"Why, what would you expect him to reply,"
laughed Alberto. "All he could do was behave like Don
Abbonio.† Bow, and murmur: 'Always ready to
obey.' I think that's more or less how he expressed
himself."

"It's Barbicinti who's to blame, I've got a feeling,"
cried Micòl from the court, whom distance obviously

* In English in the original.
† Character in Manzoni's *The Betrothed*.

hadn't prevented from following our conversation. "No one's going to persuade me it wasn't he who went and complained at viale Cavour. I can just see it happening. Anyway, we must forgive the poor creature: when people are jealous they're capable of anything. . . ."

She may not have meant the words to have any pointed meaning, but they struck me painfully all the same. I was just going to get up and go. And I might even have managed it, have really got away, if just at that moment, as I was turning to Alberto, as if to ask for help and evidence, I hadn't been pulled up again by the pallor of his face, the sickly haggard shoulders lost in a pullover that was now too big for him (he winked, as if to tell me not to take it to heart, and then was already talking of other things: of the tennis court, and the radical improvements that, in spite of everything, were starting that same week); and if at the same moment, apart from that, I hadn't seen, at the edge of the clearing, the small black sorrowing figures of professór Ermanno and signora Olga together, taking their afternoon walk in the park and coming slowly in our direction.

Chapter Five

The long period that followed, until the fatal last days of August 1939 – until the vigil of the Nazis' invasion of Poland and the phony war – I remember as a kind of slow, progressive descent into the bottomless funnel of the maelstrom. We four – Micòl, Alberto, Malnate and I – were the only people to use the tennis court, which was soon re-covered with a good layer of red earth from Imola (we couldn't count on Bruno Lattes, presumably lost chasing after Adriana Trentini). Variously paired, we spent whole afternoons playing long doubles, with Alberto, though short of breath and tired, always mysteriously ready to start again and to refuse himself and the rest of us any respite.

Why did I persist in going back every day to a place where I knew perfectly well I would find nothing but humiliation and bitterness? I couldn't say exactly. Perhaps I hoped for a miracle, for a sudden change in the situation, or perhaps in fact I actually went there in search of humiliation and bitterness. . . . We played tennis; and, in the rare intervals Alberto allowed us, stretched on four deck-chairs in a shady row in front of the *Hütte*, we argued, Malnate and I especially, on the usual subjects of art and politics. But when I suggested a walk in the park to Micòl, who was really very kind to me still, and sometimes even affectionate, she very seldom agreed; and if she did, she never came willingly, but, looking half disgusted and half con- descending, very soon made me regret having dragged her away from Alberto and Malnate.

And yet I never stopped trying, I was never resigned to it. Strung between the longing to break it off, to vanish for ever, and the other, opposite, longing never to stop going there, never to give in at any price, I ended up in practice never staying away. Sometimes, admittedly, it was enough for Micòl to look at me more coldly than usual, to make an impatient gesture or to look bored or sarcastic a moment, for me to think quite sincerely that I had made up my mind, I had done with her. But how long did I manage to keep away? Three or four days at the most. On the fifth, there I'd be again, looking gay and casual as if I'd just got back from a trip (I always spoke of trips, when I got back; trips to Milan, to Florence, to Rome: and it was just as well that all three of them looked more or less as if they believed me!), but in fact broken-hearted, and trying at once to find an impossible answer in Micòl's eyes. This was when we had our "married rows"–as Micòl called them–during which, if I got the chance, I even tried to kiss her: and she put up with it very patiently, and was never ungracious.

But one evening in June, about half-way through the month, things took a turn for the worse.

We were sitting side by side on the steps outside the *Hütte*, and, although it was already eight o'clock, we could still see. In the distance I could make out Perotti busy taking down and rolling up the tennis net; since the new red earth had come from the Romagna, he couldn't do enough to look after the surface of the court–which was odd too, for him. Malnate was

having a shower inside the *Hütte* (we could hear him
behind us, breathing noisily under the jet of hot water);
Alberto had left a little earlier with a melancholy "bye-
bye". In fact Micòl and I were left alone and at once
I took the chance to start up my dreary, absurd, everlasting courtship. As always, I kept trying to persuade
her that she had been wrong and was still wrong in
thinking it would be unsuitable for us to have any love
relationship; as always I accused her (in bad faith) of
lying to me when, less than a month before, she had
assured me there was no-one between us. According to
me there was, or at least there had been, someone in
Venice during the winter.

"For the umpteenth time I tell you you're wrong,"
Micòl was saying softly, "but I know it's no good, I
know you'll be at it again tomorrow, with the same
old tale. What d'you want me to say: that I'm secretly
sleeping around, that I lead a double life? If that's really
what you want, I can satisfy you with it."

"No, Micòl," I replied, just as softly, but more excitedly. "I may be all sorts of things but I'm not a
masochist. If you only knew how normal, how terribly
banal my longings are! Yes, laugh away if you like.
But if there's just one thing I'd like it'd be this: to hear
you *swear* what you said is true, and to believe you."

"Well, I can swear it straight off. But would you
believe me?"

"No."

"All the worse for you, then!"

"Yes, of course: all the worse for me. In any case, if
I *could* really believe you. . . ."

"What would you do? Let's hear."

"Oh, the most normal, banal things, that's the
trouble! This, for instance."

I grabbed both her hands and began covering them with kisses and tears.

For a little she let me do it. I hid my face against her knees, and the smell of her smooth, tender, faintly salty skin made my head reel. I kissed her there, on her legs.

"That's enough now," she said.

She slipped her hands out of mine and stood up.

"*Ciao*, I'm cold," she went on. "I must go indoors. Supper'll be on the table and I've still got to wash and change. Come on, get up: don't behave like a child."

"Good-bye!" she called, turning towards the *Hütte*. "I'm off."

"Good-bye," Malnate replied from inside. "Thanks."

"Be seeing you. Coming tomorrow?"

"Don't know. We'll see."

We started off in the direction of the *magna domus*, high and dark in the sunset summer air full of mosquitoes and bats, with the bicycle between us, and me gripping its handlebars convulsively. We were silent. A cart full of hay, pulled by a pair of yoked oxen, came along in the opposite direction to ours, with one of Perotti's sons, who, as he passed, took off his cap and wished us good evening, sitting up on the hay. Even though I had accused Micòl in bad faith without believing my accusation, I wanted to yell at her just the same, and tell her to stop play-acting with me. I wanted to insult her, even hit her. And then? Whatever would I get out of it?

But it was here I went wrong.

"It's no good denying it," I said, "because in any case I even know *who the person is*."

I had scarcely got the words out before I regretted them.

She looked at me seriously, grieved.

"Look," she said. "What you're expecting me to do now is dare you to spell out the name you've got in mind, if you've really got one, in large letters. But I've had enough. I don't want to hear any more. There's just one thing, now we've got to this point: I'd be grateful if from now on you'd be around a bit less . . . if . . . well, quite honestly, if you didn't come here quite so often. To be quite frank with you: if I wasn't afraid the family'd start clucking over it–why, how on earth, and so on–I'd ask you to stop coming altogether: for good."

"Forgive me," I managed to murmur.

"No, I can't forgive you," she said, shaking her head. "If I did you'd start up again within three days."

She went on to say that for some time now I hadn't been behaving decently: either as far as I was concerned, or as far as she was. She had told me over and over, a thousand times over, that it was no use, that I mustn't aim at any relationship between us except one of friendship and affection. But honestly: the minute I could, there I was all over her with kisses and what-not, as if I didn't know myself that in situations like ours nothing could be nastier or less suitable. Heavens! Couldn't I control myself? If we'd been physically bound by rather more than a few kisses, well, if that had been the case she might have under-stood my . . . have understood that she'd got under my skin, as they say. But considering the way our relation-ship had always been, my craze for kissing and cud-dling very likely meant just one thing only: that I was essentially dry-hearted, and constitutionally unable to love properly. And then, for goodness' sake!–what did all these sudden comings and goings mean, these nosey or tragic looks I gave her, these moody silences and sulks and fantastic insinuations—in fact the whole bare-faced continuous repertory of foolishness and embarrassment? If the married rows were kept exclusively for her, when she was on her own, it wouldn't be so bad: but for her brother and Giampi Malnate to have to watch them—no, no, and no again.

"I think you're exaggerating about that," I said. "Whenever have I made a scene in front of Malnate and Alberto?"

"Always, the whole time!" she retorted.

When I came back after a week's absence—she went on—saying I'd been in Rome, for instance, and laughing, as I said it, in a nervous, crazy sort of way, for no apparent reason: did I really think Alberto and Malnate didn't realize I was talking nonsense, that I hadn't been anywhere near Rome, and that my fits of *Cena delle beffe*-type laughter* were all directed at her? And in our arguments, when I leaped up screeching and ranting like a man obsessed, giving everything a personal slant (Giampi'd end up getting angry some day, and he wouldn't be entirely to blame, poor soul!), what did I think—that people didn't realize she, and she alone, was, quite unwittingly, the cause of all my outbursts?

"I see," I said, banging my head. "I realize you don't want to see me any more."

"It's not my fault. It's you who've gradually become unbearable."

"But," I stammered after a pause, "you said I could, in fact must, come back occasionally. Didn't you, now?"

"Yes."

* A play by the Italian author Sem Benelli.

"Well then, you decide. How must I arrange things
so as not to go wrong? How often ought I to appear?"

"Oh, I don't know," she said, shrugging her shoulders. "I should think first of all keep away for at least
three weeks. Then start coming again, if you really
want to: but please, *even afterwards*, not more than
twice a week."

"Tuesdays and Fridays, will that do? Like piano
lessons."

"Stupid," she muttered, smiling in spite of herself.
"You really are a stupid."

Chapter Six

Although, especially at first, it was terribly hard to
stick to it, I made it a point of honour to obey
Micòl's orders scrupulously. When I got my
degree on June 29th, and immediately had a warm
note of congratulations from professór Ermanno,
which included an invitation to dinner, I thought I
should say no, I was very sorry I couldn't. I wrote that
I had a sore throat, and my father refused to let me out
in the evening. But the real reason for my refusal was
that only sixteen days had so far passed out of the three
weeks of exile imposed on me by Micòl.

It was terribly hard, and of course I hoped that
sooner or later I'd have it made up to me: but vaguely,

and without counting on it at all, content to obey for the moment and, through my obedience, to remain bound to her and to the paradise from which I was temporarily banished. As far as Micòl was concerned, even if I'd had things to reproach her with before, I now had nothing, it was all my fault and I was the only one who needed to be forgiven. How wrong I'd been! One by one I remembered the times when, often using violence, I had managed to kiss her on the mouth, but only to think how entirely good she'd been to put up with me so long, although she'd refused me, and to feel ashamed of my satyr-like lust, which paraded as sentiment and idealism. When the three weeks had gone by, I ventured back, and from then on kept strictly to my two visits a week. But this didn't bring Micòl down from off the pedestal of purity and moral superiority I had placed her on since I went into exile. She stayed right on it, up there. And as far as I was concerned I thought myself lucky to be let in to admire the distant image, no less lovely within than without, now and then. *"Like the truth – and like it sad and lovely . . ."*: these two lines of a poem I never finished, although written much later, immediately after the war, referred to Micòl in August '39, to the way I then saw her.

Thrown out of paradise, I did not rebel, but waited silently to be welcomed back. But I suffered for it, all the same: in anguish, some days. And it was only to lighten, somehow, the weight of this often unbearable separation and loneliness that about a week after my final disastrous talk with Micòl I had the idea of visiting Malnate, and keeping up with him at least.

I knew where to find him. Like Meldolesi at one time, he lived in a district of pretentious small houses

outside Porta San Benedetto, between the kennels and
the industrial zone. It was very much more solitary and
fashionable than it is now, since the last fifteen years
have overwhelmed it in unbridled speculative building: the small two-storeyed houses, each with its own
modest, pretty garden, belonged to magistrates,
teachers, civil servants, white-collar workers on the
town council, whom it wasn't hard to see, on late
summer afternoons through the bars of their spike-
topped gates, busy watering, pruning, and weeding,
in pyjamas. The owner of Malnate's house, a certain
Dr. Lalumía, if I remember rightly, was a local magis-
trate, a Sicilian of about fifty, terribly thin, with a
shock of grey hair, and, as soon as he noticed me standing on the pedals of my bicycle, holding on to the bars
of the gate with both hands, and peering into the
garden, he put down the rubber hose with which he
was watering the flower-beds.

"What is it?" he asked, coming towards the gate.

"Is Dr Malnate here?"

"This is where he lives. Why?"

"Is he at home?"

"Heaven knows. Is he expecting you?"

"I'm a friend of his. I was just going by and I thought
I'd stop a moment to say hello."

While we were speaking, he had covered the ten odd
yards between us. I now saw only the top of his bony,
fanatical face and his black pin-sharp eyes over the
edge of the sheet-metal that bound the bars of the gate
at about a man's height. He stared at me with obvious
suspicion; but the examination must have ended
favourably, because almost at once the lock clicked and
I was able to go inside.

"Do go along in there," the judge said at last, raising

his skeletal arm, "along the path round the back of the house. The small door on the ground floor, that's Dr. Malnate's. Ring the bell. He may not be in; but my wife'll open up, as she's sure to be there just now, getting his bed ready for the night."

After this he turned round and went back to his house, taking no more notice of me.

Instead of Malnate, a fleshy blonde in a dressing-gown appeared at the door Dr. Lalumía had pointed out.

"Good evening," I said. "I was looking for Dr. Malnate."

"He's not back yet," said signora Lalumía, in the friendliest way, "but he shouldn't be long now. Nearly every evening, as soon as he leaves the factory, he goes to play tennis at the Finzi-Cortinis's, you know, those fine people in Corso Ercole I. . . . And, as I say, he ought to be here any moment. He always drops in before supper," she smiled, shutting her eyes delightedly, "to see if there's any post."

I said I'd come back later, and made to pick up the bike which I had leant against the wall, beside the door. But she insisted on my waiting. She asked me in, and sat me down in an armchair, and then stood before me and told me she was from Ferrara, "thoroughbred Ferrarese", and knew my family very well, and my mother ("your Mummy") in particular, since "something like forty years ago"–and as she spoke she smiled, and sweetly lowered her eyelids again–they had been friends at the *Regina Elena* primary school, the one beside the church of San Giuseppe, in via Carlo Mayr. How was my mother?–she asked. Would I please not forget to greet her from Edvige, Edvige Santini, and she'd be sure to remember. She mentioned the danger

of war, and, with a sigh and a shake of her head, the
racial laws, and then, having excused herself (she'd been
"without help" for a few days and had to do everything herself, including the cooking), she left me on my
own.

When she had gone, I looked round. I was in a large,
low-ceilinged room that was obviously bedroom,
study and sitting-room combined. It was after eight
o'clock: the rays of the setting sun came in through the
large horizontal windows, and caught the dust floating
in the air. I looked at the furniture: the divan, half bed
and half sofa, with a large white pillow at the head, and
a cheap, shoddy, red-flowered counterpane on the rest
of it; the black Moorish-style table, between the divan
and the room's single armchair, of fake leather, on
which I was sitting; the fake-parchment lampshades
strewn about; the white telephone that smirked flirta-
tiously on the glum black of a shabby, legal-looking
desk, all drawers; the ghastly little oil paintings on the
walls: and although I thought Giampi had a pretty
good cheek turning up his nose at Alberto's modern
furniture (how could he, being such an old moralizer,
and such a stern judge of everyone else, be so lenient
with himself and his own stuff?), all at once, my heart
suddenly wrenched by the thought of Micòl – it was just
as if she'd been there, pressing it with her hand – I made
a solemn resolution again to be good with Malnate, not
to argue with him, not to quarrel. When she heard of
it, Micòl would take it into account, too.

The siren of one of the sugar factories at Pontelagoscuro wailed in the distance. Immediately afterwards,
a heavy footstep scrunched on the gravel outside.

The judge's voice sounded very close beyond the
wall.

"Oh, Doctor," he said, in his noticeably nasal voice, "there's a friend waiting for you indoors."

"A friend?" said Malnate. "Who is it?"

"Go along in . . .' said Lalumía encouragingly. "I just said a friend."

Tall and fat, taller and fatter than ever, perhaps because of the effect of the low ceiling, Malnate came in.

"Not really!" he exclaimed, his eyes wide with surprise as he adjusted his glasses on his nose.

He shook my hand vigorously, and slapped me on the back several times, and it was very odd, as he'd always been against me ever since we first met, to find him so friendly, thoughtful, and chatty. Why on earth? I wondered, in confusion. Had he also decided to change his ways, with regard to me? Maybe. In any case now, on his own ground, he was no longer the argumentative tough I'd so often fought with under the observant eye of Alberto, and later of Micòl. As soon as I saw him I knew that away from the Finzi-Continis (and to think that just recently our rows had got really hurting, we'd almost come to blows!) every reason for quarrelling was destined to melt away, like mist in sunshine.

Malnate was talking, meantime: incredibly chatty and cordial. He asked me if I'd met the owner of the house when I crossed the garden, and if he'd been polite. I said yes, I'd met him, and laughingly described the scene.

"Well, that's a good job."

He went on telling me about the judge and his wife, giving me no time to say I'd met the wife as well. They were very nice people, he said, but a bit of a bore the way they both kept trying to protect him from the snares and perils of the big world. Though he was

firmly anti-fascist (he was a roaring monarchist), his
honour didn't want any trouble, and was continuously
on edge in case Malnate, whom he said he'd sniffed out
as just about the likeliest future client for the Special
Tribunal, secretly brought dangerous types along: ex-
political prisoners, people watched by the police, sub-
versives of any kind. Signora Edvige was always on the
hop as well, spending the whole day perched up behind
the gaps in the first-floor shutters, or turning up at the
door at the most hair-raising hours, or even at night,
after she'd heard him come in. But she was worried
about other things. Like a good Ferrarese – because she
came from Ferrara, maiden name Santini – she knew
what she knew, as she put it – which meant the local
women, married and unmarried. According to her, a
young man on his own, a stranger with a degree and a
flat with its own front door, might just be ruined at
Ferrara, his backbone turned to *oss boeucc** by the girls.
So what had he done? Well, he'd always done his best
to reassure her, of course. But it was quite obvious,
signora Lalumía'd only calm down when she'd turned
him into a dreary little lodger trailing about in his vest,
pyjama pants and slippers, his nose poked into the
kitchen saucepans.

"Well, why not?" I objected. "I've often heard you
grousing about restaurants and eating places."

"That's true," he admitted, amazingly docile: and
his docility never ceased to surprise me. "It's no good,
is it? Freedom's all very fine, but if you don't put the
brakes on somewhere" (and as he said this he winked)
"where are you going to end up?"

It was beginning to get dark. Malnate got up from
the divan where he'd been lying, turned on the light

* *Osso buco*: Milanese dialect.

and then went on into the bathroom. He felt he needed a shave, he said from the bathroom. Would I wait while he did it? Then we'd go out together.

And so we carried on talking, he in the bathroom, I in the bedroom.

He said he'd been at the Finzi-Continis's that afternoon, and in fact had just come from there. They had played for over two hours: first he and Micòl, then he and Alberto, and finally the three of them together. Did I like playing American?

"Not much," I replied.

"I can see why," he said. "A decent player like you can't see much sense in it. But it's fun."

"Who won?"

"The American game?"

"Yes."

"Micòl, of course!" sniggered Malnate. "There's just no stopping her. Even on the court she's a real streak of lightning. . . ."

He asked me why I hadn't appeared for some days. What had happened, had I been away?

Remembering how Micòl had told me no one believed it when I said I'd been on a journey, every time I stayed away, I said that I'd got fed up, that often, just recently, I'd had a feeling I wasn't welcome, and especially that Micòl didn't want me there, so I'd decided to keep my distance for a bit.

"What are you talking about!" said Malnate. "Micòl's got nothing against you. Are you sure you're not mistaken?"

"Quite sure."

"Oh well," he sighed.

He said no more, and I was silent too. A little later he appeared at the bathroom door, shaved and smiling.

He saw me examining the hideous pictures hanging on the walls.

"Well, what d'you think of my little den?" he said. "You haven't told me what you think of it."

He was grinning in his old way, waiting to catch me out, but at the same time, I could read in his eyes, he had made up his mind to keep his temper.

"I envy you, honestly," I said. "I've always dreamed of having something of my own like this."

He gave me a pleased, grateful look. Then he said that of course he too realized the Lalumías' limitations in matters of taste in furniture. But their taste, so typical of the lower middle classes ("which aren't the backbone of the nation for nothing," he added parenthetically), had something alive and vital and healthy about it; very likely in direct ratio to its own banality and vulgarity.

"After all, objects are nothing but objects," he exclaimed. "Why make yourself a slave of them?"

Take Alberto, now–he went on–holy smoke! By surrounding himself with things that were perfect, exquisite, unflawed, he too would some day end up becoming . . .

He went across to the door, without finishing what he was saying.

"How is he?" I asked.

I had got up myself and joined him at the door.

"Who, Alberto?" he said, startled.

I nodded.

"Well yes," I said. "He's seemed a bit run down, lately. Don't you think so? I've got a feeling he's not well."

Malnate shrugged, then put out the light. He went ahead of me in the darkness, and said no more till we

reached the gate, except to answer signora Lalumía's
"Good evening" from a window on the way, and,
right at the gate, to suggest I had supper with him, at
Giovanni's.

Chapter Seven

I t was no good deluding myself, Malnate knew perfectly well why I was staying away from the Finzi-
Continis', just as he knew, at least to some extent,
what point relations between Micòl and me had
reached. But both of us steered clear of the subject, in
our talk, both being unusually reserved and delicate.
And I was sincerely grateful to him for pretending to
believe what I had told him the first evening, and never
referring to it again: grateful to him for playing along
with me and supporting me in it.

We met very often, nearly every evening. Since the
beginning of June, the suddenly stifling heat had emp-
tied the town. Usually it was I who went to his house,
between seven and eight. When he was out I waited
patiently, sometimes entertained by chat with signora
Edvige. But generally I found him there already, alone,
wearing his vest and lying on the divan, staring up at
the ceiling, hands crossed at the back of his neck; or
else sitting writing to his mother, to whom, I discovered, he was united by a deep, rather exaggerated

affection. But as soon as I arrived he hurried into the bathroom for his shave, after which we went out, as it was understood we were to have supper together.

As a rule we went to *Giovanni's*, sitting outside, opposite the castle towers that beetled above us like crags in the Dolomites, and touched at the peaks, like them, by the waning daylight; or else to the *Voltini*, a cheap restaurant outside Porta Reno from the tables of which, in a row under a light arcade facing south across the open countryside, you could then see right across to the vast expanse of the airport. But on the hottest evenings, instead of going into town, we would go along the fine Pontelagoscuro road, cross the iron bridge over the river, and pedal side by side along the towpath, with the river on our right, and the Venetian countryside on our left, until, after another quarter of an hour, we reached the great isolated building of the Dogana Vecchia, now famous for fried eel, half-way between Pontelagoscuro and Polesella. We always ate very slowly. We would stay on at the table until late, drinking Lambrusco and light wine from Bosco, and smoking our pipes. But when we ate anywhere in town, at a certain point we laid down our napkins, paid our own bills, and then, wheeling our bicycles, walked up and down Giovecca, or along the viale Cavour as far as the station (Corso Ercole I we always avoided, in these night wanderings of ours). And it was he, then, generally about midnight, who offered to see me home. He would glance at the clock and say it was bedtime (the factory sirens sounded at eight for them, the "technical staff", admittedly, but it still meant getting up at seven!) and however hard I pressed him to let me take him home instead, he simply refused to allow it. My last sight of him was always the same: half-way along the street he would sit astride his bike and wait for me to shut the street door on him.

After we had eaten on two or three evenings, we ended up on the bastions at Porta Reno, where, in the open space, flanked by the gasometer on one side, and by piazza Travaglio on the other, a fairground had been set up that summer. It was only a cheap one, half a dozen shooting booths round the patched grey toadstool of a small circus tent. I was drawn to the place, drawn and moved by its usual melancholy crowd of poor prostitutes and young louts and soldiers, and wretched suburban homosexuals. I quoted Apollinaire, Ungaretti. And although Malnate, looking faintly reluctant, accused me of "cheap decadentism", in his heart he too enjoyed going up to the dusty piazzale after supper at the *Voltini*, pausing to eat a slice of melon by the acetylene lamp of the water-melon man, or to put in a half-hour's shooting at the booths. An excellent shot, Giampi was. Tall and stout and elegant in the well-pressed cream linen jacket I had seen him wearing since the beginning of summer, and very calmly taking aim through his thick tortoiseshell-rimmed spectacles, he had obviously taken the fancy of the coarse, painted Tuscan girl–a kind of queen of the castle–at whose booth, the moment we appeared at the top of the stone staircase leading from piazza Travoglio to the top of the bastions, we were imperiously invited to stop. While Malnate was shooting the girl kept up a flow of sarcastic compliments with an undercurrent of obscenity, which he answered with a great deal of spirit, using the familiar *"tu"*, and with the easy and to me inimitable casualness of a man who has spent long hours in brothels as a youngster.

One particularly sultry evening in August we landed up instead at an open-air cinema, where I remember they were showing a German film with Cristina Söderbaum. When we went in, the film had already started, and as soon as we sat down I started whispering ironical comments without paying attention to Malnate, who kept telling me to be careful, not to *bausciare**, that in any case it just wasn't worth it. And he was quite right. A fellow in the row in front of ours, suddenly jumping to his feet against the milky background of the screen, threateningly told me to shut up. I retorted with an insult, and he shouted back: "*Fóra, boia d'un ebrei!*"† and flung himself on me, grabbing my neck. It was lucky for me that Malnate, without a word, was ready to hurl my assailant back into his seat, and drag me out by the arm before the lights went up again.

"You're a fine old idiot," he scolded me, as soon as we had dashed over to the parking place to collect our bicycles. "And now *scià, gamba*:‡ and just pray to that God of yours that the swine in there was only making a guess."

This was how we spent our evenings, one after another, seeming always to congratulate ourselves for managing to talk without quarrelling the way we did when Alberto was there, and without even considering the possibility of simply ringing him up and asking him to come out and join us.

We had now dropped politics. As we both sat back in the certainty that France and England, whose diplomatic missions had been in Moscow for some time, would in the end come to an agreement with the

---

* "To make a row": Milanese dialect.
† "Get out, you filthy Jew": Ferrarese dialect.
‡ "Shove off, quick": Milanese dialect.

U.S.S.R. (this understanding, which we thought inevitable, would save the independence of Poland and peace at the same time, and so bring about the end of the Axis pact, and the fall of Mussolini at least), we now talked nearly always of art and literature. Although he stuck to his moderate tone, and never went too far in our discussions (at any rate–he said–he had little understanding of art, it wasn't his job), Malnate firmly rejected, quite out of hand, what I loved most: from Eliot to Montale, from García Lorca to Esenin. He would listen to me reciting Montale's *"Non chiederci la parola che squadri da ogni lato"** or fragments of Lorca's *Lament for Ignazio*, feeling moved, and each time hoping vainly to warm him, to bring him round to my taste. He would shake his head and say no, Montale's *"ciò che non siamo, ciò che non vogliamo"*† left him cold, that real poetry couldn't be based on negation (heavens, let's not drag Leopardi into it! Leopardi was quite another matter, and anyway he'd written the *Ginestra*, I mustn't forget!), but, on the contrary, it was based on affirmation, on the *yes* which, in the final analysis, the poet *couldn't fail* to utter in the face of hostile nature and death. Even Morandi's paintings didn't win him over– he said–: no doubt they were very subtle and delicate, but to him they seemed too "individual", too "subjective" and "rootless". Fear of reality, fear of being mistaken: this, basically, was what Morandi's still lifes expressed, his famous pictures of bottles and flowers; and fear, even in art, is always a very bad counsellor. . . . And though I secretly cursed him, I could never answer back: the thought that the following afternoon, he, the blessed, would be seeing Alberto and Micòl,

---

* "Do not ask us for the word which can define everything. . ."
† "What we are not, what we do not want."

and perhaps talking to them about me, was enough to
remove the faintest notion of rebellion from me, and
send me back into my shell.

In spite of that I chafed.

"Well, after all," I objected one evening, "your attitude towards contemporary literature, the only living
literature, is just as radically negative as its attitude, our
literature's attitude, is towards life–which is something
you won't tolerate. Now is that fair? Your ideal poets
are still Victor Hugo and Carducci: admit it."

"And why not?" he said. "I think Carducci's republican poems, the ones he wrote before his political conversion–or rather before he went back to his neo-
classic and monarchical second childhood–should all
be rediscovered. Have you re-read them lately? Try,
and you'll see."

I replied I hadn't re-read them, and hadn't the slightest wish to. To me they were, and still remained, empty
"fanfares" puffed up with factitious, patriotic rhetoric.
Downright incomprehensible, in fact. And amusing if
only for that: because they were quite incomprehensible, and therefore basically "surrealist".

Another evening, all the same, not so much because
I wanted to shine, as for some odd vague need, heaven
knows quite what or why, to confess, to pour myself
out, that I had been feeling for some time, I gave way
to the temptation to recite one of my poems to him.
I had written it on the train, coming back from Bologna
after my degree thesis had been discussed, and although
for some weeks I had been deluding myself that it
faithfully reflected my profound desolation at the time,
the horror I had inspired in myself in those days, now,
as I said it to Malnate, I gradually saw quite clearly,
feeling more uneasy than dismayed, all its falseness, all

its literariness. We were walking along Giovecca, at
the end there near the Prospect, beyond which lay the
thick country darkness, a kind of black wall. I recited
slowly, making myself stress the rhythm, my voice
filled with pathos in an effort to pass off my poor shop-
soiled goods as genuine, and, the nearer I drew to the
end, the more firmly I was convinced that my exhibition was bound to fail. But I was wrong. The moment
I finished Malnate gazed at me, looking remarkably
serious, and then, leaving me open-mouthed, assured
me he had liked my poem a lot, a very great deal indeed. He asked me to recite it again (which I did at
once); after which he declared that in his modest
opinion, my "lyric", on its own, was worth all "Montale and Ungaretti's dreary efforts put together". You
could feel real pain, a "moral commitment" that was
absolutely new and authentic. Was Malnate sincere?
At least on that occasion I would say he was. At any
rate he quickly learnt my verses by heart, and quoted
them endlessly, saying that it was possible to catch a
glimpse in them of an "opening" for contemporary
Italian poetry, which was stuck on some pretty dry,
stylized and "hermetic" shoals. As for me, I am not
ashamed to confess that I let him talk without contra-
diction. I made a few feeble protests now and then in
the face of his effusive praises, my heart filled with
gratitude and hope that, now I come to think of it,
were more touching than contemptible.

All the same, as far as Malnate's taste in poetry was
concerned, I feel bound to add that Carducci and Victor Hugo were not, in fact, his favourite authors. As an
anti-fascist and a Marxist he respected them. But his
real passion, as a good son of Milan, was Porta: a poet
to whom, before that, I had always preferred Belli, and

it was wrong – Malnate said – to compare Belli's gloomy
Counter-Reformation monotony with the varied,
warm humanity of Porta.

He knew hundreds of lines by heart.

> *Bravo el mè Baldissar! Bravo el mè Nan!*
> *L'eva pœu vôra dè vegní à trovamm:*
> *t'el seet mattascion porch, che maneman*
> *l'è on mes che nô te vegnet à ciollamm?*
> *Ah Cristo! Cristo! com'hin frècc sti man!**

he would start declaiming aloud in his thick, rather
raucous Milanese voice, on the night we wandered
near via Sacca or via Colomba, or very slowly made
our way up via delle Volte peeping through half-shut
doors into lighted brothels. He knew the whole of
Ninetta del Verzee† by heart, and it was he who revealed
it to me.

With a threatening forefinger, and many winks, and
a knowing allusive expression (alluding to some remote
episode of his adolescence in Milan, I supposed), he
would often murmur:

> *No Ghittin: non sont capazz*
> *de traditt: no, stà pur franca.*
> *Mettem minga insemma à mazz*
> *coi gingitt, e cont i s'cianca. . . .‡*

---

* There's my fine Baldassarre! There's my fine Dwarf!
  High time you came to see me, too.
  D'you know, you lousy old fool, it's nearly
  A month since you came along to f . . . ?
  Ah Christ! Christ! How cold these hands are!
† "Ninetta of the Herb Market."
‡ No Ghittina: I'm not able
  To betray you: no, be sure of that.
  Don't go classing me with the others,
  The coxcombs and the rascals . . .

Or else, sadly, bitterly, he would start up:

*Paracar, che scappee de Lombardia . . .**

emphasizing each line of the sonnet with winks, which of course referred, not to Napoleon's French, but to the fascists.

He was equally enthusiastic and committed when he quoted the poetry of Ragazzoni and of Delio Tessa: of Tessa in particular, who nevertheless – and I didn't fail to tell him so, once – hardly seemed to me to qualify as a "classic", oozing twilight decadent sensibility as he did. But the fact was that anything connected with Milan and its dialect made him quite remarkably indulgent. Everything from Milan he accepted, smiling benevolently. Even literary decadentism, even fascism, had something positive about them in Milan.

He would recite:

> *Pensa ed opra, varda e scolta*
> *tan se viv e tant se impara;*
> *mi, quand nassi on'altra volta,*
> *nassi on gatt de portinara!*
>
> *Per esempi, in Rugabella,*
> *nassi el gatt del sur Pinin . . .*
> *. . . scartoseij de coradella,*
> *polpa e fidegh, barettin*
>
> *del patron per dormigh sora . . .†*

---

* *Stones* fleeing from Lombardy, these 'stones' being Napoleon's soldiers."

† Think and work, look and listen,
   The longer you live the more you learn;
   me, when I'm born another time,
   I'm going to be born a portress's cat!

and he would laugh to himself, his laughter full of tenderness and of nostalgia.

Of course I didn't understand Milanese dialect perfectly, and when there was something I couldn't follow I asked about it.

"What's Rugabella, Giampi?" I asked one evening. "I've been to Milan, it's true, but I can't say I really know it. Can you believe it? I get my bearings there rather worse than anywhere else: worse than in Venice, even."

"But for heaven's sake!" he said, oddly emphatic about it. "Why, it's so clear, so rational! I can't see how you dare compare it with a damp old latrine like Venice!"

And then calming down at once, he explained that Rugabella was a road: the old street not far from the cathedral where he was born, where his parents still lived, and where, in a few months, perhaps before the end of the year (always presupposing the head office in Milan didn't turn down his application for a transfer) he hoped to be able to return and live. Because, let's get it clear—he explained—Ferrara was a very fine little town, lively and interesting in all sorts of ways, including politically. In fact he thought the experience gained in his two years there had been important, not to say fundamental. But home and mother—well, they were always home and mother, and as for the sky of Lombardy, "*cosí bello quando è bello*";* there was none other in the world, at least to him, that began to compare with it.

> For instance, in Rugabella,
> be born the cat of signor Pinin . . .
> . . . bags of offal, lights and liver
> and the master's cap to snooze upon . . .
> * "So fine when it is fine": Manzoni, *The Betrothed.*

Chapter Eight

As I have said already, when the three weeks of exile were over I began going to the Finzi-Continis' every Tuesday and Friday. But not knowing how to spend my Sundays (even if I had wanted to take up with old school friends again, Nino Bottecchiari or Otello Forti, or with more recent friends from the university, whom I had met during the last few years at Bologna, I could not have done so: they were all away on holiday), I allowed myself an occasional visit, apart from that, on Sundays as well. And Micòl let it pass, and never told me to stick to the letter of our agreement.

We were very polite to each other, rather too much so, actually. Conscious that we were on a fairly stable-looking but in fact precarious footing, we were careful not to spoil things, to keep in a neutral zone of mutual respect, where excessive familiarity was as much out of place as excessive coldness. When Alberto felt like playing, and this grew progressively rarer, I was quite ready to make a fourth, but if possible I avoided part-nering Micòl. As a rule, though, I was not even dressed for tennis. I preferred to umpire the long relentless singles between Micòl and Malnate, or else, sitting under the big umbrella beside the court, keep Alberto company.

The obvious deterioration in Alberto's health gnawed at me horribly, growing gradually into another secret torment, the reason for an anxiety perhaps even sharper and more painful than the thought of Micòl, however constant. I would gaze at his face, grown longer now with his thinness, and then watch the way his breathing, down his thickened neck, seemed every day more laboured; and my heart would contract with hidden anguish. There were times when I would have given anything at all to see him well again.

"Why don't you go away for a bit?" I asked him one day.

He turned and stared at me.

"Do I look run down?"

"Well no, not exactly run down. . . . Just a bit thinner, I'd say. Does this heat bother you?"

"Yes, a lot," he panted.

He raised his arms and took a long breath.

"My dear chap, I've been feeling pretty awful for a long time. Go away . . . but *where?*"

"I think the mountains would do you good. What does your uncle say? Has he had a look at you?"

"Oh yes. Uncle Giulio guarantees there's nothing wrong; and that must be true, don't you think? Else he'd have prescribed something for me. . . . According to him, in fact, I can perfectly well play all the tennis I like. And what else? It's obviously the heat that's dragged me down like this. And then I'm not eating a thing, or practically nothing."

"Well then, seeing it's a matter of the heat, why don't you go to the mountains for a fortnight?"

"Mountains in August? I ask you! Besides . . ."–and he smiled–"*Juden sind* everywhere *unerwünscht.* Have you forgotten?"

"Nonsense. Not at San Martino di Castrozza, for instance. You could perfectly well go to San Martino – or even to the Lido in Venice, to the Alberoni beach. . . . The *Corriere della Sera* said so last week."

"How ghastly. August in an hotel, elbow to elbow with gangs of jolly Levis and Cohenim – no thanks, that's not my idea of fun. I'd sooner stick it out here till September."

The following evening, taking advantage of the new friendliness the reading of my poems had aroused between us, I resolved to speak to Malnate about Alberto's health. There was no doubt about it – I said – something was wrong with him. Hadn't he noticed Alberto's difficulty in breathing? And didn't it seem to him at least odd that no one in the family, neither his uncle nor his father, had done a single thing to get him better? His uncle, the doctor from Venice, didn't believe in medicine, so that was that. But what about the others, including Micòl? Calm, smiling, seraphic: nobody moved a finger.

Malnate listened to me in silence.

"I shouldn't worry too much," he said at last, sounding faintly embarrassed. "D'you really think he's in such a bad way?"

"Good God!" I burst out. "Why, he must have lost twenty pounds in the last couple of months!"

"Oh, come on! Twenty pounds is a hell of a lot, you know."

"Well, maybe not twenty, but fourteen, sixteen. At least."

He was silent, thinking it over. Then he admitted that he too had noticed Alberto wasn't well a while ago. On the other hand – he went on – were we really sure we weren't getting worked up about nothing? If

his nearest relations weren't doing a thing, if even professór Ermanno's face showed not the slightest sign of
anxiety, well. . . . Now take professór Ermanno: suppose Alberto were really ill, could he possibly have
bothered to lug along a couple of lorry-loads of red
earth from Imola for the tennis court? And, by the
way, about the tennis court: did I know they were
going to start enlarging that famous surround within
the next few days?

Thus, starting with Alberto and his presumed illness,
we imperceptibly brought the Finzi-Continis–a subject taboo until then–into our evening conversations.
We both knew quite clearly that we were walking on a
minefield, and for this very reason went ahead very cautiously, careful not to stumble. All the same, whenever
we spoke of them as a family, as an "institution" (I
don't know which of us first used this word: I remember we liked it, and it made us laugh), Malnate didn't
spare them, and was harshly critical. What impossible
people!–he said. What an odd, ridiculous bundle of in-
curable contradictions they represented, "socially"!
Sometimes when he thought of the vast amount of
land they owned, of the thousands of labourers who
worked it, disciplined, submissive slaves of the Cor-
porative Regime, sometimes he was even inclined to
prefer the grim "regular" country landlords who in
1920, '21 and '22 hadn't hesitated to open up their
purses to set up and fatten those black-shirted squads
who went round beating people up and giving them the
castor-oil treatment. *At least* they were fascists. When
the time came, there'd be no doubt about how to
treat them. But what about the Finzi-Continis?

And he shook his head with the air of a man who
could understand if he wished, but didn't want to, just

didn't feel he could: subtleties, complications, infini-
tesimal distinctions, might be all very interesting and
amusing, but only up to a point, there had got to be
some sort of limit.

Late one night, after the middle of August, we
stopped for a drink at a wine shop in via Gorgadello,
beside the cathedral, just a few steps from where, till a
year and a half ago, Dr. Fadigati, the well-known ear,
nose and throat specialist, had had his surgery. Between
one glass and the next I told Malnate about the doctor,
whose good friend, the only one he had left in Ferrara,
I had become in the last five months before his suicide
"for love" (I said "for love": and at that point Malnate couldn't restrain a sarcastic, strictly undergraduate
giggle). It was only a step from Fadigati to homosexu-
ality in general; on which Malnate had very simple
views: proper *goi* notions, I thought to myself. To him,
pederasts were just "wretches", poor "obsessed"
creatures who should be treated only from the medical
point of view, or in order to take social precautions.
Whereas I maintained that love justified and sanctified
everything, even pederasty; indeed that love, when it
is pure, that is totally disinterested, is always abnormal,
asocial, etc.: just like art – I went on – which, when it is
pure and therefore useless, no priest of any religion,
including the priests of socialism, ever approves of. Forgetting our good intentions for once, we worked ourselves up into an argument that was almost like those
in the old days, until it suddenly dawned on us that
we'd drunk a bit too much, and we burst out laughing
together. After which we left the wine shop, crossed
the half-empty Listone, and went up San Romano, till
at last we found ourselves walking haphazardly along
via delle Volte.

A cobbled street, full of holes and without a pavement, it seemed even darker than usual. As ever, while
we practically groped our way along, guided only by
the light from the half-open doors of the brothels,
Malnate started reciting a few lines of Porta: not from
Ninetta, I remember, but from the *Marchionn di gamb
avert.**

He declaimed in a low voice, in the sad bitter tone he
always assumed when he recited the *Lament*:

> *Finalment l'alba tance veult spionada*
> *l'è comparsa anca lee dai filidur . . .*†

but here he suddenly broke in on himself.

"What would you say," he asked me, jerking his
chin in the direction of a brothel door, "to our going
in for a look?"

There was nothing very remarkable about the suggestion; all the same, coming from him, with whom
I'd always spoken so seriously, it surprised and embarrassed me.

"That's hardly one of the best," I replied. "It must be
one of the under ten lire ones. . . . Never mind,
though, let's go in."

It was late, almost one in the morning, and we were
hardly welcome. The portress, on a rush-seated chair
behind the door, started grumbling because she didn't
want us bringing in our bikes; then the owner, a pale,
dried-up little stick of a woman of indefinable age,
wearing glasses and dressed in black like a kind of nun,
started grousing about the bikes and the time as well.
Then a maid, who had already started cleaning up the

---

* "Melchior with the bandy legs."

† "At last the dawn, so long looked for, appeared through the
cracks [in the shutters]."

little parlours, all brooms and dusters and long-handled
dustpan under her arm, shot us a scornful glare as we
crossed the entrance hall. And even the girls, gathered
peaceably together and chatting away in a single sitting
room round a group of regulars, didn't look too
friendly. None of them joined us. No less than ten
minutes went by, during which Malnate and I sat
facing each other in the small separate room into which
the proprietress steered us, hardly exchanging a word
(the girls' laughter, the coughs and drowsy voices of
their customer-friends, reached us through the wall)
before a little blonde with a delicate air and hair drawn
back on to the nape of her neck, soberly dressed like a
schoolgirl of good family, decided to appear at the
door.

She didn't seem all that fed up, either.

"Good evening," she said.

She examined us calmly, her blue eyes brimful of
irony. Then she turned to me and said:

"Well, *celestino**, what about it?"

"What's your name?" I managed to stammer.

"Gisella."

"Where are you from?"

"Bologna!" she exclaimed, opening her eyes wide,
as if promising heaven knows what.

But it wasn't true. Calmly, perfectly self-possessed,
Malnate noticed it at once.

"Bologna my eye," he said. "You're from Lombardy, I've got a feeling, but not from Milan. Get along
with you, you're from around Como."

"How on earth did you guess?" the girl asked,
astounded.

* The prostitute, like Micòl, calls the narrator celestino because of his blue eyes.

The owner's sharp face popped up behind her, meantime.

"Well," she grumbled, "there seems a lot of useless
talk going on around here."

"Oh no," protested Gisella, smiling and pointing to
me. "Celestino here's got serious intentions. Shall we
go?"

Before I got up and followed her I turned to Malnate.
But he was looking at me encouragingly, affectionately.

"What about you?"

He gave a short laugh, and gestured vaguely as if to
say: "I don't come into this; I'm quite outside it."

"Don't worry about me," he said. "Get along upstairs, I'll wait for you."

Everything took place very quickly. When we went
downstairs again Malnate was chatting with the owner.
He had taken out his pipe, and was talking and smoking, finding out about the prostitutes' "economic treatment", about the way their fortnightly rota-system
worked, about the "medical check-ups", etc.; and her
answers were just as responsible and serious as his
questions.

"*Bon*,"* Malnate said at last, when he noticed me, and
got up.

He went ahead of me across the hall, towards the
bicycles we had leant against the wall beside the door,
while the owner, who had now grown very polite, ran
ahead of us to open the door.

"Good night," said Malnate. He dropped a coin into
the portress's outstretched palm, and went out first.

"So long, love," shouted Gisella, yawning, before
disappearing into the sitting-room where her work-
mates were gathered. "Mind you come back!"

* In French in the original.

"So long," I replied, going out myself.

"Good night, gentlemen," the owner whispered respectfully behind me; and I could hear her bolting the door.

Holding our handlebars, we went up via Scianze to the corner of via Mazzini, and there turned to the right for via Saraceno. It was Malnate who was talking mostly, now. He told me what he had found out from the owner of the brothel. In Milan, until a few years before – he said – he'd been a pretty keen customer of the famous brothel of San Pietro all'Orto (where – he added – he had several times tried to take Alberto, but quite without success), but it was only now that he'd bothered to find out something about the laws that regulated the "system". Christ, what a life these prostitutes led! And how abject and reactionary the "Ethical State" was, to trade in human flesh like this!

Then, noticing I was scarcely answering, and unwillingly at that, he asked:

"What's up? Don't you feel well?"

"I'm all right."

"*Omne animal post coitum triste*," he sighed. "But don't brood about it. Get a good night's sleep, and everything'll be fine tomorrow, you'll see."

"I know, I know."

We turned left, along via Borgo di Sotto.

"The schoolmistress Clelia Trotti must live somewhere round here," he said, gesturing towards the small houses on the right, in the direction of via Fondo Banchetto.

I didn't answer. He coughed.

"Well . . . how are things going with Micòl?"

I was suddenly seized by a great need to confide in him, to open up.

"Badly, that's how. I've fallen pretty hard, you know."

"Oh, we've realized that," he said, laughing good-naturedly. "For some time now. But how's it going at the moment? Is she still ill-treating you?"

"No. As you'll have noticed, we've reached a certain *modus vivendi* just lately."

"Yes, I've noticed that you're not always scratching away at each other, the way you used to. I'm glad you're friends again. It was nonsense."

My mouth twisted, my eyes swam with tears. Malnate must have noticed the state I was in.

"Oh, come along now," he urged me, embarrassed. "You *mustn't* let yourself go like this."

I swallowed, with an effort.

"I don't think we'll ever be friends again," I murmured. "It's no good."

"That's nonsense," he said. "If only you knew how fond of you she is. When you're not there and she talks about you—and she very often does, you know—no-one's allowed to say a word against you. If anyone does, she's on him like a viper. Alberto's very fond of you, too, and thinks very well of you. In fact—maybe it was a bit indiscreet of me—but a few days ago I recited your poem to them. And you just can't imagine how much they liked it: both of them, d'you hear, both of them. . . ."

"I don't know what to do with their fondness and their good opinion," I said.

We had come out, meantime, into the little piazza in front of the church of Santa Maria in Vado. There was not a living soul to be seen, either here or along via Scandiana as far as the Montagnone. In silence we went across to the fountain beside the churchyard. Malnate leant down to drink, and after him I drank as well and washed my face.

"Listen," Malnate continued, as he started walking again, "I think that's just where you're wrong. Liking and good opinion, especially in times like these, are the only values you can really rely on. What's more disinterested than friendship? Besides, I don't feel, well, at least from what I know it doesn't seem to me that anything happened between you that . . . After all, in time it may perfectly well . . . Now look, for instance: why don't you come and play tennis more often, the way you did a few months ago? Absence doesn't really make the heart grow fonder, you know! Actually, old thing, I've a feeling you don't know much about women."

"But it was she herself who told me not to come so often!" I burst out. "What d'you suggest, that I take no notice? It's her house, after all!"

For a few seconds he was silent and thoughtful.

"I can hardly believe it," he said at last. "I might even understand if there'd been something between you . . . how can I put it . . . something serious, irreparable. But what actually happened?"

He stared at me, uncertainly.

"Forgive this rather . . . undiplomatic question," he went on, and smiled. "But did you ever get to the point of kissing her, at least?"

"Oh yes, often," I said, sighing desperately. "Worse luck for me."

Then, in minute detail, I told him the story of our relationship, right from the beginning, without holding back about the incident in her room last May, the incident I felt had definitely and irrevocably put things wrong, I said. I described the way I'd kissed her, or at

least the way I'd tried to kiss her so many times, not
just that one time in her bedroom, and the various
ways she'd reacted, when she was most fed up with me
and when a bit less so.

I poured it all out, and was so much absorbed, so lost
in these bitter reminiscences that I never noticed his
sudden complete silence.

We had been standing outside my own front door
for nearly half an hour, now. Suddenly I saw him start.

"Hell," he muttered, checking the time. "It's a
quarter-past two. I've just got to be off, if not how'll I
wake up in the morning?"

He leap on to his bike.

"So long," he said, ". . . and bear up, now."

His face looked odd, I noticed, greyish. Had he been
bored, fed up, with my confessions?

I stood watching him as he shot away. It was the
first time he had dumped me there like that, without
waiting for me to go into the house.

Chapter Nine

Although it was so late, my father had still not put
out the light.

Since the racial campaign had started in all
the newspapers in the summer of '37, he had been
suffering from a serious form of insomnia, that was at

its worst in summer, with the hot weather. Whole nights he spent without a wink of sleep, reading a bit, wandering about the house a bit, listening a bit in the dining-room to broadcasts in Italian from foreign stations, and chatting to my mother in her bedroom. If I came in after one o'clock I found it hard to get down the long passage along which our bedrooms were strung in a row (first his, then my mother's, then Ernesto's, Fanny's, and finally, right at the end, mine) without his noticing. I might creep past on tiptoe, without my shoes, even: but my father's sharp ears caught the minutest squeaks and rustles.

"Is that you?"

As I might have guessed, I could not escape being checked on, even that night. As a rule his "Is that you?" only had the effect of hurrying me: without answering, pretending not to have heard, I would go straight on. But not that night. Although I could well imagine, and not without annoyance, the kind of questions I would have to answer, the same for years now—"Why so late?", "D'you know what the time is?", "Where have you been?"–I stopped, pushed the door half open and poked my head round it.

"What d'you think you're doing over there?" my father said at once from his bed, peering over the top of his spectacles. "Come along, come along in a minute."

He was not lying down but sitting in his night-shirt, his back and head leant against the carved white-wood bedhead, covered only up to the base of his stomach by just a sheet. It struck me how everything in him and around him was white: his silvery hair, his pale, emaciated face, his white nightshirt, the pillow propping him up, the sheet, the book lying open on his belly; and how this whiteness (a hospital whiteness, I thought) went well with the surprising, remarkable serenity, the expression of goodness, filled with wisdom, that illumined his light eyes.

"What an hour!" he said smiling, glancing at his waterproof Rolex wrist watch, from which he was never parted, even in bed. "D'you know what the time is? Twenty-seven minutes past two."

For the first time, perhaps, since, at eighteen, I was given the front-door key, the ritual expression failed to irritate me.

"I've been wandering around," I said quietly.

"With that friend of yours from Milan?"

"Yes."

"What does he do? Is he still a student?"

"Student indeed! He's twenty-six. He's got a job . . . as a chemist in the industrial zone, in a Montecatini factory making synthetic rubber."

"Well, just think. And there was I thinking he was still at the university. Why don't you ever ask him here to supper?"

"Well . . . I thought I'd better not add to Mother's work, you know."

"Oh nonsense! There's nothing to it. Lay an extra place, that's all. Bring him along, do. And . . . where did you have supper? At *Giovanni's?*"

"Yes."

"Did you eat well? Tell me what."

I settled down quite happily, not without surprise at my own pleasantness, to name various dishes: those I and those Malnate had chosen. I had sat down, meantime.

"Good," said my father at the end of it, pleased.

"And then", he went on, after a pause, "*duv'èla mai*

ch'a si 'ndà a far dànn, tutt du?* "I bet" – and he raised his hand, as if to stop me denying it – "I bet you've been after the girls."

We had never discussed things of the kind together. A fierce modesty, a violent, irrational need for freedom and independence, had always made me scotch his timid efforts to get on to such subjects even before he made them. But not that night. I looked at him, so white, so frail, so old, and realized, almost physically, that the old childish rancour which had always kept us apart was melting as if by magic, and now had no reason and made no sense.

"Of course," I nodded. "You've guessed it exactly."

"You went to a brothel, I suppose."

"Yes."

"Quite right," he said approvingly. "At your age, at yours above all, they're the best solution from every point of view, including health. But how d'you manage about money? Is the *sabadina*† Mother gives you enough? If not, let me know, and I'll do my best to help."

"Thanks."

"Where did you go? To Maria Ludargnani's? She was already well set up in my day."

"No, to a place in via delle Volte."

"The only thing I'd recommend to you," he said, suddenly assuming the tone of the medical profession he had exercised only as a young man, since later, after my grandfather's death, he had spent his whole time running the estate at Masi Torello and two properties

---

* Where and what have you been up to, the pair of you?": Ferrarese dialect.

† The pocket money which parents give their children on Saturdays: Ferrarese dialect.

he owned in via Vignatagliata, "the only thing I'd
recommend you to do is never neglect the necessary
prophylactic measures. It's a bore, I know, and something you'd gladly do without. But it's all too easy to
get a nasty dose of blenorrheia, otherwise the clap, or
worse. Now if you ever notice anything wrong when
you wake up in the morning, will you come to the
bathroom *at once* and get me to look at it? If anything
happens, I'll tell you how to treat it."

"I see. Don't worry."

I could see he was looking round for the best way of
questioning me further. Now that I'd got my degree
– I imagined he wanted to ask me – had I any ideas, any
plans for the future? But instead he wandered off into
politics. Before I came home – he said – between one
and two o'clock, he'd managed to get several foreign
radio stations: Monteceneri, Paris, London, and Bero-
münster. Now, on the basis of this latest news, he was
sure the international situation was going quickly
downhill. Yes, alas: it was a real *afàr negro*.* The Anglo-
French diplomatic mission to Moscow seemed on the
point of leaving (completely unsuccessful, needless to
say!). Would they really go off from Moscow like
that? He was afraid they would: after which there'd
be nothing to do but all recommend ourselves to
God.

"What d'you think?" he exclaimed. "Stalin's not the
man for moral scruples. I'm certain he wouldn't hesi-
tate a minute to come to an agreement with Hitler, if
it suited him."

"An agreement between Germany and the
U.S.S.R.?" I said, smiling faintly. "No, I don't think
so: I don't think it's possible."

* "A dirty business" in the dialect of Ferrara Jews.

"Let's wait and see," he said, and smiled too. "And let's hope the good Lord listens to you!"

At this point, there was a complaint from the next room. My mother had woken up.

"What did you say, Ghigo?" she asked. "Is Hitler dead?"

"No such luck," sighed my father. "Go to sleep, my love, don't worry, now."

"What's the time?"

"Nearly three."

"Send that boy to bed!"

Mother said a few more incomprehensible words, and was silent.

My father stared into my eyes for a long time. Then, very softly, almost murmuring, he said:

"Forgive me for talking about this. But you'll understand that. . . . Both your mother and I have known since last year that you're in love with Micòl Finzi-Contini. That's true, isn't it?"

"Yes."

"And how are things between you now? Still going badly?"

"They couldn't be worse," I murmured, suddenly realizing quite clearly that this was the literal truth, that in fact our relationship couldn't be worse, and that, in spite of what Malnate thought, I would never manage to climb up the slope at the bottom of which I had been gasping pointlessly for months.

My father gave a sigh.

"I know, it's all very sad. . . . But after all, it's very much better this way."

Head hanging, I said nothing.

"Very much better," he went on, raising his voice a

little. "What would you have liked to do? Become engaged?"

Micòl too, that evening in her room, had asked me
the same question. She had said: "What would you
have wanted? Us to *get engaged*, is that it?" I hadn't
breathed, I had nothing to answer. As now – I reflected
– I had nothing to answer my father either.

"Why not?" I said, though, and looked at him.

He shook his head.

"D'you think I don't understand?" he said. "I like
the girl too. I've always liked her, since she was a
child . . . when she used to come downstairs in the
synagogue to take the *beracà* from her father. Pretty,
in fact beautiful (even too beautiful, perhaps!), intelligent, full of spirit. . . . But to get engaged!" he said
slowly, opening his eyes wide. "Getting engaged, my
boy, means getting married later; and these days, without a secure profession, apart from everything else, tell
me how . . . I suppose you wouldn't have expected me
to help you support a family (I couldn't have, anyway,
I mean not to the extent you'd need), still less have
hoped that she would. She'll have a magnificent dowry
of course," he went on, "there's no doubt about that.
But I don't think you . . ."

"Oh, forget the dowry," I said. "If we loved each
other, how'd the dowry come into it?"

"You're right," my father agreed. "You're perfectly
right. When I got engaged to your mother in 1911 I
didn't bother about these things either. But times were
different in those days. You could look calmly into the
future. And although the future didn't turn out quite
as easy and cheerful as the pair of us had thought it
would (we got married in 1915, as you know, the war'd
already begun, and I volunteered straight afterwards),

society was different in those days, it guaranteed . . .
besides, I'd studied medicine, whereas you . . ."

"Whereas I?"

"Well, you know, instead of medicine, you wanted
to take literature, and you know that when it was time
to decide I didn't stand in your way at all. This was
what you really wanted, and both of us did our duty:
you choosing the way you felt you must choose, and
I not stopping you. But now? Even supposing you'd
wanted a university career . . ."

I shook my head.

"Worse," he went on, "worse! It's quite true that
nothing, even now, can stop you studying on your
own . . . preparing yourself for the difficult, risky job
of being a writer, a militant critic like Edoardo Scar-
foglio, Vincenzo Morello, or Ugo Ojetti . . . or else,
why not? a novelist, or"–he smiled–"a poet. But, for
this very reason: how could you, at your age, barely
twenty-three, and with everything still ahead of you,
how could you think of taking a wife, and starting a
family?"

He spoke of my literary future–I said to myself–as if it
were a beautiful, enticing dream, but not to be translated into anything real or concrete. He spoke of it as
if he and I were already dead and now, from a point
outside space and time, were discussing life together,
and everything that might have happened or not happened in the course of our respective lives. Would
Hitler and Stalin get together?–I wondered, meantime.
Yes, very likely Hitler and Stalin would get together.

"But, apart from that," my father went on, "and
apart from a whole heap of other considerations: will
you let me tell you frankly . . . give you a piece of
friendly advice?"

"Go ahead."

"I realize that when someone, especially at your age, loses his head over a girl, he doesn't stop and work things out . . . and I realize too that your character's rather special . . . and don't think that two years ago, when that poor wretch Dr. Fadigati . . ."

Since Fadigati died, we had never mentioned him at home. How on earth did Fadigati come into it now? I looked at him questioningly.

"Yes, let me finish!" he said. "Your temperament (I've a feeling you get it from your grandmother Fanny), your temperament . . . you're too sensitive, that's it, and so you're not satisfied . . . you always go off looking for . . ."

He stopped, and waved a hand at ideal worlds, peopled by daydreams.

"Forgive me for saying this, anyhow," he went on, "but even as a family the Finzi-Continis aren't suitable . . . they aren't for us, you know . . . if you married a girl like that I'm sure it would end badly, sooner or later. . . . Yes, yes," he insisted, perhaps fearing some movement or word of protest from me, "you know very well what I've always thought of them. They're different . . . they don't even seem like *judím*. . . . Oh yes, I know: maybe that's just why you liked Micòl so much . . . because she was above us . . . socially. But mark my words, it's better this way. The proverb says: 'wife and oxen from your own village.' And, in spite of appearances, that girl isn't from your own village. Not in the least, she isn't."

I had hung my head again, and was staring at my hands lying open on my knees.

"You'll get over it," he went on, "you'll get over it: and very much sooner than you think. Of course I'm sorry; I can imagine what you're feeling just now. But d'you know, I envy you just a little bit as well? If you want to understand, really understand the way things are in this world, you've got to die at least once. And as that's the law, it's better to die while you're young, when you've still got time to pull yourself up and start again. . . . Understanding when you're old is ugly, very much uglier. What can you do? There's no time to start from scratch, and our generation's taken so many knocks. In any case, you're so young, praise heaven! You'll see, in a few months you won't think it's true you went through all this. You may even be glad about it. . . . You'll feel richer, or . . . maturer, or . . ."

"Let's hope so," I murmured.

"I'm so glad we had this out, so glad to have this weight off my mind. . . . And now I've got just one last recommendation. May I?"

I nodded.

"Don't go to their house any more. Start studying again, take something up, start giving private lessons, say, I've heard there's a great demand for them . . . and don't go there again. It's more manly, apart from everything else."

He was right. Apart from everything else it was more manly.

"I'll try," I said, looking up again. "I'll do all I can to stick to it."

"That's the way!"

He looked at the clock.

"Now go and get some sleep," he said, "because you need it. And I'll try shutting my eyes a minute too."

I got up and leant over him for a kiss, but the kiss we exchanged turned into a long embrace, silent, and very tender.

Chapter Ten

That was the way I gave Micòl up.

The following evening, keeping the promise I had made my father, I kept away from Malnate; and the day after that, a Friday, I didn't go to the Finzi-Continis's. A week went by, that way, the first without my seeing anyone, either Malnate or the others. Luckily no one sought me out, which certainly helped; otherwise I would very probably not have stuck it, and would have let myself be drawn back again.

Ten days after our last meeting, though, about the 25th of the month, Malnate rang me up. He had never done so before, and as I had not answered the telephone myself, I was tempted to say I was out. But I changed my mind at once. I already felt strong enough, if not to see him, at least to talk to him.

"Are you all right?" he said. "You really dumped me, didn't you?"

"I've been away."

"Where to? Florence? Rome?" he asked, not without a hint of irony.

"A bit farther this time," I replied, already regretting the over-pathetic expression.

"*Bon.* I don't want to pry. Well now, are we going to meet?"

I said I couldn't that evening, but the next I'd almost

certainly come round to him at the usual time. But he wasn't to wait for me–I went on–if he saw I was late. In that case we'd meet at *Giovanni's*. Wasn't that where he'd be having supper?

"Very likely," he said, drily. And then: "Have you heard the news?"

"Yes, I have."

"What a mess! Do come along, and we'll talk about everything."

"So long then," I said gently.

"So long."

And he hung up.

The following evening as soon as supper was over I cycled to within a hundred yards of the restaurant. All I wanted was to check up that Malnate was there, and in fact, after finding that he actually was (he was sitting as usual at a table out of doors, in his everlasting cream-coloured jacket), instead of joining him, I turned away, and went up on to one of the Castle's three draw-bridges, the one exactly opposite the *Giovanni*. This way, I calculated, I could watch him very much better, without the danger of being noticed. And so it was. Resting my chest against the stone edge of the parapet, that reached about the height of my heart, I watched him as he ate. I looked down at him and at the rows of other customers with the wall behind them, and at the waiters in their white jackets moving fast among the tables, and, strung up there in the darkness as I was, above the glassy water of the moat, I almost felt I was in the theatre, secretly watching an agreeable, meaning-less play. Malnate had now got to the fruit. He picked at a large bunch of grapes, eating one grape after an-other, and every now and then, obviously expecting to see me, turned his head sharply to left and right. As he did so the lenses of his thick spectacles (those "great ugly specs", as Micòl called them) glittered: shuddering, nervous. . . . When he had finished the grapes, he signalled to a waiter and spoke to him for a minute. I thought he had asked for the bill; and was getting ready to go when I saw the waiter coming back with a cup of coffee. Malnate gulped it down all at once. Then, from one of the two breast pockets of his jacket, he took out something very small: a notebook, in which he started writing in pencil. What the hell was he writing?–I smiled. Poetry as well? And here I left him, busily writing in the notebook, from which, at infrequent intervals, he raised his head to turn and look left and right, or else up at the starry sky, as if searching for inspiration and ideas.

For the next few evenings I roamed the streets haphazardly, watching everything, drawn by everything quite impartially: by the great newspaper headlines plastered over the booths in the middle of town, written in huge block capitals, underlined in red ink; by the photographs of films and variety shows stuck up by the cinema entrances; by the shady groups of drunks who hung about right in the middle of the old city's alleyways; by the number-plates of cars lined up in piazza del Duomo; and by the odd variety coming out of brothels, or gradually emerging from the dark brushwood of the Montagnone to have ices, beer or fizzy drinks at the zinc counter of a kiosk lately set up on the slope of San Tomaso, at the end of via Scandiana. One night, about eleven, I found myself near piazza Travaglio, peering into the half-darkness of the famous *caffè Shanghai*, used almost exclusively by prostitutes off the street and workmen from Borgo San Luca not far away; then, immediately afterwards, on the top of the bastion overlooking it, I stood watching a feeble shooting match between two youths, played out under the tough gaze of the Tuscan girl who had admired Malnate. I stayed there, holding off, without saying a word, without even getting off my bike: and at one point the Tuscan girl spoke to me directly:

"Hey, why don't you come up and have a try yourself?" she said. "Be brave now, don't be scared! Show these softies what you can do."

"No thanks," I replied politely.

"No thanks," she repeated. "God, the blokes they turn out nowadays! Where's your friend? Now that's what I call a bloke! Tell me now: where've you hidden him?"

I said nothing, and she burst out laughing.

"Poor pet!" she said, pityingly. "Run along home now or Dad'll be smacking you. Run along to byebyes now, there's a good boy!"

About midnight the following night, without knowing why, or what I was really looking for, I was on the opposite side of town, pedalling along the unpaved lane that ran smoothly, curving slightly round the inside of the Wall of the Angels. The moon was full and splendid: so bright and luminous, in the perfectly clear sky, that there was no point in using a lamp. I pedalled slowly along. Lying on the grass, under the trees, I kept seeing lovers, and mechanically counted the couples, one by one. Some tossed about half naked, one over the other, intertwined, others already lay apart, hand in hand; others, clasped together, but motionless, seemed asleep. I counted more than thirty couples, as I passed. And although I sometimes went so near them that I brushed them with my wheel, no one ever seemed to notice my silent presence there. I felt, and was, a kind of strange fleeting ghost: at once full of life and of death; of passion, and of detached pity.

When I got level with Barchetto del Duca I stopped. I got off my bike, leant it against a tree trunk, and for a few minutes, facing the still, silvery park spread before me, I stayed there watching. I was thinking of nothing very precisely but of all kinds of things, one after the other, without pausing over any one of them in particular. I looked, and listened to the immense, thin cry of crickets and frogs, and was myself surprised at the slightly embarrassed smile that came to my lips. "Well, here we are," I murmured, not knowing what to do or what I had come to do. I was filled with a vague feeling of how pointless all commemorations are.

I started walking along the edge of the grassy slope, my eyes fixed on the *magna domus*. All the lights were out over there, and although Micòl's bedroom windows faced south, so that I couldn't see them, I was quite certain, for some unknown reason, that no light was coming from them either. When I got exactly above the point in the garden wall that was "sacred", as Micòl said, "*au vert paradis des amours enfantines*", I suddenly had an idea. Suppose I were to creep into the park, over the wall? As a boy, that far-off June afternoon, I hadn't dared to, I'd been frightened. But now? What on earth was there to be frightened of now?

I glanced round quickly, and a moment later I was at the foot of the wall, suddenly finding, in the sultry shadows, the same ten-year-old smell of nettles and dung. But the wall wasn't the same at all, it had changed. Perhaps because it was ten years older (I too was ten years older, and ten years taller and stronger) it seemed to me neither as high nor as hopeless as I remembered it. After my first unsuccessful effort I lit a match. There were all the footholds I needed, and even a big rusty nail still sticking out from the wall. I made a second attempt, and reached it at once; then, grabbing it, I easily pulled myself up to the top by my arms.

As soon as I was sitting there, with my legs dangling over on the far side, the first thing I noticed was a ladder leaning against the wall below me. I wasn't surprised; amused, if anything. "Look at that," I said. "There's even a ladder." All the same, before starting to go down it I turned round a moment towards the Wall of the Angels. The bicycle was still there, leaning against the trunk of the lime tree, where I had left it. It was an old bike, a bone-shaker that wouldn't really tempt anyone.

Soon, with the ladder's help, I reached the ground, and, leaving the path that ran inside the garden wall, I immediately cut across the field strewn with fruit trees, meaning to reach the main drive at a point more or less equidistant from Perotti's house and the girder bridge over the Panfilio canal. I trampled the grass noiselessly, my mind still quite empty: seized by what might have been a scruple now and then, admittedly, but shrugging off all anxieties before they had time to get established. How beautiful Barchetto del Duca was at night, I said to myself, how sweetly it lay in the moonlight! I wasn't looking for anything, among those milky shadows, in that sea of milk and silver. No one, however much surprised to find me there, could really have blamed me a great deal. After all, when you came to think of it, I even had a bit of a right to, now. . . .

I left the drive, crossed the bridge over the canal, then, turning left, soon reached the tennis court clearing. It was perfectly true. Professór Ermanno had kept

his promise. The wire-netting round it had been taken
down and lay in a jumbled luminescent heap at the side
of the court, on the opposite side to the one where the
audience's cane chairs and deck-chairs usually stood in a
row. More than that: the work of widening the space
round the tennis court had already begun, and on all
four sides a strip was being taken from the surrounding
meadow, at least three yards on the sidelines and five
at the ends. Alberto was ill, seriously ill. But they had
somehow, even in *that* way, got to hide how serious
his illness was! Quite right, too, I thought approvingly, and went on.

I came out into the open, meaning to make a wide
turn round the clearing, and wasn't surprised, when I
was already a long way from the tennis court, to see
Yor's stout familiar outline suddenly trotting towards
me from the *Hütte*. I stood still and waited for him, and
when he was about ten yards away he stopped as well.
"Yor," I called in a muffled voice, "Yor!" Obviously
he recognized me. His tail gave me a brief, pacific wag of
greeting, then he turned slowly back the way he came.

Every now and then he turned, as if to make sure I
was following. And I didn't follow him, or rather,
although I was drawing nearer the *Hütte*, I never left
the far end of the clearing. I was walking about twenty
yards from the great dark trees curving round in that
part of the park, and looking to my left all the while.
The moon was now behind me. The clearing, the
tennis court, the *magna domus*, a sightless buttress, and
then, over at the end, hanging above the leafy tops of
the apple, fig, pear and plum trees, the embankment of
the Wall of the Angels: all this looked clear and definite, as if in relief, in a light that was better than daylight.

I carried on that way, and then realized I was only a few steps from the *Hütte*: not the front of it, the side looking out at the tennis court, but behind, between the trunks of the young firs and larches on to which it backed. Here I stopped. I stared at the rough black shape of the *Hütte*, against the light, suddenly uncertain, no longer knowing where to go, where to make for.

"What shall I do?" I said softly, perplexedly. "What shall I do?"

I kept staring at the *Hütte*, and was thinking now—without my heart beating any faster at the thought, taking it in quite indifferently, as stagnant water lets the light play over it—thinking that yes, suppose after all it was here, to Micòl, that Giampi Malnate came every night after leaving me at my own front door (why not? wasn't that why he always shaved so carefully before coming out to supper with me?): well then, if that was so, the tennis court changing rooms might be a splendid hide-out, for them.

Why yes—I went on, quietly working it out in a kind of quick inner whisper—why of course. How could I have been so blind? He went around with me just to get through the evening till it was late; then, having put me to bed, as it were, he came dashing on his bike to her, waiting for him in the garden, of course. But of course. Now I realized what his gesture in the brothel had really meant. Oh well: making love every night, or nearly, is all very fine, but the time soon comes when you start missing your mother, the skies of Lombardy, etc. . . . And what about the ladder, there against the garden wall? It could only have been Micòl who put it there, in *that* particular place.

I was clear-eyed, calm, tranquil. As in a game of

patience, every piece fitted in, the whole thing worked out perfectly.

Micòl, of course. With Giampi Malnate. With her sick brother's closest friend. Hidden from him and all the others at home, parents, relations, and servants, always at night. In the *Hütte* as a rule, but perhaps some nights up there in her bedroom, in the room where the *làttimi* were. Was it really hidden? Or were the others, as always, pretending not to see, letting things slide, in fact deep inside them trying to help, since basically it is right and human for a girl of twenty-three who cannot or will not marry to have what nature entitles her to, just the same. They even pretended not to see Alberto's illness, in that house. It was their system.

I strained my ears. Absolute silence.

What about Yor, though? Where had Yor gone!

I tiptoed a few steps towards the *Hütte*.

"Yor!" I cried loudly.

But then, as if in answer, through the night air, from very far away came a plaintive, sad, almost human sound. I recognized it at once: it was the old, dear voice of the piazza clock striking the hours and the quarters. What was it saying? It was saying that I was very late once more, that I was foolish and wicked to keep tormenting my father, who was sure to be worried, that night like all the other nights, because I still wasn't home, and so couldn't sleep: and that at last it was time for me to put his mind at rest. Properly. For good.

"A fine novel," I grinned, shaking my head as if before an incorrigible child.

And I turned my back on the *Hütte* and went off through the trees, in the opposite direction.

Epilogue

My story with Micòl Finzi-Contini ends here. And so this narrative ought to end now, since all I might add would no longer concern her, but, if there was anything to add, only myself.

I already said, at the beginning, what her fate and that of her family was.

Alberto died of malignant lymphogranuloma before the others, in '42, dying so slowly that, in spite of the deep furrow dug through the midst of it by the racial laws, the whole of Ferrara, from a distance, was affected by it. He choked. Oxygen was needed to help him breathe, and in ever-increasing amounts. And as there was a great shortage of it in Ferrara, because of the war, towards the end his family cornered the market in gas cylinders over the whole countryside, sending people to buy them at any price in Bologna, Ravenna, Rimini, Parma, Piacenza. . . .

The others, in September '43, were taken by the *repubblichini*.* After a short stay in the prison at via Piangipane, they were sent to the concentration camp at Fòssoli, near Carpi, the following November, and thence to Germany. As far as I was concerned, though, during the four years between the summer of '39 and the autumn of '43 I never saw any of them. Not even

* The fascists of Mussolini's Republic.

Micòl. At Alberto's funeral, behind the windows of the old Dilambda, adapted to run on methane gas, that followed the funeral procession at walking speed and afterwards, as soon as the hearse had gone inside the gateway at the end of via Montebello, turned back at once, I thought I made out her ash-blonde hair a moment. That was all. Even in a town as small as Ferrara people can perfectly well vanish from one another's sight for years and years if they want to, and live together like the dead.

As for Malnate, who was called to Milan in November '39 (he had tried ringing me up in September, but without result; he had even written me a letter . . .), I never saw him again either, after August of that year. Poor Giampi. He believed – yes, truly believed! – in the brave Lombard and communist future that smiled at him, then, from beyond the darkness of the coming war: a distant future, he admitted, but one that was certain, couldn't fail. But what does the heart really know? If I think of him, setting off for the Russian front with the C.S.I.R.* in '41, never to return, I always remember vividly the way Micòl reacted every time he started to "catechize" us, between games of tennis. He spoke in his low, calm, rumbling voice; but Micòl, unlike me, never took much notice. She never stopped answering back, prodding him, badgering him.

"But whose side are you on, girl? The fascists'?" I remember him asking her one day, shaking his big sweaty head. He couldn't understand.

So what was there between the pair of them? Nothing? Who can tell.

The fact is that, as if foreseeing her own coming

* The Italian expeditionary force in Russia.

death, her own and that of her whole family, Micòl kept telling Malnate that she cared nothing for his democratic, social future, that she abhorred the future in itself, far, far preferring "*le vierge, le vivace et le bel anjourd'hui*", and the past even more, the dear, the sweet, the pious past.

And as these, I know, were only words, the usual desperate, deceptive words that only a real kiss would have stopped her uttering: let them, just these and no others, seal the small amount the heart has managed to remember.

GIORGIO BASSANI

Born in Bologna in 1916 of a Ferrarese family, Giorgio Bassani spent the first twenty-seven years of his life in Ferrara, the scene of this novel.

He was a founder of the Action Party in 1942, was imprisoned and was freed after the fall of Mussolini. From its founding in 1948 until 1960, Bassani was an editor of the international review BOTTEGHE OSCURE. For many years he was an editor for a Milanese publisher, where he brought out, among other books, THE LEOPARD, and taught history of the theatre at the Italian National Academy for Dramatic Arts. He is now one of the two vice-presidents of Radiotelevisione Italiana.

Bassani has written three novels: GLI OCCHIALI D'ORO (THE GOLD-RIMMED SPECTACLES), which appeared in English in 1960; IL GIARDINO DEI FINZI-CONTINI (THE GARDEN OF THE FINZI-CONTINIS); and, most recently, DIETRO LA PORTA. He has also written a book of long short stories, LE STORIE FER-RARESI, and a collection of poems, L'ALBA AI VETRI, as well as essays and literary criticism which have not yet been collected into a volume.

In 1956 he won the Strega Prize with LE STORIE FERRARESI. THE GARDEN OF THE FINZI-CONTINIS achieved the greatest popular success of any Italian book in recent years, and won the 1962 Viareggio Prize.